HEROINES OF OLYMPUS

RIVER BENNET

For everyone who has been wrongly villainized.

"Watch as my shattered edges glisten."
Taylor Swift

CONTENT WARNINGS

This book is intended for mature readers, eighteen years and older. It contains the following themes and situations. Please review the triggers before reading:

Abduction

Alcohol

Animal Death

Anxiety

Assault

Attempted Rape

Blood

Combat

Death

Espionage

Gambling

Gladiator-style Arena

Hostages

Incest

PTSD

Sexual Assault

Sexual Harassment

Shipwreck
Slavery
Snakes
Torture
Trafficking
Violence

NOTE FROM THE AUTHOR

Dear Reader,

Like many of you, my love of Greek Mythology has spanned decades. The complex dynamics between gods and mortals, combined with powers gifted by the cosmos is very compelling when you want to escape.

I always felt like that world had so much promise and potential, a well of stories waiting to be reimagined. It is with that spirit in mind that I crafted *my* Olympic Isles.

Many of the characters will match the established lore you know so well. However, there are equally as many times I took creative license when examining how they would fit in this world that I created.

Everyone's preferences are their own and are neither right nor wrong. This is merely to establish expectations before diving in. If you are a stickler for Homer, you might find this story isn't for you.

If you can set aside your preconceived notions, the Fates might spin a tale for you.

Temple of
the Harvest
Mt.
Eurymanthus
THESSALY
Corcyra
Temple of
the Hunt
AITOLIA
Sea
Temple
Atlas
Mountains
Mt.
Etna
ATTICA
Iron
Temple
Solar
Temple
Gulf of Corinth
Temple of
Celebration
Hhaca
THE
WASTES
OLYMPIA
OLYMPUS
Te
W
Temple of
Olympus
War
Temple
Mt.
Stymph
Temple of
Commerce
Temple of
Love
LERNA
SPARTA
Sir
Str
Temple
Harbor
Medusa's Island
Tartarus Allegiance
HEROINES
of OLYMPUS

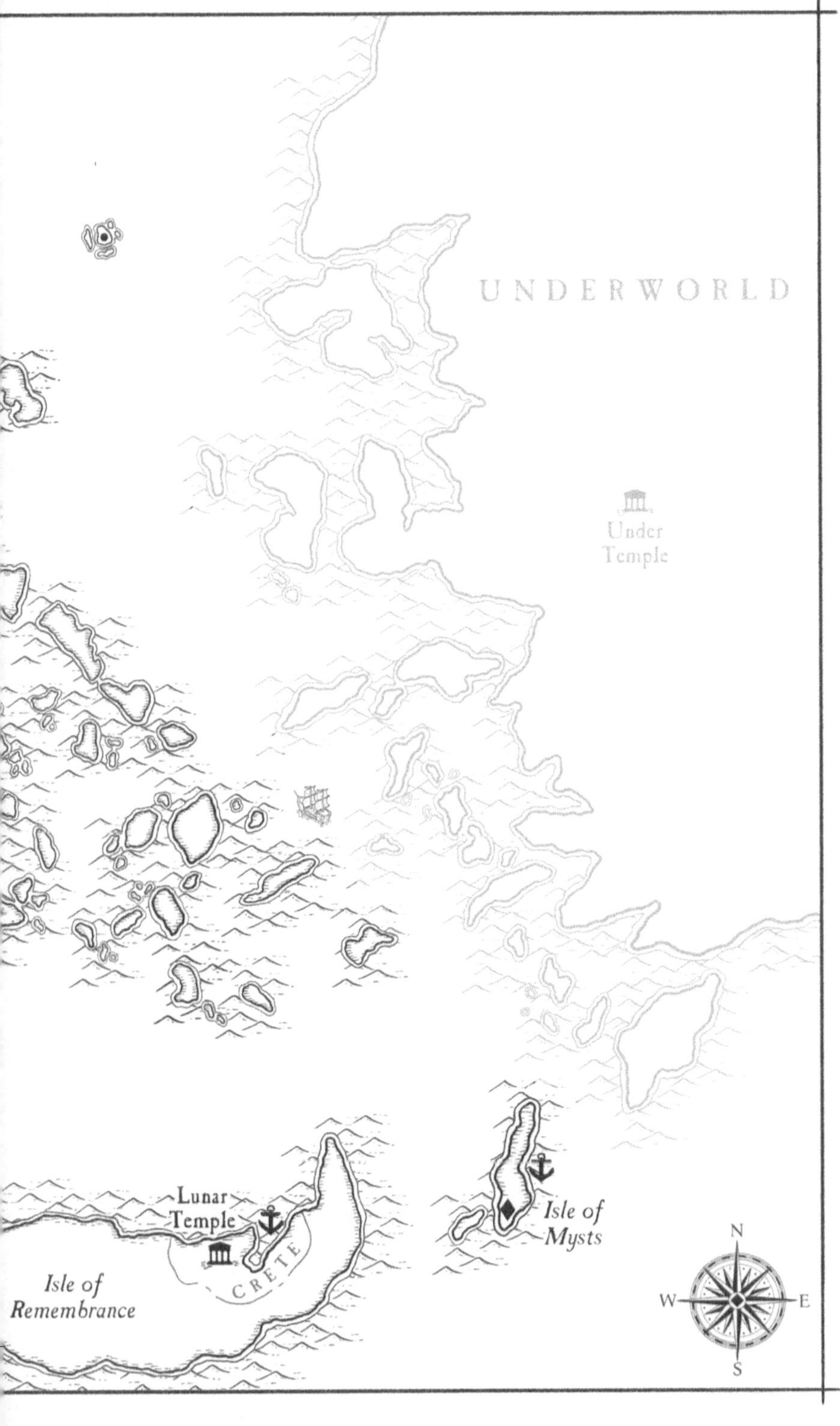

UNDERWORLD
Under Temple
Lunar Temple
CRETE
Isle of Remembrance
Isle of Mysts
N
W
E
S

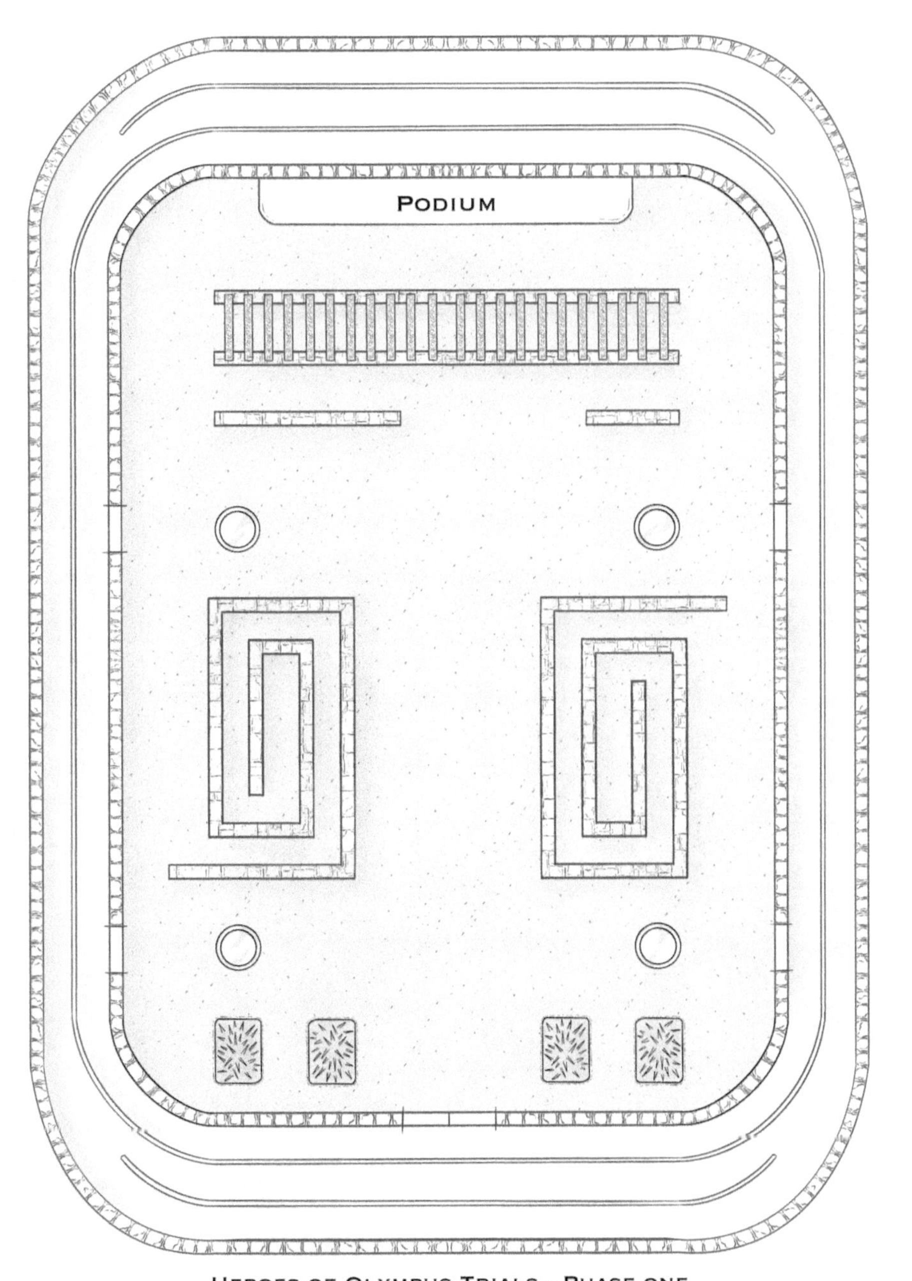

PODIUM
HEROES OF OLYMPUS TRIALS - PHASE ONE

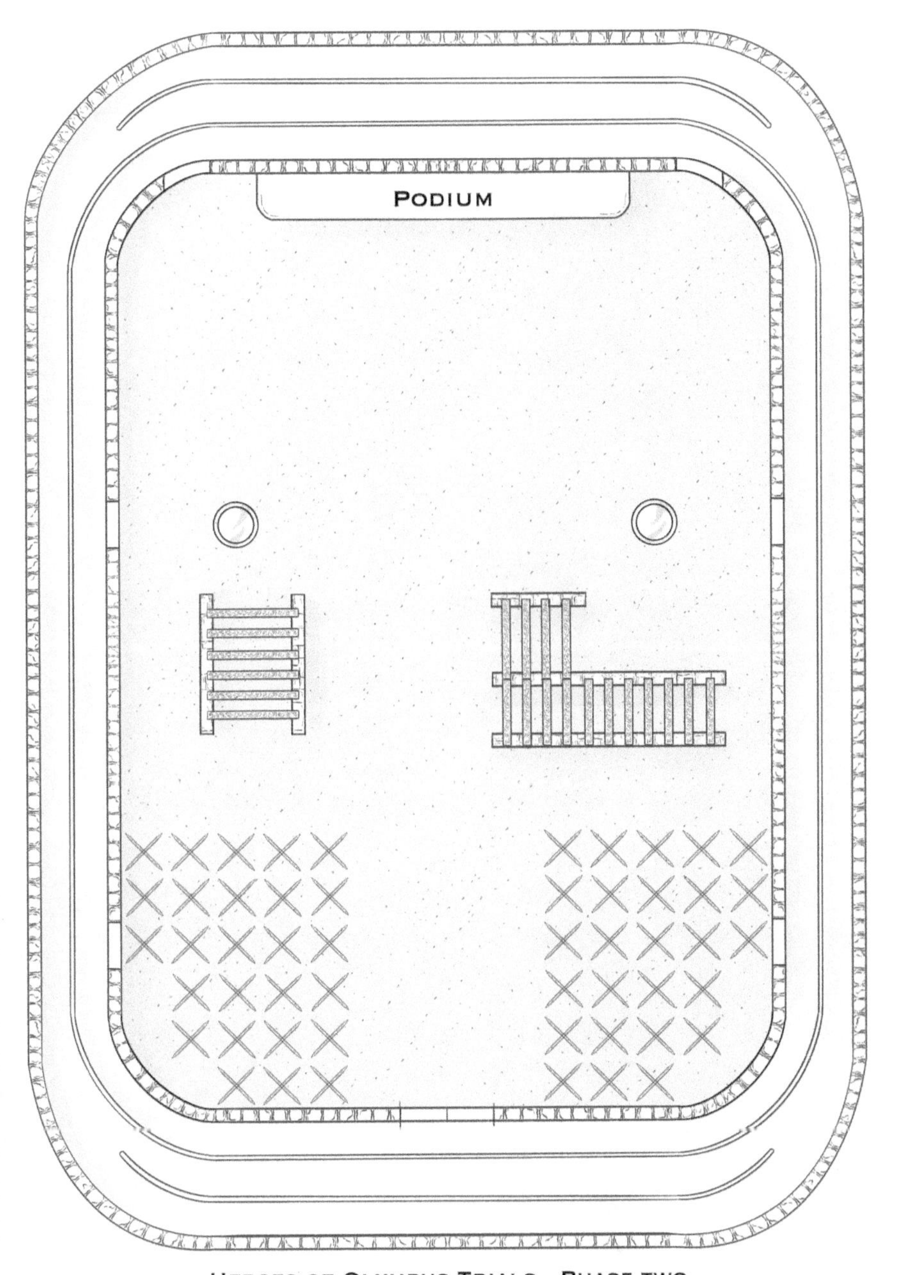

PODIUM
HEROES OF OLYMPUS TRIALS - PHASE TWO

1

MEDUSA

"Stop that!" Medusa swats at one of the infernal serpentine vermin he cursed her with.

It recoils and its small tongue flicks out in irritation. "Just leave me alone for five Fates damned minutes."

Medusa sighs as she leans her head back and lets the ripples of the hot spring caress her aching muscles. Never knowing when she will have to fight for her life again, her body struggles to relax in the therapeutic warmth of the water.

Her cavern is bright at this time of day. The noontime sun streams in through the large open areas at the top, casting beams of light around the space, often falling directly on the many statues that litter her sanctum. Do the Fates wish to punish Medusa further by spotlighting the many terrible things she has had to do to stay alive? Their faces haunt her even in her dreams when the guilt creeps into her heart - thorny vines pricking and poking every tender spot of her soul, leaving a raw open wound. These men had all come to kill her. Why should she carry the weight of their deaths any longer?

The snake from before, and an additional one, hiss in her ear, pulling her out of her thoughts. She rolls her eyes and dips below the surface, staying under momentarily to drown out the world. Hopefully, the water will quiet them down for as long as Medusa can hold her breath.

She pops above the waterline, sitting on a rock along the side of the pool. Submerged only up to her collarbone, Medusa rubs her hands along her arms to remove any lingering sweat and dirt. The patches of scales on her skin are rough beneath her fingers, ever-present reminders of what *he* did to her. For a moment, she can still see the soft pink of the skin she used to have, instead of the current reptilian greens and golds.

Her muscles are firm underneath, toned from eight years of fending off the world as it sends countless soldiers to erase her existence. She absentmindedly rubs the arrowhead birthmark on her wrist - an action that is a compulsion at this point, though she will never understand why. The nature of her survival has been gruellingly physical. The result is thighs that are thick and powerful, abs that are solid, cushioned by curves over her wide hips and a soft belly. She has the body of a warrior.

The serpents, where her long cherry hair should be, slither around aimlessly. Their hisses and tongue flicks occasionally tickle her neck and ears. Her yellow-green eyes meet her reflection, filling her with bitterness and shame as the image taunts her. Medusa splashes the water, watching as her face dissipates amongst the ripples.

Medusa soaks for a while, forcing herself to relax and unwind. Her defensive lifestyle requires her to maintain her training nearly every day, partially to keep her skills honed but also out of boredom. Sparring with poor substitutes for training dummies helps release the frenetic energy coursing through her when there is little to do.

She reaches over to the side of the pool and picks up the novel she has been reading. Books are among her most trea-sured items that she rarely gets the chance to enjoy. Medusa savors the books anytime she ends up with a new one brought in by the Heroes, but she gets so wrapped up in them she forgets and flies through them.

The latest one is a cheesy romance, and she enjoys the comfortable ease of a read like that. She raised an eyebrow when she found it amongst the possessions of a particularly burly man that she assumed was a mercenary. It reminded her that you can never judge someone's literary tastes by appearance.

Barely a chapter into her reading, more of her serpents slither intently around her face. Annoyed, she swats them away, but their insistence on annoying her is unrelenting.

"What are you doing? Stop that!"

The sporadic hisses are now in unison, building into an overwhelming cacophony in Medusa's ears. Realizing something is wrong, she pushes aside her initial irritation with them.

She is not alone. No one has ever made it this far into her sanctum without her knowing, but it can be the only reason for her serpents to behave this way.

The bubbling water masks the sound of her movement as she carefully slides to the very back of the pool. As silently as she can, Medusa lifts herself out of the water, picking up the nearby sword and pressing herself against the wall.

A flicker of a shadow catches Medusa's eye on the other side of the cavern. There. Found him.

His footsteps are silent. Had it not been for her serpents, she would have been ignorant of his arrival. She had been sitting there, completely exposed. She kicks herself for being so foolish, for letting her guard slip even for a moment. The Pantheon has made certain there is no rest for monsters.

The sand sticks to Medusa's bare, wet feet as she stealthily stalks toward her attacker, using the statues of his fallen brethren for cover. Why can she not hear him? No one is this silent.

Her serpents are wild around her head, but the hissing has stopped, recognizing her need for silence.

All at once, every serpent jerks to her right and they hiss together once more. Medusa shushes them so she can focus, only stopping when a ray of light glints off of a shield in the direction they are hissing.

With barely any time to react, the shield gets closer. It is large and bronze, easily concealing the bulk of his torso and face.

She pulls her sword back and moves into a defensive stance. Digging her heels into the ground, like Nikolas taught her all those years ago, Medusa prepares for his attack.

Her blade rarely gets any use, as her serpents usually get the job done before the attacker is in swinging distance, but this one seems to have come prepared.

When he is a few feet away, the shield moves to the side in a flash, creating enough space to allow an arm and a sword to swing at her without exposing him to her snakes.

She parries and blade meets blade, the reverberation traveling up her arm, but she holds firm. He quickly retreats behind the shield and circles her. She turns with him, never letting her sword drop. They play this game for a few more minutes before Medusa has had enough. She will not be toyed with.

She lunges at him suddenly and grabs the bottom of the shield, flipping it upward with every ounce of strength she has. He must not have been expecting her to come at the bottom of the shield and it flies up and over his head easier than anticipated.

The man squeezes his eyes shut to avoid being turned to stone. Medusa uses the split second to her advantage and moves behind her attacker. She grabs his black hair by the fistful and forces him down to his knees. He swings his sword aimlessly, keeping his eyes as tightly closed as possible, but she knocks it out of his hand with a blow to his forearm with the hilt of her weapon.

He may have had some grand speech prepared, in his back pocket, that he planned to use to beg to be spared if it came to that. She doesn't wait to find out. In a clean stroke, Medusa neatly severs his head from his shoulders, his body slumping to the ground at her feet.

Blood runs down her fingers as she inspects the head of the fallen warrior. He had been another in a long line of Heroes of Olympus, sent to rid the world of all of its unsavory beings, such as the gorgon who has just felled him. Another to come along reeking of arrogance, drowning in assumptions that their prey would be of little concern.

Eyeing his uniform, she notes the golden stars on his leather epaulets and the red cloak. Heracles Legion. Poseidon must be getting desperate to end her if the Pantheon is allowing him to send their most elite fighters after her. His shoes are not standard fare for a Hero though. They are gold, like the stars of his rank, but also interwoven with vines of silver. Bronze wings on the outer side of each shoe stop her in her tracks as she stares at the sandals of Hermes.

She walks a few feet away and picks up the shield the man carried, dusting it off to inspect it further. The carvings and symbols look older than any language commonly used, but languages had been one of Medusa's passions as an Acolyte. Translating the script that is legible takes a few minutes.

A weapon forged with steel is mighty indeed, but a weapon formed through wisdom cannot be matched.

Athena's shield. Images flash through her mind of the goddess of wisdom and war in her ceremonial garb for official functions, her shield always on her left arm. Medusa has seen it many times but never so close as to read its inscription.

What does this mean for her? This man shows up with gifts from two gods to aid him on his assassination mission. Does the hunt for her extend farther than Poseidon now? Is the entire Pantheon hunting her down?

She sighs as she begins the tedious work of removing the body of her latest would-be assassin. Dwelling on these thoughts leads nowhere productive. No, Medusa must keep her chin up and be grateful that she is both alive, and that this man is not another statue, immovable, frozen in place to torment her along with all the others.

Today is supposed to be her day off from training and the never-ending list of tasks required of her to maintain her living environment on her own. She is single-handedly responsible for making and finding all her own food, and sourcing all her drinking water.

She realizes every day that she took so many things for granted as an Acolyte. That does not diminish the misery she experienced at the hands of that institution. Still, she had fresh food any time she needed it, clean running water, fireplaces, access to enchanted items that made day-to-day tasks easier.

Today, though, she was going to sit by the fire pit at the entrance to her cavern, lounging on the pile of blankets she has foraged over the years. The plan had been to enjoy the delicious jasmine tea that she never gets to drink, and read her cozy book. If the Heroes could time their assaults with the days, she is already doing annoying shit, that would be great.

Medusa stares into the burning coals as the blaze from the pyre dies down to simmering embers. Burning his body may be harsh, but she has limited options. It is this, or toss him over the back cliff side. Fire seems like the least messy choice. Plus, does she want to make her home any more gruesome than it already is?

His boat still needs to be searched, but her body sags beneath the weight of another death. Her clothing is sticky with the Hero's blood as she peels it off, and the pungent smell of the smoke from the fire assaults her as she pulls her tunic over her head.

The warmth of the pool has lost its appeal, and Medusa hastily washes away the evidence of her latest victim. In mere minutes, she is out of the water again. She will ever be able to fully relax here.

MEDUSA MAKES her way to the shore of her tiny island. The only benefit to the steady stream of warriors dispatched to end her has been the constant replenishment of supplies.

She always takes a dark solace in examining the items each Hero felt were important enough to accompany them on a death mission. Tiny glimpses into the lives of people free to live amongst society. Of people who did not have to hide from the gods. She is quite careful, though, not to let her daydreams get too lofty. Picturing these men walking amongst their day-to-day lives is one thing, but envisioning herself doing these things was something she cannot dare to entertain.

When Medusa allows herself the freedom to pursue this traitorous line of thought, it makes the lonely nights here on the edge of the world seem almost unbearable.

It surprises her to find a dinghy on shore, as opposed to the small one-man vessels that tend to be the transportation of choice for her assassin tormentors. As her eyes scan the large outcroppings of rocks that ring her island, she sees a slightly larger boat with what appears to be a proper cabin. Realizing a vessel that size would need more than her recent kill to operate, she stops to assess her next steps. Should she wait for the men on the boat to realize her assassin has not returned and lie in wait? Take advantage of the element of surprise and get the jump on them? The first option would require the disposal of more bodies, whereas option two allows for simply loosing the anchor on the ship when the tide was on its way out. Option two it is.

The boat's proximity to the rocks aids in Medusa's stealthy approach, with the dusky hour of the day ensuring a seamless blend into the shadows. Once she is alongside the modest hull, she secures the dinghy to a metal ring, her rogue knowledge of knot tying making the task quick and efficient. Slowly, she stands up, adjusting her balance with the gentle rocking of the water until she is can stand and see through the slats of the railing. She spots two men on the deck. One a scrawny old man who looks like he has spent his life on the open water. The other, as if a caricature of opposites, is a boulder of a man. At least triple the muscle on the so-called elite warrior that was tasked with hunting her down. Quickly formulating a plan, Medusa silently mouths the words she says every time she has to kill. Every time she has to run. Every time she has to make an impossible choice.

This shall not break me

She silently slips onto the deck, going for the smaller man first, thinking she could knock him unconscious and focus entirely on the mountain of a man who would be the real threat. Using the metal gauntlet that commonly adorns her right hand in combat, Medusa brings it down on the back of his head and he collapses at her feet. The sound has the other man whipping around, but quickly remembering the target of the current mission, he tightly shuts his eyes. Despite not being able to see, he readies himself into a fighting stance and welcomes her attack without a hint of fear. She cocks her head in confusion and approaches him slowly, trying to assess the swiftest way to attack. She is halfway to him when his head tilts slightly, and Medusa spots a birthmark behind his left ear. The familiar shape halts her in her tracks, then her vision goes dark, and a hood is pulled over her head from behind.

A loud silence washes over her. Where she normally can hear her snakes slithering and hissing, it is quiet, as if they are sleeping. The absence of their presence makes it clear how accustomed she has become to them. Small hands pull her arms tightly behind her back and they spin her around. She can hear shuffled movement, they replace the small hands on her arms with large ones with a grip like iron. Light peeks though as they pull the hood up enough for Medusa's face to be visible – including her eyes. Her confusion is impossible to hide, as she looks into another person's eyes for the first time in eight years. How is this happening? As the shock recedes, she realizes that person is a woman.

The deep laugh in her ear tells Medusa she is being held by the larger man, and she stiffens at the thought of someone yet again touching her against her will. The rage simmers in her eyes but does not rise to the surface–she refuses to let it. She has to stay calm and keep her wits about her. He spins Medusa around once again and she meets his gaze, taken aback when he does not even fear her, much less turn to stone as he should. "I knew that over-puffed peacock Perseus would underestimate ya. I was hoping for it."

Medusa does not know what is happening, but the best option is to keep him talking. "He was hardly even a challenge. If you were so confident he would fail, why didn't you assist him?" He chuckles again and the unease in her gut churns. "Because, Lyra, we are here to talk to you."

The deck feels small as she hears the name she was born with. The name her mother gave her before Medusa's conscription to Temple service. It was the name Nikolas used whenever she was on the verge of despair. A fresh start, as the Council used to call it. And her name became yet one more thing that could not be her own. The last time Medusa heard that name, she was twelve. When Nikolas died.

"I don't understand. How do you know that name? How does this hood make it safe for you to look at me? If you are here to talk to me, why did you come with the Hero sent to kill me?"

The woman finally speaks. Her voice is like honey, a contrast to the gruffness of the man's.

"I know you have so many questions, Lyra, and we are more than happy to answer them. We only ask that you keep this hood on. It is through its magic, my magic, that we can see you as we do, and not suffer the fate of so many who have been before us."

Medusa considers carefully, cursing herself for being distracted by the beauty of this woman. She quickly dismisses the thought as a random moment from a lonely mind. No one would have interest in a monster like Medusa.

"I will keep this hood on and hear what you have to say under the condition that you remove your hands from me immediately." Medusa says, glaring up at the man, who still has a death grip on her upper arms.

"Happy to oblige now that we are all in agreement that the lovely hood Psyche has provided will stay on, so that I don't end up an accidental, or intentional, statue." He releases her immediately, his tanned hands dropping to his side, and she relishes the sudden lack of contact. Not that she dislikes being touched, but she cannot accept the violation of her consent. Which is precisely what had gotten her into the mess that is her current situation — wait… did he say Psyche?

Her gaze returns to the woman, and her eyes widen. "Surely he's not implying that you are, Psyche?" She intends to say that with a scoff, but the glint of the rising moon on her dark hair overwhelms her and it comes out in more of an awed whisper.

At that, the woman's equally dark lips curve into a smile. Medusa finds herself once again distracted by her radiance. The contrast of her copper skin to the darkness of her eyes, lips, and hair is absolutely captivating. Medusa curses at herself internally for losing her focus on what are more pressing matters. These people have rocked her world, but all she could think about was how soft her skin might be, her lips. *Stop it.*

The woman takes her time answering, as Medusa tries to hide her flustered reaction. "I am indeed Psyche. This is Alec, and the unfortunate victim of your gauntlet is Yiorgos. However, that is not what's important. The time has come for you to remind the gods who *you* are. Are you truly content to live in exile, constantly fighting for your life?"

"Of course not, but it was this, or let them hunt me down, looking over my shoulder even more than I do now. Does that seem like the better option to you? Has your immortal lifespan made you so out of touch to the mortals and the demitheos like me?" It surprises Medusa how quick she is to anger. As an Acolyte, she never would have dared to speak to a god like this. Perhaps it is the isolation, or the part of her that has always fought against everything, even when it comes with consequences. Likely a combination of the two, and only one of those is within her control. Medusa cannot deny that she is truly intrigued now, and she feels these people have brought great change.

2

The air is thin and cold, causing her pale pink skin to pebble as Aphrodite walks through the maze of catacombs beneath The Temple of the Owl, Athena's temple. Using the guise of a visit to her dear friend, she made the journey here as quickly as she was able.

They spent the day together laughing, dining, and enjoying each other's company. Aphrodite only slipped away once Athena retired for the evening.

While the diversion had been quite pleasurable, it had been impossible to keep her thoughts from wandering to her plans.

Weeks of poring over scrolls and texts had finally produced a promising lead.

Aphrodite pulls out the folded map she inconspicuously tucked into the folds of her dress and holds it close to one of the lit torches along the walls. The flames give off a slight green tint and she smiles at the first confirmation that the dusty old book she found was right.

The presence of the fabled everflames down here indicates the use of ancient magic, exactly what Aphrodite has been looking for.

She is not sure what she will find down here. The book had merely said that *a crucial key has been placed within the catacombs of the athene noctua. May the accompanying map guide those who seek it.*

There had also been warnings and declarations of the horrors any mortal would face in these tunnels, but Aphrodite is no mortal.

After almost an hour of twists and turns, she comes to a dead end, its only occupant, an old wooden door that pulses with magic.

Aphrodite reaches for the handle, hissing when it burns her hand.

A voice fills her head that is both male and female, both high and low. "Daughter of the theos, what do you seek here?"

Prepared to face obstacles such as this, Aphrodite recites the words from the book that will allow her access, "I come for knowledge and knowledge alone."

A wave of consciousness slams into her and courses through her body in an effort to detect her true intentions. She grits her teeth against it as she forces her will to be nothing other than what she stated, a bead of sweat running down her face with the effort.

The presence rushes out of her as quickly as it had entered, leaving her gasping from the exertion.

The sigh of the magic is palpable as the door creaks open, granting her entry to a tiny, dark chamber. Against the back wall is an altar with three exquisitely decorated bowls, three ceremonial daggers, and a book that looks older than time itself.

With a few quick steps, Aphrodite crosses the room and reaches for the vial that hangs from her neck by a delicate gold chain - its contents another fortuitous find from the old tome.

The potion inside of it makes her hesitate for a single

moment, assessing if the risk would be worth the knowledge she is not even sure she will gain.

Throughout her quest for power, Aphrodite has been watching over her shoulder, waiting for the Guard to be at her door, waiting for the Oracle to see her plans and pass them along to the king of gods. This potion, however, should prevent that.

Every action committed by a person, god or mortal, is tied to their eternal soul, making it extremely lucky that the book also contained the recipe for a potion. Made of the rarest plants found all across the realm, it puts the soul to sleep for a short period of time, and any actions during that window cease to exist. If not mixed properly though, paralysis will set in, leading to a very slow and painful death, even for a god.

Aphrodite's lips tingle as soon as they touch the top of the vial, and she braces herself for the bitter taste of the nightshade, valerian, and foxglove. The powerful odor has her fighting off a gag as the last of the contents empty into her mouth.

The sensation in her lips spread to her entire body, and for a moment she is fearful her measurements may have been erroneous, but she breathes a sigh of relief when it fades and she feels almost normal again - minus a hollowness in her chest that she assumes must be the absence of her soul's consciousness.

Satisfied that she can proceed, she glances at the table once more, looking at notes so she can follow the very specific instructions on how to open the book.

The bowl in the middle is first, its rose quartz color almost imperceptible in the low lighting of the dank room. She picks up the matching dagger, feeling the smooth mineral beneath her fingertips. Holding her left palm out, she slices it open until blood runs freely from it. She quickly holds her bleeding hand over the bowl, allowing a generous amount of her life force to fill it.

The second bowl and dagger are next and located to the left of the first set, the moonstone they are made from shining brightly. She repeats the prior steps, slicing open her right palm this time, barely sparing a thought for whatever story she will need to come up with to explain these away to the healer.

For the last offering, she collects the tools on the right. The final cut, a vertical slit between her breasts, stings as she holds the bowl beneath it.

Setting the obsidian bowl down, Aphrodite wipes her hands clean on her skirts. Dipping a finger into the different bowls, she uses her blood to write runes all over the front and back cover of the book.

As soon as she is done with the runes, the book flies open, appearing satisfied with her sacrifice.

The pages are old and brittle, but she flips through indelicately, and is almost in a rage when she sees nothing of importance. Academic sketches fill a majority of the pages, depicting many of the magical flora found in the realm, and some that have long since left their world.

Her eyes land on a blank page and she pauses for a moment before having the idea to mark the page with blood from each bowl.

Within moments, words appear before her, shining in a gold glittering script that emanates power.

Aphrodite scans the page, taking in the lines of cryptic verse, recognizing the vague nonsense of a prophecy almost immediately.

THE SERPENT SLUMBERS,
 where it ought not be.
 And is strongest yet,
 when it is three.

The Hearts of the Fates,
will unlock the way.
The mighty will fall,
ferrying the realm
to peace for all.

APHRODITE PINCHES the bridge of her nose in frustration, but is at least grateful to have something to go on. She kicks herself for not bringing any kind of writing utensil to jot down what she found. Trying to commit it to memory, she reads through it several more times.

As she turns to leave, Aphrodite gazes on the book once more. She cannot bring it with her and she doubts anyone else would find it and have use for this gibberish, but a lingering feeling in her gut says she should not leave it.

A self-satisfied smirk spreads across her lips as she grips the corner of the page and rips it straight out of the book, pleasantly surprised when the words remain visible.

It is almost as if Aphrodite can hear the book screaming as she folds up the stolen page, tucking it back into her dress with the map.

AFTER A BRIEF STOP at Aphrodite's island, she will return to the Temple of Olympus. As soon as she steps out of the healer's door, an Acolyte informs her there is a visitor in the dining room. The imposition is grating, but Aphrodite paints on a smile, ever the cordial hostess.

The table is already filled with foods that she did not ask for, glasses of wine already poured. Dozens of candles scattered about illuminate the room in a warm glow. At the end of the table, in the head seat she usually occupies, is her son Oedipus, his Heroes helmet casually sitting on the table. Was she the best mother? No, but surely Aphrodite taught him better manners than this?

"What are you doing home? I thought you were on a rotation to Apollo's Temple?" Aphrodite asks him, trying to keep her tone neutral. A mother is supposed to love her child, but something about him has always sent her instincts screaming. He has done nothing she can say is wrong, per se, but she cannot deny that she has caught his gaze lingering on her a little too long.

When he was growing up, he would try to peek into her dressing area when she was changing, or trying to spy on her with her lovers. It was always chalked it up to a natural, youthful curiosity, but the older he has gotten, the more she avoids him, as it seems to only be getting worse.

Never has Aphrodite been ashamed of having her body on display and it was only ever an issue with one of her children, so she is not to blame. Something is off about him.

Now, she wishes that her clothing concealed more. Aphrodite is dressed for the warm weather found on her island year round. The sticky humidity making less clothing the preference. What she wears consists of thin, sheer fabrics that hide little.

"Aren't you pleased to see me, Mother?" He asks, his face forming into a pout with puppy dog eyes that have a pang of guilt shooting through her. It *should* please her to see her child.

Aphrodite dismisses it with the wave of her hand, "Your presence simply caught me off guard, that's all."

Sitting down at the opposite end of the table, Aphrodite attempts to keep some distance between them. Oedipus gets up and walks over, sitting down by her. She almost misses the predatory look that crosses his eyes as he stares at her breasts through her dress.

With a hope of a distraction, she asks, "Darling, what have you been up to?"

Oedipus sits back in his chair, pausing before answering as her skin prickles under his gaze.

"Since when do you care?" He bites, all friendliness vanishing from his face.

Aphrodite shifts nervously in her chair, clasping her hands together. "I have always cared for my children. Don't pretend otherwise just to be hurtful," she replies.

He leans forward, and picks up the knife from its place setting, twirling it around. He wouldn't hurt her, would he?

With her focus on the knife, his right hand under the table moves until it is on her inner thigh, sliding up rapidly.

Aphrodite jerks away, standing up as her chair falls over behind her.

In a flash, Oedipus is in front of her, pushing her back until she is against the wall of the dining room, the knife pressed firmly against her throat.

"What are you doing?!" she shouts, but he pushes the knife harder, until it draws a trickle of blood, silencing her.

His left hand is suddenly on her collarbone and slowly making its way down to her breast, cupping it aggressively. His touch repulses her; her disgust apparent on her face.

"You fuck everything and everyone, seem to have no line you won't cross." He breathes, his voice void of any emotion. Aphrodite truly fears that he might harm her, but she refuses to mince her words to placate him.

"You disgust me. My own son? I would never touch one of my children that way and I don't know where I went so wrong with you that made you turn out this way."

The hand that is groping her drops and the rage returns in his eyes builds with the pressure of the knife. She can feel a steady stream of blood trickling down her chest now as it heaves with fear.

A shout comes from the hallway as several of her Acolytes runs in, screaming at him to stop.

He drops the knife to the ground, annoyed at the interruption, and storms out.

An Acolyte rushes over to help her as she falls to the floor, back against the wall, sobbing.

3

HESTIA

Sweat trickles down her forehead as Hestia makes her way to see the Oracle. She reaches up and wipes it on her sleeve before it can run down her glasses. The sun is unrelenting, and she has to squint against it as it glares down on the crowded streets of Olympus, and her normally cool alabaster skin is tinged pink. The capitol city of the Olympic Isles is bustling with activity, a mix of merchants, pilgrims, acolytes, all intersecting in a mixing pot of life.

With the upcoming Hero Trials, there are more visitors than usual. It never ceases to amaze her how far people will travel to watch the brutal bloodshed. The Heroes are supposed to be the protectors of the realm, chosen by Ares and Athena, but somewhere along the way, the recruitment process has become a source of entertainment and revenue.

Hestia's patience is tested as she moves at the sluggish speed of the masses, and she is getting increasingly more frustrated the longer it takes. Her shoulders bump from side to side between the surrounding people, and the heat of so many bodies pressed together is stifling. If she were Athena or Aphrodite, she would drop her hood, make the crowd part

20

before her, and tell them a god walks amongst the mortals. She sneers at the thought of moving through this world with that level of audacity, and pulls her hood lower, ensuring her anonymity remains.

At last, she is upon the white marble steps of her destination. The golden dome of the building glints in the sunlight, standing out amongst the white buildings that make up the sprawling city. She sends a quick prayer up to the Fates that this will be a fruitful endeavor.

The six months that her dear friend, Hera, has been missing have tested Hestia's sanity. Where has she been? How is there no one looking for her at all? Why is she the only one who seems to care? Nobody expects Zeus to be bothered, but Fates damnit. Someone has to be concerned with what happened to her.

Once inside, she drops her hood and the acolytes immediately drop into bows of recognition.

"No, please, none of that is necessary with me." She gestures for them to stand. "I was wondering if I could see the Oracle today?"

They glance amongst each other before one of them answers. A young girl, with beautiful dark hair in tight braids from her scalp to her waist, accentuated with golden beads and charms that matched the silken golden robes Oracle acolytes wear. "My goddess, you must make an appointment."

"I was wondering," Hestia continues. "If it would be possible for me to have a private audience with the Oracle, off of the official record."

They bristle, and the same girl continues to speak for the group.

"We do not wish to displease you, goddess, but this request is highly irregular."

"I understand, and do not wish to put you in a difficult position. However, the nature of my business with the Oracle is highly sensitive and quite urgent. I beseech you to reconsider."

They huddle together and whisper amongst themselves before the girl reluctantly nods her head and instructs Hestia to follow her.

The hallways are bright despite the lack of windows. The pale color of the marble reflects the glow of the sconces that are peppered along the wall, washing the entire space in a golden aura.

"Wait here, please, goddess," the girl tells Hestia, and then slips into one of the large double doors before her.

Much quicker than expected, the door opens again, and she gestures Hestia inside.

The golden hue is gone and replaced with a room as dark as the night sky on a new moon. The only illumination is a faint glow in what is presumably the center. Hestia drifts close to it, careful not to bump into anything in the blackness.

Somewhere on the other side of the light from her comes a voice. "Sit, goddess, I've been expecting you."

Now that she is closer, she can see the light is coming from a basin on a table. The swirling liquid inside glows and sparkles as if they scooped from the cosmos. In its light, she can barely make out a chair, and she takes a seat.

A hand reaches over and takes one of Hestia's, revealing bronze skin that has seen many decades of life. How much of that time was spent in this dark room of prophecy and divination? The Oracle dunks Hestia's hand into the basin with no warning and it feels like time is standing still. The hairs on her arms stand on end and the air feels both stagnant and electric.

"Think of that which you came here seeking. Perhaps the Fates will answer."

Hestia closes her eyes and pictures Hera, her warm smile, the laugh that lit up every banquet hall and gala. Her heart aches at the absence of her friend, and her anger bubbles to the surface as she replays the inaction of the Pantheon in the wake of Hera's disappearance.

"Hmm." The Oracle huffs in frustration and pulls Hestia's hand out of the basin.

"What's wrong?' Hestia asks, only slightly distracted by her hand being completely dry.

"The Fates cannot see an answer. Something is amiss. They were unaware Hera is no longer at Zeus's side. You must return to me. This is very alarming indeed, and the Fates and I will commune intensely as we try to find our missing goddess. They told me this, though, Knowledge Keeper. You will soon have an unlikely ally in your quest, so they strongly caution you to not be too quick to dismiss anything too hastily. Keep your eyes open, goddess, trouble is brewing."

As soon as the last word leaves the Oracle's mouth, every lamp and sconce lights up, revealing a near empty room. The table and single chair are still there. The basin is now clean, no longer filled with the glistening light of the universe. Hestia gets up from the table and leaves through the door she came. The young acolyte is waiting to see her out of the building.

THE HALLS of the Olympic Temple are much more tranquil than the chaos of the city itself. Besides the occasional Acolyte going about their duties, Hestia has barely seen anyone in the complex.

She makes her way past the open courtyards, their beautiful blooms signaling that Persephone must be on this side of the Mysts.

The long corridor of meeting rooms and planning spaces feels eerily silent until she hears voices coming out of one of them. Her instincts are tingling as she ducks into an alcove.

As the conversation gets closer, she listens intently.

"What makes you think Perseus can't handle her?" Hestia immediately recognizes the voice as Athena.

"I think you underestimate her, and overestimate him. I'm going after her myself. This has taken long enough." The gruff voice in response is that of Poseidon.

"He's one of my best warriors. We sent him with my shield, the sandals. We will kill the beast once and for all and be done with this. You've interfered with my plans enough with your lust and lack of self control. End. This. Now."

"I don't know who in Tartarus you think you're talking to, you shrew, but don't worry. I'm on the next ship. As you know, the tides are always in my favor."

Two sets of footsteps retreat in different directions as Hestia digests what she overheard. Poseidon is going after Medusa. Hestia pokes her head out of the alcove and heads straight for her library as soon as the coast is clear.

Her pace is brisk, the silk fabric of her skirts swishing against her generous thighs as her heart pounds with every step. The light from the sconces flickers along the walls and floors. Combined with the soft echoes of her footsteps, the shadows almost seem to take on a life of their own.

The Allegiance has to get this information. The risk of working with them is immense. If she were to be discovered, it would be straight to a god cage. Every time she has to transmit something to the rebel group, her body is held hostage by the barrage of nervous energy that never fails to present itself. The cost has never been enough to make her reconsider, however.

Hestia may not have the same reasons to be there as most of the members of the Allegiance, but she feels that her heart is equally committed. It has been decades, possibly even a century, since she has been close with anyone, but that does not mean her eyes have been closed. No, they have been very much open throughout the orchestrated famines, the secret executions, the trafficking.

Watching in horror as the power imbalance has grown alongside the arrogance of the Pantheon, she would look around and wonder why no one was saying anything against it. Is she truly the only one appalled by their actions? Surely not. But was Hestia to do? Be a lone vigilante? That is the fastest way to end up in a god cage... but they aren't supposed to know about those. Another lie the Pantheon has perpetuated to keep the citizens falling in line. If they believe the gods are truly invulnerable, they are much quicker to kneel.

Her frustration with the malicious cruelty of the gods has been growing, and Hestia is positive she would have done something stupid if not for an encounter that had to have been orchestrated by the Fates themselves. By all logic, she never should have discovered the Allegiance operation in the Temple of Olympus four years ago. The rebels had planned their mission immaculately, but somehow their paths still crossed, and they made the decision to trust each other.

So now, once a week, she uses a communication stone to relay anything important she overhears during her many meetings and duties. Hestia's lip curls as she remembers a conversation she overheard today between Aphrodite and Athena. They had been fawning over each other's cosmetics and clothes, the handiwork of the enslaved nymphs - which are supposed to be illegal. How they can so callously own a being and make them work for them is beyond her comprehension. She has to remind herself that her silence is much more helpful to the nymphs, and the Allegiance, than a hot-tempered outburst would be.

Usually, Athena would be off at her own temple, but this week there is a flurry of visiting gods here for the spectacle of the Trials.

As she reaches the final stretch to the library, Hestia runs back through the week's events and recalls if there is anything relevant she may need to add. The meetings she sat through this past week had been incessantly dull and yielded little useful information.

How anything ever truly gets accomplished here, Hestia will never know. In every meeting, she sits and listens. She listens to the information that is always being droned on and raises an eyebrow when someone inevitably interjects an argument. Watching as the gathering descends into bickering, internally rolling her eyes as they shout over one another - egos preventing them from not weighing in with their undoubtedly priceless opinions. Occasionally something useful will innocuously slip out but they are easy to miss if she loses focus. So, despite her attention trying to wane, she diligently listens and watches.

Locking the doors to the library behind her, she breathes in her space. This is her domain, her sanctum. With a flick of her wrist, the torches along the wall and candles in the chandeliers spark to life, illuminating the grand room that houses the most important tomes, scrolls, and artifacts in all the Olympic Isles. As the God of Knowledge, this is her temple.

Tasked by the Fates to be the Keeper of the Immortal Flame, it is her duty to make sure the spark of knowledge and enlightenment lives and thrives. Chuckling, she remembers the time a small child inquired why she was in charge of books if she was a flame god. Hestia crouched down to his level and explained that the flame is a metaphor for knowledge and learning, for living with our eyes open and seeing the world for what it truly is. As such a god, turning an ignorant eye to the current state of the world is something she would never have been able to do.

Sighing, she finally reaches her desk on the library's top floor and plops down into the velvety chair sitting behind it. She ducks under the desk and opens the compartment hidden in the floor, designed to only recognize Hestia's magical aura.

The board slides out of place, and she takes out the smooth blue stone. The marbling on it swirls around like a storm cloud trapped inside. Psyche's magic has always been beautiful. It is incredible to have an asset such as Psyche on their side. Hestia wishes she had known them all in time to have prevented the chain of events that led to Psyche's involvement, the heartbreak that led her to the Allegiance's doorstep.

Hestia shakes away the thoughts. Guilt and sadness for past events help no one. Shutting her eyes, she closes her hand around the stone and envisions the message she wants to send and its recipient, Alec. Her mood lightens slightly when she pictures the handsome man who will receive this. It sours again when she remembers he might be in Poseidon's path of rage. She has done everything she can. The rest is in the hands of the Fates.

When she is alone like this, she allows herself the indulgent moments to recall the dark gray eyes that matched the salt and pepper color of his hair and beard. She remembers the warm smile on the kind face of the man who took a chance on her and saw in her someone who would fight with them and for them. Maybe she can tell him that someday once they bring this world crashing down around them… if they live to see the other side.

4

MEDUSA

edusa brushes the sand from the mythical shield of Athena, running her fingers over the metal owl, as its bronze eyes stare at her, judging her. She agreed to hear what these people have to say, but under the condition that it would be back in her home. Everything about this day has been off and the need to be in a familiar space was palpable.

Psyche and Alec followed her back up the hill to her sanctum while Yiorgos stayed behind to keep watch. Or maybe it is to avoid her. Guilt tries to continue its reign of terror in her mind, but she shuts it down.

She does not know any of these people. What was she supposed to have done?

Reaching up, Medusa touches the hood, amazed at their unwavering confidence that it will not fail. The silence of her serpents still unnerves her.

"My gods."

Alec's voice jerks her out of her daze and back to the task at hand.

He is staring into the eyes of one of the statues, and Medusa hangs her head in shame. It is the one that haunts her the most -

he was so young. She looks around her cavern and tries to imagine it in the eyes of Psyche and Alec. What do they see when they look at the gallery of frozen faces, forever fated to hang in her halls as permanent portraits? Do they see the small army's worth of hatred that Medusa has had to wade through to survive? Or do they see the victims of a monster?

Medusa's strength falters as she feels the pressure of their judgment on her soul. Shame and helplessness flood through her. She never wanted this to be her life. To be hunted and forced to slice away at her soul, little by little, with every kill. And now to be judged by it as well.

Alec reaches out and touches the smooth stone cheekbone of the statue. "He was just a boy."

"I know, I-"

"The gods sent a child to come after you? What in the name of the titans were they thinking?" He rubs the back of his neck and grits his teeth.

Psyche holds up a hand to silence him. "We need to get back to why we are here. They can do nothing for him now. The only path in front of us that will help boys like him in the future is to continue the mission." She turns to Medusa. "I'm sorry if I was blunt on the deck. I knew if I hadn't been you might not listen to us and I couldn't take that chance. You are more important than you could possibly know."

Heat floods Medusa's cheeks. How can she be important? All she offers is death and ugliness.

"We have left the Pantheon unchecked for far too long. They have too much power and think that anything that displeases them should be removed from existence. Families have been torn apart, and that's not even touching the atrocity that is the Acolytes," Alec's gravelly voice accentuates the rage in his words. She does not know what this man has lost, but she has a feeling it was great indeed.

Unsure how to respond, Medusa returns her focus to the

shield. As expected, it is soul locked, keeping anyone from wielding it who does not have permission. She grunts under the weight of it as she rolls it against one of the cavern walls.

Pulling Medusa's attention back to her, Psyche asks, "What do you know of your parents and how you came to be chosen to be an Acolyte?"

Confused by the drastic change in topic, she sets the shield aside. It takes her a moment to recall what she had been told by the Masters, by Nikolas, by the Council. They said Medusa was to be given an explanation one time and then she was never to speak of her parents again. She was so young and fortunately, Nikolas has taken pity on her and allowed her to talk about her family in quiet whispers when they were away from prying ears.

"My mother was a mortal woman who had caught the eye of a rakish god. He was not cruel, but he was also not kind. My mother loved me dearly, and that she was so honored when Athena herself chose me to be one of her Acolytes." She does not feel the need to state her feelings about her forced fate. There is no reason to share any more than necessary until the visitors reveal their true motive. Medusa is not expecting Alec and Psyche to exchange surprised but worried glances. Is her history not even her own? Is it yet another part of her that the Council has carefully crafted?

"This will be hard to hear, but there is so much more to your story." Psyche says with a forlorn gleam in her eye. Despite Medusa's unease at the world shifting information she is sure to receive, something about Psyche's expression is exhilarating.

"I can't share much with you yet, but I will reveal what I can. It was your mother who was the god. Your father was a mortal, and he loved her so very much. Your mother was part of the Pantheon, and it angered them greatly when she fell in love with your father. After she discovered a plot to have him assassinated simply for being an inconvenience to them, she vowed to never let the Pantheon harm him, and they fled that night. They somehow eluded the trackers sent to follow them, but only for so long. By the time they had caught up to your parents, you were already born.

"The trackers captured your parents and brought them and you back to The Temple of Olympus. They quietly executed your parents, overseen by the god your mother considered her closest friend, Athena. Before your parents died, Athena told them she was choosing their daughter to be an Acolyte for her temple and she would grow up confined to the very life they had sought to escape."

Medusa's chest tightens, and she finds it hard to breathe. "How can this be true? They extensively instructed me on the history of Olympus, the Pantheon, and there was no mention of this." Her brain struggles to process this information. Has her entire life been designed to exact revenge on her mother? Who was a god? It is Alec who responds this time, his voice taking on a tone that is both dark and soft.

"Your mother's betrayal angered the petty gods, especially Athena, and they ordered all records of your mother to be eradicated from the history books. They repainted murals, tore down statues, and cast an elaborate glamor, causing her to fade from people's minds. All because your mother and my brother had the nerve to fall in love."

Medusa's jaw drops. "You mean you're my uncle? My family?"

She has always been alone, and the hope that blooms in her heart at the prospect of having family has her absolutely terrified. Every Acolyte spends almost their entire Initiate period wistfully daydreaming of the family they might have hailed from. In the dining hall they would boast amongst themselves, their tales getting grander and grander as they claimed to have come from the families of Guards, Heroes, and even the gods themselves. She had never taken part in those fantasies, instead clinging to the small piece of knowledge that someone had loved her.

"I am. I was one of the few people who knew where they were hiding. I helped them get supplies and tried to keep an eye out for the trackers." He looks down and his voice gets very low as he says, "The trackers knew to watch me. They figured out where you were and waited for me to leave on a supply run that day. I didn't know you were gone until I returned the next day. I don't know how the glamour didn't take. Maybe my grief had been too strong, but I remember them fiercely."

His obvious guilt weighs heavily on him. Medusa is not sure what to think, which way is up, but there is one thing her gut tells her is certain. She reaches across the table, feeling the rough wood brush against her arm, and places her hand over his.

"Uncle..." Medusa says tentatively. "You can't blame yourself. I don't know entirely what happened that day, but it sounds like you were brave enough to defy the Pantheon to help them. That tells me you loved them very much, and that is what matters." It surprises her to see a slight glint in his eyes from tears that are peeking through but will never fall.

"Thank you," he responds with a breath that sounds like relief.

"I'm glad to begin to know some of the truth about my life, and I know there is so much more that I don't know yet, but my most pressing question brings us to the present. Why have you come to find me now? Why am I so important?"

"We are part of a group that has been working in the background to save as many people as we can. People who have been crushed beneath the boot of the unforgiving tyrants who run our world. All will be revealed in time. I know we must seem so cryptic, but this level of secrecy is the only thing that has kept us out of the Pantheon's hands."

Medusa understands being hesitant to trust. She doubts her guard will ever be fully down again and kicks herself for ever dropping it to begin with.

"Come with us," Psyche says. "Join us and help us make a difference."

Medusa pauses, looking around her home of the last eight years. She sees nothing that brings her any comfort or joy. Only faces haunting her every waking moment. This invitation could be a setup. A trap. Maybe the Pantheon is getting more clever with their approach.

Her gaze at last lands on the young boy once more. So young. Forever frozen. Robbed of decades' worth of living and for what? This may be impulsive, but she does not care. She has nothing to lose at this point.

"How soon do we leave?"

THEY ARE ALMOST BACK to the ship, Medusa and Alec rolling the shield down the hill, while Psyche carries Hermes's sandals and the small bag with Medusa's meager possessions, when they hear Yiorgos calling for them. He is waving his arms frantically and pointing to the horizon. A ship.

"We've got company. We need to move!"

They scramble aboard, tucking the precious artifacts down in the cabin.

The sky is a breathtaking mix of vivid sunset colors giving way to the soft pastels and deep blues of night. The sun sinking on one horizon, in a burst of pinks and oranges, while the moon rises on the opposite one, the soft lavender haze fading into the twinkling navy sky.

Medusa scans in all directions, trying to spot any more threats but cannot see anything else. She turns and sees Yiorgos handing Alec a scope that he focuses toward the sunset. She rushes over to him to glean any clue what they face. He sees the panicked look in her eyes and hands her the scope, pointing her in the direction he had been viewing.

She squints tightly against the glare of the sun. There, off in the distance, a ship. Not a large vessel, but still bigger than the small boat the four of them currently occupy. They are still too far off to assess how many people are on board, but based on the size alone, it is too large to be the usual party of one, two Heroes at most usually sent to dispatch her. Why is this time different? And why is another group here so soon? She knew that was always a possibility, but their increased attention on her indicates that at last her whereabouts have finally made it back to the Pantheon. She gulps in dread and tries remaining focused on getting through whatever is headed their way.

Alec raises the anchor. Yiorgos preps the solitary sail as they make haste to depart. A gust of wind fills the sail and they are in motion faster than she would have thought possible. She hurries over to the back railing, desperate to see a gap opening up between them. The bright, golden light shining from the setting sun makes it hard to judge the distance between the vessels and she holds her breath until she knows if they are clear or not.

After a few minutes, the ship gains on them, and she knows they cannot slip away. Once again, she will have to make choices that never stop weighing on her soul. She may tell herself that she holds no guilt over having to kill to protect herself, and that is true to an extent. However, guilt or no, she can feel the mark it leaves every time. Marks that will follow her around forever escape from them too unrealistic to even be a dream.

She uses what little time she has left before the ship overtakes them and assesses her defenses. Removing her hood would endanger her companions. If they have fallen though and it is down to her, at least she has that. Maybe these cursed serpents will be her salvation for once.

In this moment, as in so many others, she is grateful for the weapons training she had growing up. Medusa instinctually reaches for her sword on her right hip, the steely grip a familiar comfort in her left hand, the weight of it making the muscles in her arms flex beneath it. While they do not serve as the security forces at the Temples, and have a much more academic purpose, Acolytes have to be ready to drop their books in defense of their gods should the need arise.

Alec and Yiorgos are still frantically trying to increase speed - to no avail. They shout back and forth to each other, but Medusa cannot hear them over the wind and thrashing water. She looks around the deck for Psyche, but does not see her anywhere. Before Medusa can question where she went too closely, the other boat gets close enough for her to see its deck.

Three men are on the deck of the two-sail ship, but she still has to squint to make out their features.

"Fates be damned!" A wall of sea mist hits Medusa's face, its saltiness stinging her eyes. She wipes at them with the hem of her tunic, blinking away the blurriness until it clears.

They are closer now and her blood turns to ice in her veins - Castor and Polydeuces. Like Perseus was, the Twins are part of an elite battalion of the Heroes. Overseen by Poseidon, their deep blue cloaks of the Oceanic Legion fluttering on the sea breeze. The Twins have a reputation for being inseparable and immeasurably cruel. They aren't as terrifying as who undoubtedly accompanies them. *HIM.*

She does not even bother to look at the third man, as she already suspects who is heading this mission. The world spins.

Breathe. This shall not break me.

Heat flushes her neck and face as she grips her sword tighter, until it hurts, using the only thing that can sometimes pull her out of a spiral - pain. The bite of the cold metal does nothing to bring her back to solid ground, however. Heart pounding and face numb, she continues to descend into a full anxiety attack as Poseidon steps out onto the deck.

5

ICARUS

There are so many people here. The thought thrills and slightly intimidates Icarus as she stands on the ship's railing that brought her to the city of Olympus. There has to be at least twice as many people milling about here than when she got onto the ship at her home port of Thessaly. The opportunities before her seem endless as she takes in the pulse of the busy metropolis.

The early evening air is brisk, as the sea breeze rolls into the harbor, causing her to debate if it is worth the hassle of digging her shawl out of her bag.

After disembarking and making it a few steps into the dense crowd, she appreciates her decision not to bother. Body heat envelops her, and her pulse quickens as she steps into the busy streets. Following signs for the nearest inn, she takes in the hum of activity - musicians playing for coins, the occasional person dancing along, merchants hawking their wares. The unfamiliar smells hit her as she progresses. Spices, then perfumes, and so many types of food.

It would shock her poor mother to see her baby girl wandering through all of this alone.

A stall full of glittering trinkets catches her eye. *Do not stop.* Still needing to get settled into the inn, now is not the time to dawdle.

As Icarus walks past, she realizes it is her mother's voice in her head keeping her from perusing. She is almost twenty-five years old, and tomorrow she competes in the Trials to become a Hero. It is time to let herself live a little.

Rows of glitzy knickknacks greet her when she approaches the stall - little hippocampi encrusted with faux emeralds, chimeras covered in multicolored glass, things she would have adored as a child but do not speak to her now. She runs her fingers over a pegasus carved out of moonstone. Perhaps the white horse can be a good luck token, to help her manifest a spot in the Pegasus Legion? But where would Icarus even put it? Moving on, she browses through the sparkling menagerie. Icarus may be treating herself, but reminds herself not to be too carefree with the meager amount of money in her possession.

Toward the back of the stall, hanging by a delicate thread chain, is a small, fiery gem that feels like it is pulling Icarus. In a trance, she walks over to it and gently picks it up. The reds and oranges that cover the many facets of the stone are semi-transparent, as if they are merely windows. Inside, its core is flickering, but not from the light of the torches on the street, from within.

The woman working the stall approaches to assist her. She takes the gem from Icarus and gently puts the chain over her head. The length of the necklace puts the gem directly over her heart, casting rays of light across her golden skin. It must be the heat from the crowds, or her adrenaline, but Icarus would swear that it heated up.

"How much for this?" Icarus asks, knowing it will be too expensive. Already, the idea of being parted from it has her slightly panicked. This cannot be normal. It has to be because this is her first time leaving home. Just the adrenaline from so many new things all at once.

"The Fates smile upon you tonight. It is a gift."

"Really? But why?"

"This item has been in my family for generations. Kept on display, never looked at twice by anyone who browsed. We always thought it was just an old legend, but my grandmother told us a day would come when the stone would call to someone. She said we would know when that time came, and apparently she was right."

Icarus is speechless. She holds the stone again in her palm.

"Are you sure?"

"I think my Yaya would return from her rest just to smack me if I didn't give this to you." She closes Icarus's hand around the stone and covers it with her own, staring into her eyes. "Go now, Sunshine. Destiny awaits. Be fearless."

A few blocks away, the shock of what just happened wears off. Icarus continues to replay the cryptic conversation and, with every step, doubt creeps in.

Is Icarus really this gullible? Fresh off the ship from the farmlands and immediately falls for some higher destiny nonsense. But how did she know her nickname from her mother?

Her cheeks flush as she looks at the gem again. This thing is probably just cheap glass. The woman likely has an entire crate of these and gets her kicks by tricking naïve country people into thinking they are special. But, it cost nothing. If she were being targeted for being gullible, surely the goal would have been to at least lighten her purse a little. It makes little sense.

Still mulling this over, not really paying attention to where she is going, Icarus slams into a man's back.

He turns around to seek out the source of the collision and catches a jaw to the fist.

Icarus narrows her eyes, as her internal sense of justice peeks its head out.

Because of her distraction, she finds three men squared off against the man who was just struck. The middle closest one flexes his fingers after the punch.

Don't get involved. She doesn't even know why they are attacking this man. He could have done something horrific. *Leave it alone.*

The man rubs his jaw, and Icarus can already see a red mark forming along his strong jawline. One of his angular eyes is already swollen closed and his fawn colored skin is discoloring from bruises. She imagines, when not recently punched in the face, multiple times, that women attracted to men would swoon over him.

A glance at his opponents shows more than one bruise blooming and at least one bloody nose. He has been putting up a fight, at least. Two of the attacking men close in on the man she bumped into, as the third man slips over to the side unnoticed.

Stay out of it.

Still unseen, the third man is circling behind the man they are attacking, while his focus is on the other two.

Stay out of it.

He grabs a board and prepares to strike the man in the back of the head, and Icarus cannot take it anymore.

Her long legs have her over to him in seconds, and she spins around to gain momentum before kicking the man in the face. He falls backward into some empty mead barrels. Ah, so they are right outside of a tavern.

The man she assisted looks at her confused, as do the two attacking men.

She shrugs and stands next to the man, putting her fists in front of her face to welcome the next challenger.

Either they do not want to fight a woman, or the playing field being even takes the fun out of for them, but the men just roll their eyes, collect their friend, and leave.

She turns to the man and extends her hand, and they clasp forearms in greeting.

"Name's Lysander. I would have been fine, but thanks, nonetheless."

"Ha. Yeah, you definitely had things under control. But you're welcome. I'm Icarus. What did you do, sleep with one of their sisters?"

Lysander laughs loudly at that. "More like one of their sister's husbands."

"Oh." Icarus says sheepishly. "I was joking. I wasn't trying to judge you."

He waves her off. "Look, the night is young and my face requires mead. Let's grab a drink and see what fun the city has in store for us tonight!"

This is it. The kind of thing Icarus has always dreamed of doing once she was out of the house and on her own. Experiencing life and finding adventures.

She chews on the idea for a minute before answering. "I am entering the Trials tomorrow. I really should go get settled and try to rest up."

"Oh, no way! Me too. The Trials, that is, I have zero desire to go rest. If I don't go blow off some steam, tomorrow I'll be too wired and off my game."

That's a good point. What would Hector say about that? She runs through all the lessons she received from the retired Hero.

When she was ten, he moved to their village, much to Icarus's delight - and her parents' dismay as soon as they saw her eyes go wide at his stories of adventure.

At twelve years old, she finally worked up the nerve to ask him to train her. He simply said, "a lady always needs to have the ability to defend herself" and she began training with him every other day.

Lysander raises his eyebrows, and nudges her with his elbow questioningly.

Her smile beams wide. Hector's advice is for tomorrow. Tonight, she gets to be alive for the first time.

6

MEDUSA

He's here. He's HERE.

Medusa drops to her knees on the deck as she is confronted with the god who plagues her dreams, twisting them to into nightmares. The conductor of the vicious cycle that keeps her trapped in the trauma that altered the very fabric of her being, literally, down to the genetic level.

Even under the magic of the hood, she can feel her snakes getting agitated.

This isn't merely another Hero she has to face. This is a god that she only escaped previously because she had the element of surprise. Her brain screams at her to keep searching for a solution, but her resolve crumbles, knowing it's hopeless. For someone so strong, and skilled with a blade, she should be shocked at how quickly the fight leaves her entirely when confronted by him.

She sits and leans her back against a supply crate as the corners of her vision pepper with stars that are only magnified every time she looks back in his direction by the final remnants of the setting sun glistening off of his polished armor.

As the ship at last pulls up beside them, she has no choice but to meet his stony stare. One look at her, resigned and dejected, and his face is alight with a cruel glee. She assumes he is here to finish the job of killing her himself, but the look in his eyes makes her fear he won't be quick about it. She shudders at the thought of being at his mercy and vows it will never come to that, no matter the cost.

This shall not break me.

"Well," Poseidon begins with a smirk. The fading sun casts his high mahogany skin into shadow. "It seems we meet again, my dear."

He says it like it's a casual occurrence, stumbling upon each other at the market, or at a Temple. It can almost be mistaken for genuine politeness, but she knows better. She knows how quickly that charming smile can turn cold.

Medusa pushes down all the thoughts of his iron grip on her upper arm when he would leer at her, tries to quiet the voice replaying in her head that lowly whispered about how the only thing keeping his hands from being extremely adventurous was because she "belonged to Athena." She had always mentally bristled at the thought of 'belonging' to anyone but if it kept his touch from wandering she would not argue, instead choosing silent compliance throughout every aggressive come on, threat, promise, whatever he wanted to call it that day.

"Now, we could have avoided all of this mess," he says, gesturing around. "If you, and Athena, had merely been more… shall we say… agreeable?"

Medusa's eyes widen, then narrow. She is having trouble focusing on what he is saying. Her breathing refuses to slow, and she is getting lightheaded, her panic dangerously close to sheer terror. "What does Athena have to do with all this?"

Poseidon's eyes widen with gleeful surprise that makes Medusa hesitate if she wants to know the answer. "I had been in negotiations with Athena to take you into my possession at my temple. She was hesitant to consider it at first, but we were in the process of final negotiations. Negotiations I had just arrived for when I saw you in the garden. You looked so lovely, Medusa. I didn't think there was any reason to wait to claim something that would soon be mine. Surely you can't blame me for being drawn to you?"

The weight of what he told her is crushing down on her. She has many questions, but lands on the only one she can fully form. "Why then, would you do this to me?" She gestures to her head, indicating the serpents laying in wait under the black hood. "Why would you make it so no one could look upon me if you wanted me to serve your temple?"

His answer is his ultimate violation. Shattering the fragile grasp remaining on her anxiety, he says, "Oh my dear, the snakes? I think they look lovely. You'll have to explain how your companions are safe around you. I'm assuming the hood, but we can cover that on the voyage to the Sea Temple. You were so rude to me in the garden. My feelings would have been very hurt if I had any." She hears the Twins chuckle at that in the background. He delivers the final blow with a self assured grin. "I told you no one else could look upon you without turning to stone. You must have assumed I meant no one other than your-self. No, lovely girl, I meant no one other than *I* would be able to look upon you."

He continues talking, but Medusa hears none of it. She is finally succumbing to her panic as he raises his trident into the air. The water around the boat swirls, the beginnings of a whirlpool forming. Her vision blurs and regains focus, and she is unsure how much is because of the setting sun, and how much is because of her darkening peripherals. Turning her head to the side, she sees Psyche stepping onto the deck. She opens her mouth to warn her, but no sound comes out. Psyche's beau-tiful dark eyes lock onto hers. As they stare at each other, the boat sways from the turbulence building around them. The wind gusts, whipping the ebony strands of Psyche's hair around her face. She glows with a light that resembles the silver of the moon that crests on the horizon.

Psyche says to her, "Close your eyes, Lyra."

Medusa listens but slowly. As the last sliver of light is visible, Medusa sees a blinding beam from where Psyche was standing and the entire world goes dark.

MEDUSA'S HEART is pounding as she races through the garden. Despite needing her entire focus to be on escaping, her thoughts cloud and her stomach churns as she remembers his hands on her. His hot breath on her neck while he whispered something as his eyes glowed had finally snapped her out of her terrified compliance. Even a god's nose can be broken.

She cannot deny that the feel of his cartilage meeting the heel of her hand had been satisfying, but Medusa is also too aware that her impulsivity started the countdown to her death. She had taken off running before she could see the rage in his eyes, or enjoy the blood running down his face.

She rounds a corner sharply, the vines from the topiaries smacking her face. The loose gravel makes her footing less stable than she would like, the flimsy sandals required of her to wear as an Acolyte slipping as she struggles for traction.

A SLAP of sea water up her nose jars Medusa awake. The salt stings her nostrils and her head is pounding as she realizes she is clinging to a large piece of wood, part of a ship, and afloat in the sea.

Everything comes rushing back into Medusa's mind- Poseidon. The blinding light. *Psyche.*

Medusa whips her head around, and there's barely enough light left in the sky to see scattered debris everywhere. *No.* Did anyone else make it?

She reaches up and discovers the hood is still perfectly in place. There is no time to be mystified by the magic as voices carry to her from her right and she rubs her burning eyes, trying to get a better look. *There.* She can just make out a couple of people on a larger piece of debris.

She reluctantly lets go of the board she is using to stay afloat and swims in their direction. Her right arm has a long gash along her bicep, and she winces through the pain of the salt water and exertion.

Halfway to her destination, a groaning sound comes from a cluster of boards to her left.

The piece at the top of the pile is heavy and she grunts, using as much strength as she can muster to get it to fall to the side.

She stares at the unconscious form before her, mouth agape, blinking. A *Hero?*

Clinging to debris, with a sizable wound above his temple, is a Hero of Olympus. His eyes are closed and his mouth is clenched in pain. His tawny skin is clammy and ashen.

What to do? The moral dilemma looms over her head like a storm sent by Poseidon. This man was here to help that monster take her, keep her, *control* her.

He is also unconscious, helpless. Has she become so callous that she would leave a defenseless person to die? Even with the hood on, she still stares death in the face, forced to be the grim reaper against her will. But this time... this time she has a choice. Can she, for the first time in eight years, have a conflict not end in death? The thought is so sweet, so lovely. But is it a reality?

Fates damnit. Maybe she can put down that scythe this once? If she can do it this time, maybe she can in the future too.

Despite her pain, despite the wreckage, and her enemy before her, for the first time in a long time, hope truly blossoms before her with the genuine possibility that she may yet have days filled with life and joy, not frozen death and horror.

She loops one of his arms around her shoulders and swims the rest of the way. With his added weight, she really has to put her legs to work. She sets her sights on Yiorgos and Alec at her destination, trying not to focus too hard on the still form lying beside them.

Keep moving.

This shall not break me.

"Lyra!"

She hears Alec's voice when he spots her headed his way, but she stays focused on getting there. The weight of this man is so much to bear. She should have removed some of his armor, but too late for that now.

When she is finally within reach, her two companions pull the man up from her by his chest plate, freeing her of his mass. They drop him unceremoniously and focus on helping Medusa out of the water.

"What happened?" Medusa asks, sputtering and coughing up seawater. "Is she alright?"

"Psyche's fine." Alec answers. "She's resting after going nova. It saved our hides with Poseidon, but it really takes a toll on her."

"So, what do we do now?" She asks.

"The Leviathan is coming to pick us up. Should be here soon, and then we can discuss the next steps when Psyche wakes up."

"And what do we do about him?" She gestures to the man.

"Eh, I say we keep an eye on him. If he stays out cold, Captain Nicodemus will have him brought on board, given medical treatment, and then assessed."

Medusa raises an eyebrow at the casual treatment of someone who sought her death.

"Will you keep him in a cell at least? He's the enemy!"

"Not my call, kiddo." He puts his hand on her shoulder and she huffs, but decides it is not worth the argument. Plus, if she has to, she has already proven that she can handle a lone hero on her own.

A light appears on the horizon. A ship.

She closes her eyes and silently pleads to the Fates that this is the Leviathan and not Poseidon.

Did they hear her? As the ship draws nearer, she has to wonder.

When the vessel is finally in full view, she heaves a sigh of relief, and thanks the cosmos… just in case.

When a rope ladder down to them, Medusa steps back and allows Alec and Yiorgos to help get Psyche and the Hero up. Once everyone else has cleared the railing, she makes her ascent.

The ship is large, its deck a flurry of activity as people rush about manning their stations. Once she has both feet down soundly, she straightens her shoulders and faces what she knows will come.

As expected, mouths drop open, and a few gasps make it to ears. She even spots one man, out of the corner of her eye, backing down the stairs he had just come up, careful to get out of her line of sight.

So this is how it is going to be. Everywhere she goes. Stares. Shock. Horror. Was this worth leaving her island?

Medusa's gaze drops, and she hangs her head. Does she not she have every right to be amongst people now that she has this hood? Her condition is not one of her own making, but can she blame people for assuming she is a horrific beast? A monster? It does not matter who she was before, how kind she was, or how large her heart was. Poseidon ripped that from her in the same breath that he stole her beauty.

A man walks up to her, a smile from ear to ear and, somehow, not a hint or whiff of judgement or condescension.

"Hi there! You must be Medusa. My name is Deonn. I'm going to take you to get settled into your cabin."

She opens her mouth to respond, but he continues talking non-stop and she smiles to herself. She will happily listen to his chatter if he treats her like an actual person, even if she doesn't deserve it.

"Yeah, the cap'n has 'em all riled up, like you're a ghost story or something. All I know, there's no way Psyche would have told us to come get you if you were evil."

She follows the sound of his conversation across the deck and over to a set of stairs.

Before they can descend, a tall man with bronze skin and black hair approaches them. He is dressed in a thick linen overcoat over his tunic, with rings on his fingers glistening as the precious gems catch the moonlight. So this must be Captain Nicodemus.

"Captain, I presume. Thank you for your swift rescue. We are so grateful to you and your crew." She almost extends out her hand but decides against it. There is no reason to expose herself to his recoil when his hand touches her touch scales. She can see him yanking his hand back, sneering in disgust.

He stares at her for a moment before speaking. Their eyes meet and there's a hatred there, a loathing, that she cannot place. She is certain she has never met this man.

He abruptly turns and walks away.

She looks to Deonn for any explanation, but he shrugs, and they continue their walk to her cabin, as she cranes her head looking into every room they pass with an open door. Maybe one of these will be Psyche's?

He turns into a room at the end of the narrow corridor, and she follows him into the tight space.

"I know it's not much, but there's a bed and a table for you. Someone will bring you some fresh clothes. I doubt much made it out of the wreckage."

"Thank you. This is more than enough. I haven't slept in a proper bed in eight years. It's perfect."

His smile falters momentarily, and she sees the sadness in his eyes. For her, and what she has been through. More pity for the monster.

"Get some rest if you can. Alec will be by as soon as possible."

A jovial voice interrupts from the hallway.

"Alec will be here now. Thanks, Deonn, for getting her down here while I talked with the captain."

Deonn pats Alec's shoulder, his broad smile returning. "Anytime, my friend. I'll leave you to get settled."

He walks out the door, and she finds herself alone with the only family member she has ever met.

"What was done with the Hero? Is he secure?" she asks Alec.

"Two guards are outside his door, but trust me, he's in no condition to be of any concern. He'll be lucky to survive if Psyche doesn't wake up soon. The healers on the ship have done all they can for the moment."

She nods, but cannot help feeling uneasy.

A thought lingers on the edge of her mind, and she debates whether she wants to ask him. She agreed to have a little trust in them until they can answer her questions more fully, but this one is nagging and she decides she cannot settle her thoughts until she has at least asked it.

"If you knew I was in Athena's Temple this whole time, why

did you not seek me out? Why did you leave me alone?" She asks, trying to keep her voice even, but it cracks along with her heart at that last word. She hopes he has an explanation ready, something to explain it all away, refusing to think he abandoned her.

His head hangs in shame and she's worried that his response will cleave her heart in two, but he says quietly, "I can't give you the entire answer to that yet."

He pauses as if he is pondering his next words.

"I didn't know what your new name was. All I knew was which temple you would be initiated into. I tried a few times throughout the years to sneak in and retrieve you, but the Guards nearly caught me every time. I wish I could tell you more, but that's really all I can say right now."

She nods her head in acceptance and is desperate to know more, but is grateful for even this bit of information. Her uncle had come for her, more than once. Someone had cared about her. Her heart warms with that knowledge, even as her inner child grieves with regret over the loneliness she had felt without that knowledge.

AN HOUR LATER, after drinking enough water to drown even a naiad, and idle chat with Alec, he asks Medusa if she wants to poke her head in on Psyche and see how she is faring. Butterflies fill her stomach at the thought, but she nods yes with as much nonchalance as she can muster. The last thing this situation needs is her fawning over a goddess just because she has been lonely.

He extends his elbow to her, and she swings her legs over the side of the bed and loops her arm through his. Medusa closes her eyes and breathes in contact with another person who is not tethered to death and violence. It has been so long that now that she faces it again, it is overwhelming. She did not realize how starved she was for contact or how unsettling it would feel.

Her eyes well with tears and Alec opens his mouth to say something, but Medusa puts a hand up to stop him before he can pity her or, worse… comfort her. As much as she loves the concept of someone holding her while she cries, it has been so long that even this small touch is too much.

She removes her arm from his and explains, "No, please. If we talk about it now, my wall will come crashing down, and I desperately need to keep it up right now. This is going to take time for me, and I'm going to be a mess along the way. I'll do my best to keep it from spilling out."

"I understand, Lyra. Allow me to say one thing, and then that'll be the last you hear from me on the matter until you're ready." He pauses, waiting for permission to go ahead, which she gives with a nod. "I will not pretend I know what your journey has been like. I can only imagine it's going to be stuff that it will take you a lifetime to process. When you're ready, though, that processing *can* spill over and we will be here waiting to help you through it. There's no reason for you to isolate your feelings. They aren't an inconvenience or imposition, nor are they anything to punish yourself over. We will do this together." He adds again for emphasis, "Together."

All she can do is nod and blink back the tears that are severely threatening to fall now. She closes her eyes tight, takes a few deep breaths and then tucks the pain away to deal with later. Her ability to compartmentalize at this point is almost as sharp of a defensive weapon as her serpentine locks.

7

HESTIA

Why could the Oracle not see anything about what happened to Hera? There has to be heavy duty power at play here. Her anxiety spikes at how far the ramifications of something like this could echo throughout their world. Who is involved? Is she to assume that every god in the Pantheon who is turning a blind eye to Hera's disappearance is complicit in her absence?

She paces in her library, reviewing what little information she has about her missing friend. Her eyelids droop from the late hour, but she still can't help but be restless. She feels like she is losing her mind. If any of the other gods went missing, would the rest of them still act as if it is business as usual? Zeus would likely cleave the world apart with lightning looking for Ares or Poseidon. Would he do the same for Hestia? Demeter? Probably only Aphrodite, and that would depend on his libido at the time.

The Oracle told her to keep the door open for an unlikely ally, but how is Hestia supposed to trust anyone at all? Between needing to hide her search from watching eyes and being an informant for the resistance, there were plenty of traitorous acts for them to uncover. Are they truly traitorous acts, though? If she does them for the sake of the morality of the realm, does that cancel out the betrayal and espionage? That will be for the Fates to determine.

Hestia thumbs through the pages of Hera's journal. She has been over it so many times already. It is a miracle she managed to slip into Hera's quarters unseen long enough to find it. Her eyes scan the pages as they say the same thing they always say. It only goes back a few months before she went missing and tells the story of a caged bird. One who knows that she is unwanted, but Zeus's selfishness cannot allow her to be let go. Hera and Zeus would not have been the first gods to decide that eternity married is a long time to commit. Perhaps she ran away. Saw a window and slipped out to go live amongst the dryads, or in a cabin on a seaside cliff. Hestia's gut still screams that her friend needs her.

She drops into the chair at her desk and pulls off her glasses, massaging her temples to work out the headache she can feel forming.

Her mind wanders to the Allegiance, and as it always does, Alec. Hestia's heart catches in her throat as she thinks about him and the danger he faces every day for standing up to the Pantheon. She wonders if there is any news from him yet, but she tries to not be constantly checking for updates. The more time she spends opening and closing her hiding spot, the more likely she will get caught. Hestia cannot afford that right now.

Medusa is such a curiosity. Hestia has heard all the rumors throughout the years about their altercation, but has always been hesitant to believe Poseidon's official story. She always felt it was very convenient that only one side of things was presented and wondered what Medusa would say about his claims. She had only met the woman a few times, as an Acolyte, when Hestia visited Athena's Temple. Medusa always seemed polite, respectful, and nothing like the duplicitous, conniving snake Poseidon claims she is. Supposedly, that's why he transformed her into a gorgon, but Hestia will hold off on believing that pile of utter donkey dung.

The Allegiance had finally gotten a lead on her location and convinced Perseus to bring Alec and Psyche with him. They speculated it would take some convincing, but the buffoon didn't even hesitate. Hestia believes he may have even muttered something about having an audience. He might have plenty of brawn, but his head must have been made of sawdust.

Hestia pulls the stone out and sees that it is glowing.

She takes one last look around her quiet library to ensure she is alone and is greeted by silence. Content with that, she focuses her attention back on the stone.

Fearful the message will tell her she was too late, especially since Poseidon already had at least a day's head start by the time Hestia overheard his plans. She takes a breath before closing her eyes to open her mind and receive the message.

Her heart is in her throat as his voice fills her head. Normally, the second his presence is in her mind, her nerves settle, and hearing him soothes some of her worries. Today, it does none of those things until she hears him utter the words that finally allow her anxiety to recede.

"We got her. We're clear and we are safe for now. There was a close call with Poseidon, but Psyche sent him running with his tail tucked between his legs."

She chuckles at the imagery that brings forth and breathes a sigh of relief.

They are safe.

His message continues and Hestia sits back in her chair to get comfortable. They never discuss the unspoken routine between them, the messages that follow the updates. Once their duties are set aside, there is always a small tidbit on how they are doing personally. They talk about food they tried, a joke they heard and wanted to share. She always hopes their messages lighten his heart like they do hers.

Hestia listens as he recounts the specifics of the altercation and when he is through, she is so grateful Psyche was there and that the Leviathan was close enough to recover them before they had succumbed to the hazardous ocean waters.

He ends the message on a much more personal level, catching Hestia off guard. Any intimate conversations have been light-hearted, meant to ease the troubles of the day, not pack an emotional punch. Today is different.

"A face flashed into my mind when everything was going to shit. I would be a coward if I don't tell you that face was yours." His voice full with emotion.

She sucks in a sharp breath and her heart nearly skips a beat, an impressive feat for a god, and he continues.

"I tell you jokes and laugh about my day when I just want to tell you that your voice carries me through until I hear it again the next week. I fear for your safety there. I know you're a god and I'm just a mortal man, but I worry what they will do if they find out you're helping us. Please be safe."

The silence that fills the room when the message ends is deafening.

He cares about her. A smile spreads across her face as her heart warms at the thought. She has never so much as hinted to him she may have feelings for him all these years. There was no point. What kind of love could they share through a stone? Can a chance encounter that led to the briefest weekend with the Allegiance be enough to form a relationship?

She had returned to the Temple of Olympus as a spy. Every day since then has been tense with worry of being discovered or, even worse, being unable to prevent some of the truly horrific actions of the Pantheon.

Hestia sits down and mindlessly rearranges the papers on her desk, unsure of what to think or how she wants to respond.

Questions keep nagging her. How long has he cared for her? Does he love her? Does it even matter if he does?

Her traitorous heart screams at her at the last question. Despite the separation, danger, and futility of any dreams of love with everything going on, it matters.

8

ICARUS

The crowd roars and the echoes of it bounce around the chilly stone tunnel, making Icarus's head throb. She should have gone straight to the inn and to bed last night, but she can't remember when she had that much fun. In front of her are fellow potential Heroes, competing in the Trials as they stand in line and wait their turn to enter the arena.

Three identical tunnels hold the remaining recruits, one tunnel on the same side of the arena as hers, the other two across. She wonders which one Lysander is in.

Icarus had sailed through the preliminary recruitment rounds, bruising quite a few egos along the way. While she has no delusions about escaping this process without making some enemies, their fragile self esteem is not enough to make her second guess her goals or dreams.

Only one more round, with forty competitors in ten waves of four, stands between her and becoming a Hero of Olympus. Another round with the final ten to show that she belongs in an elite legion - hopefully Pegasus. If she closes her eyes, she can feel the wind blowing through her hair as she flies through the clouds, her steed's feathers glistening under the warm light of the sun.

The ill-fitting armor of her breastplate digs into her collarbone, and she rolls her eyes at the design meant for a male chest. Women may be few and far between in the Heroes, but surely they are at least given proper armor? The gendered hinderance is irritating, but she shakes it off, confident she can carry her weight in the arena even if she had no armor.

The delicate chain of her pendant is smooth against her fingers as she pulls it from beneath the thin tunic she is wearing beneath her armor, the stone at the end of it glimmering as soon as she touches it. She should have asked the woman what kind of gem it is, but Icarus is positive it must be one of a kind. Her sunstone. That's what her instinct tells her it wants to be called. As if it has a life force of its own and was made for her. Tucking it away again, emboldened by its presence, Icarus brings her focus back to the arena.

It may be untested arrogance carrying her confidence, but she feels at home with a weapon and trusts her instincts and training. As long as she does not panic, she will be fine.

The line shuffles forward, and she steps up to fill the gap in front of her. Her heart flutters as she gets closer to the entrance.

There are only two people in front of her now, and her pulse quickens. Lost in focus, trying to keep her head in the game, she almost doesn't hear the man in front of her.

"Must be nice to be in *her* group, so's you know at least one person will do worse than you," He laughs.

Her grip around the pole-arm in her right hand tightens in anger, but she refuses to turn her head, does not acknowledge him. Gregor had taught her long ago, to let her training do the talking for her anytime someone's mouth gets ahead of them. She whispers the mantra he taught her under her breath.

This shall not break me

She smiles to herself as she imagines the looks on their faces when she is the victor of her group.

The next rounds are over much faster and before she knows it, she is standing at the threshold of the arena, up next, in the last wave. The metal gate comes sliding down into place in front of her. She does a last minute mental rundown of the weapons on her. Pole-arm in right hand and shield on left arm, check. Sword sheathed as a backup, and her boot daggers, check. Icarus is ready for it.

A horn sounds and her heart threatens to leap out of her chest as the gate rises again and she steps out into the arena. Cheering erupts from the stands from people who don't know her- or likely anyone participating here. The noise is deafening, but she tunes it out. It surprised her to learn that the general public could spectate the recruitment trials, but after finding out the Pantheon charged them for the tickets, it made a bit more sense.

As Icarus gets closer to the metal disc marking her starting point, the smell of blood and sweat assaults her. At least half of the groups have already gone, and what started out as pristine white sand now has splotches of pinks and reds from the blood of the Hero hopefuls.

Squinting against the sun, she cranes her neck to make out who is on the platform in the places of honor. Ares, in red for the Heracles Legion, is a given, but she wants to see who else will be watching her today. She is on the opposite side of the arena as the podium with the Pantheon, and she has to strain to see anything.

Athena's fiery red curls are distinguishable, and the goddess is dressed for the occasion in what can only be considered an armor and dress combo. The deep green of her Pegasus Legion cloak matches the rich emerald tones of her dress. Icarus wants to roll her eyes, but it looks pretty bad ass.

Zeus's silver cloak glistens and Icarus has to wonder how

many of the combatants today are hoping to end up in his personal guard - the Lightning Legion. Poseidon is there, as well as Artemis - in blue and gold for the Oceanic and Hind Legions.

Only one other face stands out, Dionysus. It is no surprise that the party god would be at a spectacle like this. He waves his hands around excitedly while he talks and she can hear the deep belly laugh that escapes his lips.. He appears to be making a reputation of always being drunk. Instantly dismissing him from her thoughts, Icarus focuses on the challenge before her.

The only visible opponent is directly across from her. He is smaller in stature, but she will not mistake that for weakness, especially since he looks like he knows how to use the knives he is wielding.

To her left is what looks like a small labyrinth made of stone walls, running along the side of the arena between her disc and one of her other opponents. The maze also looks to be mirrored on the other side of the arena. To her right is an open pit. She stretches her neck, standing on her tiptoes, and can see the sharp points of spikes in the bottom. Like the maze, a copy of this trap is also on the opposite side. Going left then.

"Ready!" calls the overseer of this spectacle, the head of the Heroes, Ares, his booming voice amplified with magic, and the participants ready themselves into their fighting stances.

This shall not break me.

The horn sounds again, and the trial begins.

She immediately makes for the labyrinth, wanting to inspect it and the other end of the arena more thoroughly.

The stone walls are about 6 feet high and she cannot see over the top of them. A gap exists between the arena wall and one of the stone walls making up the maze. Deciding against getting cornered in the tight corridors of the maze, and preferring more line of sight and ability to look over her shoulder, she stalks along the corridor. When she is almost halfway to the other side of the obstacle, an opponent comes running toward her.

Icarus digs her heels into the ground, anchoring her stance and preparing for battle. Her opponent, however, runs right past her. She cocks her head in confusion, watching his retreating form. The padding of heavy footsteps from the way the man came whips her head around, finding her face to face with a massive lion.

For as long as anyone can remember, the Trials have used illusions. One of Athena's cunning contributions to the process. Unfortunately, these illusions are still deadly.

Worked into a frenzy, the crowd in the stands just above Icarus is eagerly watching the show, waiting for her blood to spill. A few of them are throwing things down at the lion, trying to rile it up even further.

A roar from the lion reverberates off of the stone walls before it takes a swipe at her, and she jumps back to avoid its claws. Guilt pulls at her over the thought of harming such a beautiful creature. It feels wrong. She huffs and pulls at the collar of her armor.

Get it together. It's an illusion.

Her empathy might literally be the death of her one day.

Icarus rolls on the ground, under another attempt to slash her, impaling the creature from beneath with her pole-arm. She continues her roll until she is no longer at risk of the lion's body collapsing on top of her.

Cheers erupt from the crowd, and Icarus cannot tell if the noise increase is just because they got to see bloodshed, or if it is disappointment for the lack of her death. It does not matter. She detests it. Do these people not realize she is doing all of this so that she can protect them, not for entertainment?

Looking at the enormous cat as it lay there dying, Icarus walks over to the lion's head and puts her hand on its forehead.

"I'm sorry. I know you're not real, but I'm sorry."

The lion looks up at her with those words. Does it understand her?

Looking deep into its eyes, she could swear there was something more there before the light left them permanently.

She strokes its forehead a few more times, despite the streaks of blood she leaves in its fur.

Laying the lion's head back on the ground, she continues her original path toward the other end of the arena from where she started.

As she reaches the end of the length of the labyrinth from outside, the arena opens up before her briefly before there are more stone walls and corridors, but not quite a maze. A few of the walls have slats over the tops of them.

The wall of the arena in front of the podium is lined with spikes. Icarus scans for opponents but sees none so far. A look up at the podium shows all eyes on her. Smirking, she brings two fingers to her forehead in a salute, garnering a few stony stares and a cocked eyebrow from Athena.

A large man comes around a corner and sets his sights on Icarus. The handle of his greatsword is almost completely lost in his burly hands.

Quickly eying one of the stone corridors, she comes up with a plan.

The hair on the nape of her neck stands on end as she backs down one of them, weapon drawn and ready as the man follows. She continues this way until, as anticipated, he gets fed up and charges her, letting out a loud battle cry as he does.

When he is almost right on her, she leaps up and grabs the slats above her, using them to lift her body. With both feet, her heels slam into his throat and face.

He falls to the ground, grasping at his throat, but by the time Icarus drops back down, he is out cold, and the crowd is roaring.

Icarus makes her way back to the middle of the arena, ready to bring all of this to a head.

She makes note of the small spiked traps that litter the ground, barely noticeable in the sand.

A mountain of a man comes out of the labyrinth opposite the one she passed. His flail has blood dripping from it and she wonders if it is from the last opponent, or an illusion.

He spots her, taking in his last obstacle to becoming a Hero, and grins when he sees the golden braid sticking out of her helmet.

They circle each other momentarily before he raises his arms and swings his weapon at her. Her left arm sings with pain as her shield absorbs the hit. Moving around behind him to take advantage of his size, but he is not as slow as she expected and he shatters her pole-arm with his sword as she attempts to get it inside his defenses.

In a fluid motion, her own sword is out. He swings his sword at her again and this strike she meets with her weapon instead of her shield. They trade hits back and forth, parrying and swinging, until she falls complacent at the rhythm. He switches it up, delivering one blow immediately after the other, and she buckles under his strength, falling to her hands and knees.

He blocks out the sun as he crouches over her, grabbing her by the metal collar of her chest plate and yanking her helmet off.

"Yield," he orders.

"Not a chance." She answers.

He rears back and punches her in her face hard enough to have her seeing stars, and she is pretty sure her nose is broken.

She turns her head to the side, spitting out blood, noticing that hers now joins the macabre abstract painting that has become the arena floor.

Her fingers grip in the sand beneath her, and she flings it up in his face. He jerks up to full standing with a roar and she rolls between his legs and climbs onto his back. In a blink, she has him in a chokehold, one of her daggers directly below his chin and it is her commanding him to yield.

He thrashes for a moment, trying to throw her from his back, but her grip is iron and she puts enough pressure on the dagger to make blood run down his neck.

"Fine, I yield!" He bellows.

She immediately releases him, dropping from his back. She tosses her dagger on the ground next to her discarded sword and turns to face the podium and her assessors, only now hearing the fervor of the crowd over her victory.

Ares beckons for her to come forward, and she walks over.

9

MEDUSA

Medusa pushes into the room, overjoyed with the news that Psyche is finally awake. Sitting up in the bed, in a cabin that is a mirror of the one in which Medusa had awoken, Psyche gives Alec a tired smile that brightens when she sees Medusa behind him. With a blush and butterflies, Medusa approaches her bedside. Psyche crosses her legs and pats the foot of the bed for Medusa to sit there.

"I am elated to see you both!" Her grin is beaming, and it makes Medusa's heart race. "Lyra, you must have so many questions. There's a reason I can't give you resolution yet."

"I do, but they can wait until you're a little more rested," Medusa replies with a patient smile, surprising even herself.

Alec suddenly exclaims, "You both must be starving!" Before either of them can even answer, he is out of the room, words about stew and potatoes trailing behind him with the promise of a swift return.

Medusa and Psyche look at each other in his absence, and Medusa struggles with what to say. She meant it when she said her questions could wait. She spent eight years with nothing but her regrets and self-loathing to keep her company, no hope of

67

answers or closure in sight. A few more hours or days is nothing.

The longer Psyche stares at her, the more Medusa thinks about what Psyche must be thinking, what she sees. Is she taking the time to pick out every single scale and imperfection? Is she trying to decide how much of a monster Medusa is? Psyche is the god of the soul, after all. Is she assessing if the heart inside Medusa is also monstrous?

Before being hideously transformed, Psyche may have been staring for a different reason. Perhaps Psyche would have been just as captivated by Medusa's rosy pink lips as she is with Psyche's dark ones. It is moot though. Who would want to kiss lips that are deep green?

Fortunately, Psyche puts her out of her misery and speaks first. "How does it feel to be off your island?"

"Honestly? I have no idea," Medusa replies. "Coming to your cabin was the first time leaving my quarters. I don't think I will fully even process that I've left until I see land on the horizon."

Psyche's response is gentle. "There's no correct timeline for processing things. That's one of those things we don't have control over that we can only hope happens when we are strong enough to handle it. But no matter when it happens, even if it's when you don't feel you can bear it, those feelings are valid and nothing to be ashamed of."

It was not the reply Medusa expected. When she was upset at the Temple, people would brush off how she felt and explain to her why she shouldn't feel that way, or scold her, hoping to shame her into at least being silent about it. She learned to keep her problems to herself, to keep them close. Why does Psyche care how Medusa feels? These people likely want to use her curse as a weapon and then drop her at the farthest island imaginable - keeping the Olympic Isles clear of one more monster.

Wanting to change the subject to anything other than her feelings, Medusa asks, "How do you feel about the Hero being on board with us?" She picks at the edges of the blanket, not looking at Psyche.

"His presence doesn't bother me," Psyche answers. "I'm sure Alec told you he's not one of the Heroes known for being callous and cruel. I don't know why someone like him would be a Hero, let alone in the Oceanic Legion, but that's a question for him, not me."

At that, Medusa scoffs, "That would mean talking to him and having a conversation. I can name a long list of things I would rather do than converse would my would be assassin or kidnapper."

Psyche laughs in response. "No one is asking you to speak to him, so no need to worry there. I also don't worry about him being on board because I think that almost every person on this ship can stand toe to toe with him and hold their own or... at the very least, slow him down enough for assistance to arrive."

There is a quick knock at the door and Alec is back before Medusa has to fumble for a new topic of conversation once again. She sees the tray in his hands at the same time the smell wafts over to them. The aroma of the savory foods makes her mouth water and her stomach grumble. Psyche looks like she might be just as famished as Medusa as Alec puts the tray on the bed between them.

"We cannot give you all the answers you seek just yet. Before we can give you any of them at all, though, an oath must be sworn. This oath declares that the secrets of our group won't be revealed to outsiders, on threat of a punishment no one should take lightly. This is an oath of the soul, one that looks deep inside you and inspects your heart closely. It walks with you always, waiting for your heart to betray it." Psyche pauses and takes a moment to consider her word choices. "Once you take the oath, many answers will be on the other side, waiting for you. You have a choice. You are not being compelled to take this oath, but it is what is required to move forward with us."

An oath? Her skin feels tight and her face tingles as the panic of such a commitment smothers her like a blanket. She did not expect to make such a weighty decision so soon after already choosing to leave her island. Does she have curiosity about this group of people who claim to be rebels? Of course. Does she want to strike back against the gods who have allowed, and caused, so much to happen to Medusa? She wants them to pay. Her need for revenge is a storm of anger that would even give the Furies pause. But she does not know this group. Their reasons for vagueness have merit, but how can she trust they are genuine? It is too late to go back to her island, but maybe she can find another one.

The thought of an exit plan calms her nerves as her heartbeat returns to normal. As the panic recedes, she assesses the situation with a slightly clearer head.

If nothing else, Alec is her family. She would never betray her family even if she decides their cause is not for her. Her instincts are telling her though, that would not be the case. Saying yes and agreeing seems easy and logical despite the weight of the monumental step.

The commitment can't be ignored, however. Was her life great before they found her? No, but it was hers. She turned it into something of her own. Does she really want to do this? Be this far down the path of rebellion? She has no loyalty to the Pantheon, but this would change everything.

"As I'm sure you're aware, I am a god of many things, the soul being one. I administer these oaths, and I will be with you for every part. I don't pretend to know the path you wish for yourself, but I know this journey is being urged on by the Fates. I can feel it."

Medusa looks at Alec and then back at Psyche. "I don't want to go back to an island. To isolation. I want to fight back, resist. I will take your oath."

Alec smiles wide and stands to lift the food tray off the bed while saying, "I'm going to run this back to the galley. I'll see you on the other side, Lyra." With a wink, he is again out the door in a flash.

Sitting on the bed facing each other, Psyche takes Medusa's hands in her own and they lock eyes. Medusa hopes Psyche can't feel her pulse quicken. She knows it would repulse the beautiful god to learn that she makes Medusa's heart flutter.

In a blink, Medusa's stomach drops. Everything goes black for a split second and when her vision returns, she and Psyche are no longer at sea. She quickly spins around, scanning in all directions. The surroundings are a flat desert at night, no hills or mountains as far as the eye can see. The sky is filled with more stars than Medusa has ever seen, illuminating the sandy terrain around her in a dusky twilight haze. She continues to spin around, coming to an abrupt halt when Psyche is suddenly right in front of her.

"Where are we?" Medusa asks, brows furled in concern. Psyche merely smiles in response.

10

MEDUSA

"Relax," Psyche says. "We are still on the ship. We are just in the Oasis." She gestures around and continues, "I needed someplace I could administer the oaths. Somewhere my magic could come and examine their soul. I created this Oasis as a place to meet in the person's mind I'm oathing."

"My mind?" Medusa asks. Now that it has been brought to her attention, she notices there is a light breeze blowing sand around, but she her skin feels nothing. She tries to breathe in deeply, but there is no scent of any kind. "I understand. This place is absolutely lovely." Turning back to Psyche, she asks, "will this hurt?"

"Not at all. As long as you feel deep within your soul, this is a secret you can keep. This oath will never harm you."

"What happens to those that break the oath? Under what conditions is it bound?" Medusa asks tentatively.

Psyche's response comes with a smirk, "The punishment is tied into the name of our group - one that I cannot tell you until you have sworn the oath for yourself. All I can say is that if the oath is broken, you won't just be damned in this life and will be consigned to eternal suffering."

Medusa's eyes widen at that, taking in the true weight of what she will promise. Her chest tightens again, but she is not going back.

Trying to change to focus to something lighter for a moment, Medusa asks, "Do you only come here for oaths, or is this somewhere you can access anytime you'd like for an escape?"

Psyche tilts her head at the question, as if the answer is not one she had ever considered. "I only come here for oaths, but I imagine I could go within myself and come here on my own. The oath only takes a few minutes, so it always looks the way you see it now. However, if I'm in someone's mind for longer periods of time, I believe the Oasis will modify, changing the scenery to become a merging of what it believes our two subconsciousness will find pleasing. I've never tested the stability of this, though, and surprisingly, you're the first person ever to suggest such a thing."

Medusa shies away from the look of surprise on Psyche's face, keeping her external expression as neutral as possible. Of course, why would she expect a monster to be intelligent? Psyche is probably grateful that Medusa can still speak with other people.

Psyche takes Medusa's hands, and the wind blows around them, whipping the fabric of their clothing against their skin and causing Psyche's hair to billow all around her. The wind's effect can be seen, but Medusa notices she still feels nothing.

What she can feel, however, are the slumbering minds of her serpents. She does not know what they are thinking or dreaming, but she can *feel* their presence so much more vividly than she ever could in the real world.

"It's time," Psyche states and takes Medusa's hands, causing her to feel an electric hum suddenly coursing through her. Psyche looks surprised by this but then is quickly back to business. "Repeat this oath after me."

"Wait!" Medusa interjects, "how will I know if it worked?"

In annoying, vague fashion, Psyche merely answers, "You will know. Repeat after me, Lyra." She nods in agreement and they begin.

"I pledge upon my soul,
to hold these secrets told.
I bind myself to this truth
and hereby swear to never
betray or expose
The Tartarus Allegiance
lest I commit my fate
to eternal suffering"

Medusa repeats the oath as the wind continues to swirl around them. The gusts pick up speed and she fears the oath failed. She is about to ask Psyche in a panic when the gale dies down. The stars streak across the sky in the most dazzling display, the night lighting up as if it is bejeweled.

When Medusa looks back down, she sees bioluminescent fireflies dancing around them. All Medusa can think to say when she looks at Psyche is, "So... I'm guessing it worked?"

"Yes, it did, and well. My magic believes your soul is to be trusted, and my magic doesn't let me down often."

Medusa blinks and is back in the small ship cabin, sitting across the bed from Psyche, with Alec now back in the room, sitting in the chair.

He asks, "It's done then?"

"Yes," is Psyche's reply.

"The Tartarus Allegiance? So when you say eternal damnation you *really* mean it, don't you?" Medusa inquires, appreciating the directness of the name. Every utterance amongst themselves about it surely reminds them all of what will happen if they betray what they have built.

Alec stands up, leans over to give Medusa a hug, then pauses and asks, "Would it be ok if I hugged you?"

Medusa winces at the thought of the contact, but also craves it, and nods with a weak smile. He wraps his arms around her and she again fights tears. Such a small acknowledgment of a boundary should not be so moving, but after a life at the temple followed by one of isolation, how does she handle such gentle consideration? The only person who ever respected her boundaries had been Nikolas, and even then, it was only when the restrictions of the Temple life would allow. If his job as a Pantheon Guard required him to discipline her, he did so even if it warred with his conscience.

They settle into their seats as Alec begins, "Tartarus Allegiance, as you now know we are called, has been around for about twenty years, but only in the last five years has it really gained momentum and expanded to what it is now. You know firsthand of the atrocities the Pantheon is capable of, but I doubt you know the full extent."

"I'm eager to learn more about the Allegiance, but what can you tell me about my family? My parents?"

At that, Alec looks a little defeated and Psyche answers, "The Allegiance has an Oracle. The Pantheon doesn't know of her existence, which is why we couldn't mention her before you had been oathed. She demanded that we refrain from answering too many questions pertaining to your personal history. I hate to withhold information from you still, Lyra, but as you are well aware, if an oracle is insistent about something, it's best to listen to them."

"I suppose," Medusa can feel weariness taking over, her head swimming with so much information that just leads the way to more questions. "So, how do we get to this oracle?"

Alec continues, "The Allegiance established itself on the Isle of Mysts, far from the watchful eyes of Olympus and the other temples."

Medusa's eyes widen. "But the Isle of Mysts is an old legend. There's no record of it anywhere in the Temple Library."

"It's real," Alec says. "We're headed there now."

11

APHRODITE

Aphrodite slams the doors to her chambers closed. She is fuming, mostly at herself for being so careless. Hestia almost caught her leaving the library. There is no doubt that nosy bitch would have come sniffing around, wanting to know why Aphrodite was in her precious domain.

She rolls her eyes in annoyance at her long-time rival. Being the Keeper of Knowledge does not mean she is entitled to know what Aphrodite had been researching. It still stings, whether or not she will admit it, that Hestia denied her access to the restricted section. Aphrodite's status should allow her free access to anything in that dusty old sanctum of boredom.

Oh well, Aphrodite has to get more creative about her snooping, slipping in when she knows Hestia will be away for a while.

She walks over to the vanity and sits down, absentmindedly caressing the smooth stone of it. The dark marble is beautiful, to be sure, but she misses the softness of her preferred decor in her own temple. She spends so much time here at the Olympic Temple, though, that this one feels almost as familiar to her.

A rolled piece of parchment with a wax seal catches her eye. Who would have the nerve to enter her personal chambers?

The emblem on the seal sends a wave of frost all the way to her toes. The three crossroads symbol set into the red wax. Oedipus. Realizing he had been in her personal space, she shudders. Tossing the letter to the side, she tries to think of something else. She will have a talk with her guards tomorrow about allowing this intrusion.

The moonlight streaming in the window highlights the sharpness of her cheekbones and bounces off her light blonde hair, making it almost glow. She has to chuckle at the near celestial look it gives her, so innocent and saintly. She is pretty sure the Fates themselves would shudder in horror over many of the things she has done - some simply because they were fun.

Not to be free and liberal with sex is difficult when you are the God of Love. Everything about her is designed to lure a person into their most forbidden desires. Her soft lips are always pursed into a delicious pout, her small breasts always perky and enticing, a narrow waist that gives way to softly curving hips. Even her voice is silky and sweet, drawing one in as if she is part siren.

If Aphrodite allows herself, she can still too keenly feel the overwhelming pain that comes with each new phase of grief. So she refuses to let herself feel the heart-shattering pain of the loss of *her*, the hopefulness and optimism of remembering her curse, that she would come back to Aphrodite - possibly in a few years, but she could be patient. She could wait - for *her*.

That hope was slow to fade, but after a hundred years and no sign of her spirit being born into another, she had resigned herself to never seeing Andromeda again.

Another four hundred years pass and by then, now, Aphrodite's shell is practically impenetrable, and she is convinced no one will ever truly make her feel again.

She opens the top drawer of her vanity and pulls out a silver box that is intricately decorated with bronze filigree shaped into brambles and thorns surrounding it like a cage. The long pearl-tipped hair pin is sharp as she pricks the end of her index finger on her left hand. Blood rises to the surface, and she turns her finger over and the blood falls onto the brambles.

In recognition of her life essence, the vines and thorns start to morph and shift until the lid of the box is accessible and the magical lock successfully opens.

Aphrodite reaches inside and pulls out the bronze medallion, running her fingers over the ridges of each zodiac marking. The center is empty, and she gets lost staring into the vacant space.

She snaps the box closed; the vines sliding around it until it is impenetrable once more without Aphrodite's blood.

A creaking sound from the direction of her bed stills her. Someone is in her room. Her heart stops at the thought of Oedipus being behind her.

Turning around, she lets out an exasperated sigh when she sees Zeus, completely at his leisure, in *her* bed. Internally, she is shaking. How much did he see? At least it isn't Oedipus. Zeus is easy.

Aphrodite rolls her eyes to mask the anxiety she is shaking off and gets up, walking over him with every intention of thoroughly distracting him from her secrets.

"What's that box there?" He asks curiously, but she is already walking over to him, switching her mood to one of demure seduction.

"Nothing important," she says. "Just some little trinkets that I've collected, notes of things I enjoyed." For effect, she adds, "Sometimes I keep notes from Andromeda with me. I occasionally find myself missing her, even after all this time." She shrugs her shoulders, content to let that be the end of it.

He follows with, "Why go to such lengths to hide them then?"

The blankets of the bed are soft and decadent as she drops down to sit on the foot of the bed, keeping her distance from him, knowing how to play the cat-and-mouse game that lets him think he is in charge.

Her voice is soft and falsely vulnerable, lashes batting, "I was embarrassed, of course. We can't have people knowing I can be sentimental." Her finger trails along the v-neckline of her dress, drawing attention to her breasts in a subtle hint to change up the conversation.

It works, his gaze instantly turning molten.

He's handsome, even if she can't stand him. A long time ago, Aphrodite learned that shutting off emotions and focusing on sex is easier, eliminating the pesky need to actually care for someone to enjoy the act. Someone can be the bane of her existence, yet still be able to make her come so hard she sees stars. Lightning magic does not hurt either... or maybe it does, and that is kind of the point.

The moonlight is dimmed in this corner of the room, but it bounces off his muscular chest, her nipples going hard in anticipation of the hours she knows are heading her way. This is hardly the first time she has found him waiting in her bed, but it is the first time she was so preoccupied that she failed to notice it immediately.

She knows exactly what he wants when he waits for her like this. Their activities vary in moods, positions, and number of partners. One of her many talents that comes with her domain is the ability to sense what her partner is looking for, what kind of mood they are in, and cater to that. When he is in her bed lying in wait, he is in a feral mood that needs to dominate and control. An illusion she is happy to grant him, allowing herself to get lost in it as well.

He crooks his finger, and she crawls across the spacious bed on all fours until she is straddling him.

Reaching out, he rips the top of her dress open, exposing her breasts to the chilly air of the room. The sight of Aphrodite's body reacting to him paints his face in a self-satisfied smirk as he runs a thumb over her right nipple, making her suck in a breath at the sensation.

Lust pools in her center and she needs him inside her, but knows not to do anything until instructed.

His thumb continues to move in circles, making her need blossom. He eyes her mischievously, as if challenging her to break and touch him or herself.

Aphrodite does not give in, her body rigid aside from her gasps of pleasure that are increasing in frequency. It always amazes her how quickly she can reach this state, with so little touch, simply from being restricted in her responses. To her, it makes every touch magnified, and creates a wicked yearning that begs to be penetrated.

Zeus pulls her closer to him, growling, "Good girl."

In a fluid motion, he is under her skirts, one arm around her waist, holding her close, the other getting closer and closer to its destination.

When he finds her already dripping wet for him, his arrogant grin almost sours the mood but before it can, he thrusts two fingers inside of her, immediately hooking them and finding her g spot.

The moan that escapes her is wild, feral as he hits that sacred place. She rocks her hips and grinds against his hand, yelping when he grips her hair and yanks her head back, while rising onto his knees, sliding his fingers out of her.

"I didn't say you could move, did I?" He asks, his tone gravelly and laced with desire.

She shakes her head no, a smirk forming, knowing he will dislike that, but also knowing that he *wants* to punish her.

The hand that is still fisted in her hair moves her head toward his erection. She opens her lips, pleasure rippling through her as he drives himself into her mouth, her eyes watering as he hits the back of her throat.

It sometimes catches her off guard, the way she enjoys being used in the quiet private of the bed they sometimes share. Her best guess is that her disdain for him guarantees she will never develop feelings for him and, therefore, can let this to be something she allows herself to get lost within.

Abruptly, he pulls out of her mouth and releases her hair. She stays where she is, back on her knees as he climbs out of the bed and walks around behind her. He stands at the edge of the bed and yanks her backward toward him until her core is inches away from his erection.

He runs his hand along her back, up and down in strokes that a naïve girl might confuse for intimacy. She knows he is doing it to tease and build up to something, to throw her off guard.

His right hand slides up her back and around her neck as his left hand clenching her left hip firmly, his grip on her throat tightening as he teases her entrance with his cock.

Aphrodite whimpers with need, almost shaking with it, and he keeps delaying her pleasure until she's about to disobey and tell him to fuck her already.

As she opens her mouth to do that, he slowly presses into her until he fills her, causing her to cry out.

Zeus deliberately works in and out, his grip on her throat never wavering. Her body is singing with ecstasy as he moves in a rhythm that is slow and torturous. After a few more thrusts, he flips her around, the soft bedding caressing her back as she spreads her legs for him, with barely enough time to adjust to the new position before he is inside her again.

She moans with pleasure and he simply says, "now."

The orgasm that tears through her is almost blinding as she rides its waves. Just when she thinks it's done, his thumb is on her clit and a zap of his lightning has her rolling again.

Several hours later, Aphrodite lies in her bed staring up at the ceiling. Zeus is drifting off to sleep next to her. She will never be stupid enough to mistake him sleeping in her bed as intimacy. He is simply too lazy to go back to his own chambers. It often to works to Aphrodite's advantage, allowing her to slip in what are hopefully innocuous questions as his consciousness is fading.

"Where is Hera?" She asks quietly.

He yawns before answering her. "Traveling."

Aphrodite wrinkles her forehead. "No one has seen her. What if the rebels have her?"

"They don't."

"How can you be certain?"

He sighs in annoyance. "If you think I don't have my own spies, you're as naïve as they are."

12

MEDUSA

Medusa checks that her hood is still in place before stepping out of her small cabin. The last thing she wants is an accident of that magnitude. It surprises her to find it still perfectly secure, the same as it has been the other hundred times she has compulsively made sure it was safe. Maybe whatever magic allowing it to work also enchants it to stay on? Next time, she'll try to remember to ask Psyche.

She looks left and then right, coming through the door. The hallway is empty and a few feet to her right are stairs that she hopes will take her topside. Each board creaks loudly as she steps on it, no matter how delicate her foot placement and Medusa hopes it does not disturb Psyche, assuming it is actually night time. Her internal clock is telling her it is, but she will not know until she sees the sky.

The staircase does in fact lead to the decks, and the dark purple sky says her estimate was correct. A thick blanket of clouds covers the sky, preventing her from using the moon to gauge the time. The skeleton crew running the ship tells her the hour is much later than she initially thought and she is grateful for the opportunity to come out here when the fewest amount of people will be around.

She is uncertain what to expect from them. Everything has been happening so fast and being thrust into the public eye is very overwhelming. What will people think when they see her? What do they know about her? Are there whispers spoken at night to warn their babies of the serpentine horror? Do the children run through hills chanting a morbid nursery rhyme about her? Or have they hidden her existence, like they did to her parents?

Lost in a sea of her own thoughts, she nearly misses the man standing on the deck. Nicodemus, the captain.

His face is pulled into a grimace, as if he has a foul taste in his mouth. What did he just slip into his pocket?

Turning, he sees Medusa watching him, his gaze icy and full of loathing.

Flustered at her mistake, she rushes to apologize. "I am so sorry. I was in my head and should have been watching where I was going."

His dark eyes stare back at her- judging her, assessing her.

Medusa rubs the birthmark on her wrist as she stands there awkwardly for a moment and is about to leave when his face turns into a sneer that she has seen too many times. One laced with hate and loathing.

"You're awake, I see," Nicodemus says, his deep voice low but with a threatening undercurrent to it.

"Um. Yes," is all she replies, still unsure where the hostility is coming from.

Shaking his head, he scoffs as he brushes past her and walks away.

Before leaving, he turns back and calls out, "Let's see if we can get back to our home without you adding to your death count, Viper."

He turns on his heel and walks off, leaving Medusa speechless. Her brow wrinkles in frustration as she tries to work out the source of his anger. Does she have a reputation, falsely perpetuated? Lies to make anyone who might offer her aid be hesitant to trust her? The thought has often crossed her mind that Poseidon may have spread lies about her, and she always circles back to feeling insignificant, making it impossible that he would care enough to spread rumors about her. Her run-in with the captain means she needs to re-evaluate that possibility.

Not wanting to bump into him a second time, Medusa walks in the opposite direction that the captain went, and resumes her endless tirade of thoughts and questions, swirling and roaring in her head all demanding priority over the others.

The salt smell on the breeze is familiar and Medusa closes her eyes to relish the feel of the wind. It feels so much sharper than normal and she has to wonder if the absence of those senses in the Oasis is the reason. The railing is smooth beneath her hand as she glides it along as she walks, giving way for breaks where the sails are tied.

When she makes it to the bow, Psyche is there, facing out toward the water. Medusa just waits for a minute and observes. The bit of moonlight occasionally peeking through the swiftly moving clouds reflects off of her onyx hair as it blows in the breeze. When Medusa realizes she has been standing there for longer than is polite, she returns to her cabin and not intrude, and turns to leave abruptly. Before she can make an undetected exit, her foot gets tangled in a coil of rope and she falls over, making an ungodly amount of noise before catching herself at the last second on the railing.

She looks up and sees Psyche now watching her, doing her best to stifle a laugh. Despite the urge to feel embarrassed and storm off, Medusa plops down on the deck and falls into a laughing fit that steals the air from her lungs. She laughs so hard her stomach muscles are cramping and tears are streaming down her face. As if a floodgate and years of isolation are melting away and in that moment, and there might be ways to enjoy life once again.

Psyche walks over, also laughing, because laughter like this is contagious. Psyche takes a deep breath to calm herself and extends a hand down to Medusa. She reaches up to take Psyche's hand but pauses as the moon reflects off the scales on her wrist. Is she going to be disgusted by Medusa's touch?

As Psyche pulls, her hand slips, and she falls backward onto the deck, leaving them entangled in the rope, and each other, laughing again. The cycle renewed.

The moment is finally dying down as they wipe tears from the corners of their eyes, and Medusa almost forgets how monstrous she is. A middle-age woman comes running up to them out of breath. Her all white attire identifies her as a healer.

The woman notices Medusa and stares for a moment before remembering why she is there. "Psyche, goddess, we need your assistance urgently. We have done what we can with the Hero's head injury and he has been asleep but stable. This afternoon, a fever was making itself known, and we have been trying to get it back down. It just keeps climbing. We did the best we could while you were recovering, but if you can help us, I think he needs it."

Psyche responds, "I'll be right there, Agatha."

Agatha nods and leaves. Psyche turns back to Medusa, extends a hand, and they help each other up. "I must head straight down there," Psyche pauses. "You're welcome to come with me, but I can understand if you don't want to."

Medusa hesitates and thinks about her reply. Fear plays no part in it by any means, but the thought of being around Hero unsettles her.

How will she ever move past it unless she faces it head-on? "Let's go. I can't promise I'll ever be friendly with someone like him, but I imagine I can be civil." Medusa half laughs but knows deep down that this will be a test of her patience and restraint - asleep or not.

WHEN THEY REACH CADMUS' cabin, Psyche immediately enters. Medusa hesitates at the threshold, watching from the back as Psyche walks up to the still figure laying in the bed and places the back of her hand against his forehead. Agatha steps aside and lets Psyche take the lead.

"He's burning up. I'm going to need you to grab me several things," she instructs Agatha. Psyche recites the list to her, and she silently slips out of the room.

The smell of hot sweat hovers in the room and the air is thick from humidity., either from his fever or their efforts to bring it down.

Psyche turns to Medusa and adds, "I have to go get something from my cabin. It's a magical item that can help him. I hate to put you in this position, but I can't leave him alone right now. I need you to keep an eye on him."

Medusa's mouth falls open in shock and she is ready to refuse when Psyche interrupts, "It will be but just a moment, I promise. All you need to do is watch him and if anything at all happens, come shouting and myself or Agatha should hear it."

After reluctantly agreeing, Medusa takes slow steps across the room and takes a seat in the chair next to his bed as Psyche leaves. Medusa studies the walls, the floorboards, the flickering low flame in the lantern... anything to avoid looking at him. The small room provides little distraction, and Medusa studies the Hero's face. The pallor of his skin is concerning and drained of color as beads of sweat roll down his forehead.

She continues her silent study of him as his brow occasionally furrows. The gash on his forehead is impossible to miss. It looks deep, about four inches long, crossing from his temple to the top of his eyebrow. The surrounding skin is red and inflamed. If infection has not set in yet, she imagines it will be soon.

His dark brown hair curls and falls just below his ears. Right now, it's stringy and clinging to his skin. Her thoughts wander and she remembers why he is there in the first place. Medusa has every right to be angry. This man had to know Poseidon is a monster and yet he was there, anyway. She is fed up with always turning the other cheek, trying to imagine the best of intentions from everyone. Is this rage in her because of the years of isolation? Or is it the result of every injustice Medusa has suffered?

Wringing her hands, she attempts to distract herself from the torrent of angry thoughts that pour into her consciousness. Even under the weight of the hood's magic, Medusa can feel her serpents waking up, their agitation coursing through her. One of the scaly patches on the back of her left hand is rough beneath her fingertip as she uses the texture to ground herself, but it is no use. So much has happened in such a short time. The contact and conversation has been overstimulating and draining. It is all too much after eight years without it. A constant push and pull, the war of emotions in her head and in her heart. The tug of craving affection, anything to stave off the unbearable loneliness, and pushing those things away once she has them. She hopes it will balance out and she can experience life again, but Medusa has to get to the other side of this adjustment with her sanity still intact.

As she sits there, staring at his face, in her mind it morphs into the face of every Hero and mercenary who has come for her, every Master who has punished her. Angry tears well in her eyes and the hardened part of her soul wants this man to pay for all of it.

Medusa talks herself into this aggressive sense of justice

with an ease that should alarming. This man will pay even if she has to hold his eyes open. Before she even realizes she has decided for certain on this course of action, one hand is moving toward his face and the other up to remove her hood. His face is only inches away when his eyes fly open and Psyche walks in.

13

HESTIA

"What are you doing here? She managed to elude you once again?" Hestia hears Athena say to someone, as she is listening outside of a council room. It had surprised her to hear a commotion coming from one of these rooms so late in the evening.

"That bitch Psyche was there," a deep voice spits out. Poseidon. Her heart leaps for joy at hearing further confirmation that Medusa and the Allegiance members made it out safely.

Another male voice chimes in: Zeus. "What does your little pet project have to do with the rebel thorns in our side? Why were they there?"

"I don't know, and I don't care. She's still MINE," he says, roaring the last word. His obsession with Medusa goes to depths none of them could have foreseen.

"Aww, is someone upset they can't keep their pet in line?" Aphrodite teases.

The sound of a fist slamming into the table echoes throughout the courtyard. "Just because you like to get on your knees for Zeus these days doesn't mean you have any right to speak to me like that."

"That's enough!" Zeus bellows. "We can circle back to this whenever I feel like it and that's not now."

"But you know the role she-"

"Silence!"

They begin mindlessly chattering with each other, all content to drop it for the moment. Hestia seriously doubts that Poseidon is even remotely done with Medusa, but for now, the Allegiance is safe, and so is the man that seems to hold her heart.

Hestia stays seated as she hears them get up from their chairs, saying their goodbyes to each other as they walk out into the courtyard. Without looking up from her book, she can feel their eyes on her as the conversation temporarily stops. She keeps pretending to read and they make the usual assumption that she is just engrossed in whatever today's knowledge pursuit is.

After a few minutes, Hestia feels safe enough to move from her spot, trying to remain as inconspicuous as possible.

She walks to the kitchens to put together a tea tray for herself. Despite pretending to read for hours today, she wants to spend this evening doing some actual reading.

When Hestia is almost at her destination, she hears a shrill shouting accompanied by pained shrieks. Running toward the sound and around a corner, she takes in the scene before her.

Aphrodite is glowing, powers on full display as she stands over a maenad on the floor. The spiked heel of her shoe presses into the maenad's cheek as her body convulses in pain. Hestia can barely hear what Aphrodite says over the young woman's poor screams, but what she does hear makes her blood run cold in fear and hot with rage simultaneously.

"How dare you not bow the moment you see a god? Do you think I won't end your worthless life just because it pleases me?"

The woman's screams have turned to groans and Hestia fears she will go into shock.

She rushes into Aphrodite's view and shoves her off of the maenad. Aphrodite falls on her ass and skids a few feet, the look on her face going from shock to rage in an instant.

"You fucking bitch," Aphrodites says, her voice nearly reaching a pitch that only dogs can only hear.

Aphrodite stands back up quickly and lunges for Hestia, arms extended as if she means to strangle her. Hestia easily sidesteps her, causing Aphrodite to fall face-first into the stone pillar Hestia had been standing in front of.

Shrieking again as blood runs down her face and onto her blush pink dress, Aphrodite rips a cloth from her skirts and looks at Hestia, seething.

"This isn't over." Aphrodite's tone is low and serious as she turns on her heel and stomps off.

"It never is," Hestia says, returning to the maenad who is sitting up now and her breathing is leveling out.

"What's your name? Can you talk yet?"

The maenad breathes deeply, visibly wincing as her body continues to recover. On an exhale she answers, "Elena."

"Well, Elena, wait here? I'm going to go grab tea and something for you to eat. We will take a few minutes together and get you feeling settled again," Hestia offers with a kind smile.

Elena seems hesitant to trust another god immediately, but nods her head.

Hestia gently places her hand on Elena's shoulder, stands up, and heads to the kitchens.

When she arrives back with a tea tray, Elena is nowhere to be found. A scan of the vicinity only reveals a small piece of parchment, neatly folded and tucked into the branches of a fern. Quickly pocketing the note, Hestia heads to her library. She hopes Elena is alright, and can hardly blame her for wanting to be somewhere else if she was feeling better.

A wave of comfort and belonging hits her as soon as Hestia enters the library. Every time she walks through these doors, she gets this feeling, and she doubts she will ever tire of it. After gathering a few book titles of interest, Hestia settles into a cozy chair with her tea and takes out the parchment.

Dionysus will help you find Hera.

Dionysus? He seems like the least trustworthy person to divulge secrets to. This makes little sense. How did Elena know Hestia has been looking for Hera? She has been so discreet. It is worth taking a peek around him and his entourage, she supposes.

Grabbing a cloak, Hestia abandons her tea to go seek out the god of wine.

The halls are empty and she does not have to wander too far before she finds him. All gods with a seat at the Pantheon have extensive chambers in the Olympic Temple. Hestia can hear the music and raucous partying several minutes before she arrives at his chambers.

The doors are wide open as partygoers wander in and out at their leisure. Should she go in?

Hestia stands on the outside, debating, before sucking in a nervous breath and entering the room.

The music from the lute and lyre players is pleasant, and the smell of the food makes Hestia's mouth water. Even the mead is appealing. The aroma of the blend of fruits and honey is almost enough to make her consider partaking. The party atmosphere is infectious, as if the haze of herbal smoke filling the room makes her lose her inhibitions.

A tap on her elbow has her spinning around, eyes wide.

Dionysus is standing there, an amused expression on his bearded face. The room's low lighting dances off of his honey skin, the rich amber color so similar to the sweet nectar he uses to make his meads and wines.

"Eat this." He extends his open hand. There are small red berries in his palm, and Hestia looks up at him with disbelief. He can't think she will stroll in here and take magic berries?

Before she tells him to go shove them up a griffon's behind, she remembers the Oracle's words.

You will soon have an unlikely ally in your quest, so the Fates strongly caution you to not be too quick to dismiss anything too hastily. Keep your eyes open, goddess, trouble is brewing.

Hestia cannot believe she is doing this.

The taste of the berries is bitter as Hestia pops one into her mouth. Not at all what she was expecting. Her face twists in distaste and Dionysus laughs. She is about to abandon this entire ordeal when she realizes her senses are getting sharp again, the effects of the haze receding until they are gone entirely.

"What's going on?" Hestia asks. "What was that? Those berries?"

"People come to me, my temple, my circle, when they want to feel better about themselves. The incense I use is a special herbal blend that immediately fogs the senses and allows people to release their troubles."

"And the berries?"

"The berries are my own secret stash. I only grown them in the gardens of my temple in Athens. They allow me to see through the fog of the incense and keep my wits. I know why you're here, and I thought it might be better to talk with clear minds under the cover of the vapor."

Genius. A brilliant cover. Maybe Hestia will finally have someone to help her find Hera. It is still challenging to jump into trusting him. His reputation precedes him, but how much of that is merely what he wants people to see?

"Why do you want to help me?"

"I... uh, I owe Hera a favor and it doesn't sit right with me that she's missing."

Hestia raises an eyebrow behind the wire frame of her glasses, but throws her trust in with the Oracle and crosses her fingers that she interpreted that message correctly.

"How did Elena know I was looking for Hera?" She asks the lingering question.

"Her husband works on the docks, and told her about the day you were there asking questions about Hera."

"Oh." Hestia says, but her brain sticks on Elena having a husband. "A husband? I… hmm, never mind."

"Ask your questions, Hestia. This is a safe place for them. I won't judge you and everyone else here is too zonked out of their mind to even remember you were here."

"Don't you and maenads have, um, sexual relationships?" Her cheeks flush with heat.

"We do." Dionysus replies flatly, revealing nothing in his tone.

"But she has a husband. Does he not get jealous? Is this merely a place for people to have illicit affairs without accountability?"

"He is usually here with us. Hestia, I know you have spent your life amongst the books, but do you truly know so little about the many different facets of sexuality and expression?"

She frowns. She has always thought of herself as enlightened, open-minded. But he is right. Her only relationships have been people she would consider friends. Her relentless pursuit of knowledge never had her stopping to consider love, or even lust. At least, not until she met Alec. Maybe one day she will find out what is so special about the physical side of love.

14

MEDUSA

Medusa jerks her hand back and gasps. She looks at Psyche in horror and shame. *Oh no. What has she done?*

Cadmus, still groggy, glances from Medusa to Psyche and back to Medusa. They lock eyes and she hopes hers convey an apology and regret.

He looks over at Psyche again. "Hello, goddess. I would kneel in your honor, but as you can see, I'm somewhat incapacitated." His gaze meets Medusa's once more. "Thank you for tending to me so diligently and thank you for not letting me die out in the water. I owe you my life."

Is he covering for her? Why is he doing that? Does he know she was about to kill him? Guilt gnaws and picks at every fresh wound opened up by his kindness. Or is this so she will let her guard down? Maybe he will hold it over her head when Psyche is not here. Medusa cannot believe she had been so impulsive. Why is she so delusional as to think that she is anything but the monster they make her out to be? Year after year, every death, she told herself she was only doing it to protect herself. Everything was in self-defense. But this? This was too far. He was

97

helpless, and Medusa was safe. Surely, she would not have gone through with it.

Psyche looks like she does not buy the story, but moves on.

As she gains distance from what almost happened, she becomes more appalled by her actions. Would she really have done it? She seemed awfully close and Medusa is ashamed that she let her emotions take control that strongly and guide her. Her guilt has her reaching for the cup and pitcher on the table, identical to the ones in her cabin. She pours a cup and sets it on the table. Picking up the folded blanket from the floor, she places it behind his pillow, helping him sit up. He groans in pain at the shifting movement, but seems glad to be in a slightly different position. Medusa sits back down and brings the cup to his lips. He hesitates for a moment and Medusa says, "You need water and you and I both know I don't need to poison you."

At that, he opens his mouth slightly and closes his eyes as the cool water rushes in. Making sure to only give him small sips to start, they do this until the cup is empty. He looks over at the pitcher as if to ask for more, but Medusa shakes her head no. "Take it slowly with your injury. We'll do more in a few minutes. Just rest and try not to do anything stupid. I don't want healing you to be harder than it has to be. Especially when it's debatable if you are worth the effort."

"Well, your bedside manner is lacking, but at least you haven't killed him yet," Psyche says.

Cadmus looks at Medusa and she looks away in shame, pretending to be neatening up the pile of bandages on the table.

How could she have been about to kill a defenseless person? Yes, he had arrived with Poseidon, but he was not wearing his Heroes' armor when she almost crossed that line. When she has the time to think, she always chooses the kinder option. Maybe all she has been through has slowly started killing that part of heart. She can still feel it there most of the time, but then the bitterness creeps back in. Is her heart is slowly turning to stone like the statues of the dead who came to claim her life? Will this side of her slowly be the part that wins and takes hold?

Psyche pulls a stone from the pocket of her robe-like attire. It looks like a moon opal, the speckles reflecting in the flickering candlelight. As she removes the folded blanket from behind him, Psyche gently lays him all the way down.

"Stay still, close your eyes, and let the moon magic in when it knocks. It will bring your fever down, but you will probably sleep again until we reach our destination. When we arrive, you will be blindfolded and taken to a secure, but comfortable, room until we can assess what level of a threat you pose to us."

He acts like he is about to protest and then either is too fatigued or thinks better of it. She places the stone on his head and chants in a language Medusa does not understand and has only interacted with in some of the most ancient texts in the Temple library. She knows it to be a language of the gods and the softness of Psyche's voice as the words come out in a hushed whisper soothes the part of Medusa that still refuses to settle down. A calmness washes over her and she closes her eyes and relishes it while Psyche finishes her incantation. When she stops, she feels his forehead and looks pleased.

"A drastic improvement already," Psyche says, relieved. "Hopefully this will be a restorative sleep and the magic will accelerate his healing."

Agatha appears with a bucket of water in one hand, a stack of cloths in the other. She lays the cloths on the table, sets the bucket beside the bed and grabs the first strip from the pile. Once dampened with the cool water, she presses it to his forehead and wipes his brow. Psyche and Medusa leave her to it.

THEY EMERGE BACK on the decks of the ship. Medusa once again breathes the fresh sea air in deeply, pushing out the last remnants of the stuffy, feverish cabin from her system. Another wave of guilt floods Medusa over what she almost did, and she is still grateful that it seems her shame remains a secret.

As they walk to the back of the ship and look over the edge. Medusa watches the water that the ship churns up in its wake. She finds the water tumbling over itself mesmerizing and easily slips into a state where all her thoughts fade away. She thinks about absolutely nothing as she loses herself to the oblivion for a moment.

When she brings herself back to reality, she finds Psyche staring at her. Psyche quickly looks away and almost looks embarrassed to have been caught. It's rare for one to get a chance to observe such a dangerous creature so closely. Psyche's curiosity must have gotten the better of her. Medusa pulls her cloak closed tighter to make as little of herself visible as possible. Was this oath a mistake? Is she ready to be the center of attention as everyone stares in horror, hides their children?

Psyche breaks the silence before things can get truly awkward. "We should get to the Isle close to sundown tomorrow. I know you will want to rush to see the Oracle but that will have to wait until the next morning. In the meantime, tomorrow evening I could show you around the Isle, give you a tour?"

"After a couple days at sea, walking around sounds great."

Psyche smiles at her response, and continues, "Oh, I'm so glad. While we are out and about, we can also make sure you have some essentials. You didn't exactly have the opportunity to bring very much."

"That's fair. Although I'm emotionally and physically exhausted, I can safely say I would prefer here with you and having nothing to being back on my island with my meager foraged possessions."

Psyche's eyes widen, and Medusa realizes what she said. Shame washes over her, and she amends her statement, "I mean here with *all* of you, not *you* you..." she trails off as opposed to digging a deeper hole. Despite the stares, Psyche has been kind to her. The last thing Medusa should do is chase her off by scaring her into thinking Medusa is attracted to her, even though she definitely is. But could she bear it if Psyche's gaze turned to one of disdain and horror?

"Whatever you say," Psyche responds with a wink and a chuckle. "However, for what it's worth," she says as she turns to walk away. She takes Medusa's hand and says, "I very much like being here with *you* you. I look forward to more opportunities to get to know you." And with that, she drops Medusa's hand and walks away. Medusa looks at her hand in awe. It still looks the same but tingles, as if Psyche has Zeus's electric touch.

What was that? What game is Psyche playing? Maybe Medusa is doing a poor job of hiding her attraction, and Psyche is toying with her.

Her heart aches as Medusa wishes she had met Psyche before. Would she have reciprocated this attraction? She does not want to have feelings. They serve no purpose for Medusa. No one will ever be willing to look at her and see beauty. Even in the cases that someone looks at her without hate or fear, their expressions are always full of pity or curiosity instead. How could anyone get past her scaly exterior to find out who she is without this awful curse?

Is whatever this is blooming in Medusa's heart against her will, for Psyche, just going to get ripped away when Cadmus decides he wants her to pay for what she was about to do? Has she thrown away her chance to be with people again before she even really got it started?

15

ICARUS

Icarus, and her definitely broken nose, stand in a tunnel beneath the seats of the arena once more. This time, she is on the opposite side. Only the two sets of tunnels closest to the podium are being used for these rounds. Five waves of two. Just Icarus, an opponent, and whatever illusions and traps the gods throw at them. Lysander also made it to this stage, and she is hopeful he did well, and that it will not be him she faces in the arena.

When she is up next, Icarus tries to make out the layout of the arena through the bars of the gate. Anything to give her an edge when she is standing on that disc and has to formulate a plan.

Dust falls from the ceiling as it shakes from the crowd jumping above, celebrating the latest carnage.

The horn sounds, the gate slides up, and it is showtime again.

She has gotten a little more used to the roar of the crowd, so she plays it up. No matter the outcome, she has made it into the Heroes. She lifts both of her arms, palms up, encouraging the crowd to get even louder. Taking off her helmet and tucking it under her left arm, Icarus waves to the people of the Olympic Isles.

"Ready!"

The cool metal slides over her hair as Icarus puts her helmet back in place, and she faces her opponent on the other side of the arena. Not Lysander. Her shoulders sag with relief before she tenses them again to ready herself.

The horn blows, and she heads directly for her opponent. No easing around the edges, taking her time.

He must have had the same thoughts because he comes straight for her.

Let's go.

As they get closer together, she dodges her head to the right as a knife comes whizzing straight for her.

They face each other, circling for a moment, waiting to see who will strike first.

A sound to her right pulls their attention, as two large metal gates like the ones on the sides open.

For a moment, there is nothing. Icarus and her opponent glance at each other, unsure whether to resume the attack or wait for whatever is surely about to come out of these tunnels.

Their uncertainty is short-lived as a pack of wolves comes running out. Not just any wolves, massive ones.

The crowd cheers for the beasts louder than they cheered for her. They want to see blood, they care little about from whom it spills.

The familiar weight of her sword is steadying as Icarus pulls it from her scabbard, cutting down a wolf as it lunges for her. She climbs up onto the slats covering a nearby stone alleyway, hoisting herself until she is standing on them and has her balance just right.

Her opponent pulls his sword out of a wolf. Two more lying dead on the arena floor around him. That is all the wolves, then.

He walks through the corridor that Icarus is standing over,

oblivious to her presence above him. He continues stalking around the corner of the stone walls that make up the structures she is standing on. Her pulse is thundering in her ears as she silently drops into the sand behind him and tiptoes, making the crowd laugh.

She whistles, and he jerks around to face her.

They parry their weapons but her element of surprise gives her the upper hand and, in moments, she has him on his back with her sword to his throat. He yields, and she steps back, offering him a hand up. He swats it away.

"Suit yourself."

She turns to walk toward the podium. Where is the horn to indicate her round is over?

A large black bull comes barreling through the arena, trampling anything it can. It eyes her, seeing her red cloak - the same one all participants have to wear, a Heracles Legion cloak.

The bull huffs and steam comes out of his nostrils as he stomps his front hoof into the ground. Icarus takes off, running to the back of the arena, hopeful that the spike traps are still there. The bull gives chase, hot on her heels and thoroughly incensed.

Rounding a corner, Icarus almost falls into the traps she was looking for. She sees the ones on the other side and races in that direction, hoping the bull will still follow her. How far across is that pit? Five feet? Maybe? She can jump that. Right? Time to find out.

Closing her eyes, Icarus says a quick prayer to the Fates before sprinting to the edge and soaring across it easily. The bull is not as fortunate.

The horn sounds, and the crowd erupts.

THAT NIGHT, after several rounds of drinks at the tavern celebrating with her fellow new Heroes, including Lysander, Icarus is sitting at the small table beside her bed in the barracks writing a letter to her parents.

She leaves out the broken nose, and the bruises, and simply tells them she did well in her trials and is now a Hero.

Pride swells in her chest, and her smile is from ear to ear.

She seals the letter and sets it next to a similar letter to Hector, both to be dispatched in the morning on her way to her first day of training. Every recruit will do a rotation in each Legion. At the end of the rotations, two recruits will join each Legion. Initiation there has its own set of trials, but she will cross that hurdle when she gets there.

16

MEDUSA

"It just doesn't feel right. The closer we got to it, the more my bones scream to run."

Medusa leans over the railing and watches the dolphins that have been swimming alongside their ship for the past hour when a conversation between two deckhands drifts over to her.

The Mysts.

For most of the day, they have been sailing within sight of the Mysts and the crew of the Leviathan have been increasingly vocal about their distrust for the barrier between the Olympic Isles and the Underworld.

Medusa never feels that way, though. To her, it has a dark beauty. Maybe she knows deep down that one day her soul will match and sees a kindred spirit through the window of time. She assumes the Mysts are off-putting to most as a fight-or-flight instinct. They know that crossing the Mysts improperly will leave you trapped in the Underworld forever. Sure, there are plenty of people who live, work, and even commute there, but they go through the proper channels. The clearance needed

106

is mystical and ancient but, if granted, allows safe passage to and from the Underworld and its Under Temple.

Medusa has seen it a few times growing up. As one of the few Acolytes that could travel with Athena once she ascended, she thought she had been special. She had worked so hard in her training, but what little information the Allegiance has already given her leads her to believe that maybe there were ulterior motives.

Seeing the Mysts again, now, is like looking upon an old friend. She smiles at it and spends a large part of the day just staring out into the dark haze.

Standing back upright, Medusa surveys the deck. Aside from those manning the ship, there are people bustling about, prepping for their arrival. No one is hostile to her, but most are hesitant to return her smile or greeting.

Medusa spots Alec and Yiorgos talking and makes her way over to join them. Another couple rejected salutations and by the time she makes it the short walk over to them, she feels dejected and tired. Maybe this was a mistake.

Alec is his usually jovial self and informs her they should arrive within an hour, a few hours earlier than anticipated, apparently thanks to favorable winds. Unfortunately, it will still be too late to meet with the Oracle, but Medusa does not entirely mind. While she is eager to unlock the secrets of her past, the shock of leaving her island is still an adjustment. Plus, she is looking forward to her time with Psyche. Does this mean they will start their tour earlier? Best not to dwell on it, lest she get her hopes up.

MEDUSA SPENDS the last of her time in her cabin, taking a moment to be alone and recharge and recenter. Yiorgos kindly loaned her a book. Not wanting to offend after such a kind gesture, she spends the next thirty minutes getting absorbed in its pages. It is a folktale book that takes her by surprise. The illustrations are beautiful and she enjoys the short fables that succinctly tell tales of monsters being slain, heroes saving the day, but also mistakes being made and tales that show how someone's uniqueness makes them special, not strange.

Where was a book like this when Medusa was growing up? However, it does not match the Acolyte narrative of feelings not mattering and being best kept to yourself.

A few pages into a story about a hydra, a bell ringing comes from the hallway.

"Land spotted! Land spotted! Going ashore!"

Closing the book, Medusa takes a deep breath and braces for being publicly scrutinized once more. Being comfortable around people again will take time. It makes sense for them to be cautious around her, but hopefully that caution does not turn into fear.

They are about to go through The Mysts and she makes her way up to the deck for the last time on this voyage. Ignoring the whispers and stares as she makes her way to the bow, Medusa focuses on the mass of land is visible not too far on the horizon. It is just as Alec said so far - a deserted rock formation. The proximity to The Mysts surely adds to the lack of appeal from afar, and Medusa appreciates the cleverness of the location. The edge of the Mysts that they will sail through is visible and close.

The boundary of the charcoal-colored fog ebbs and flows with the water like a living entity. Glancing back at the crew, no one seems concerned and everyone is still going about their preparations. It's risky testing the limits of the safety of the abyss, but the Allegiance does this regularly. She has to trust they know what they are doing. Looking at the edge of the

Mysts, Medusa braces herself as she and the front of the boat cross over.

Suddenly, a calm that she has not felt in at least eight years washes over her. Every time she passed through as an Acolyte, she cherished the moments she spent crossing through the Mysts. The time was always too brief, but felt more like home than any place she can remember.

Her eyes close as she breathes in the peace. A slightly electric sensation builds as her skin tingles, a new but not unpleasant sensation. A gasp behind her, followed by a thunk, brings her crashing back to the present and shattering her tranquility.

When her eyes open to investigate, Medusa does not have to look far. Faint shimmers swirl around her skin, extending down her arms. Gaping at her hands in disbelief, she does not understand what to make of it. Looking around the deck, all eyes are on Medusa. Their expressions span the range from horrified to curious. What is happening? It can be nothing good. Another question for the Oracle.

They are through the Mysts and the shimmers disappear. There is no time to linger on the weird experience, because the view that meets her takes her breath away. Who could ever have imagined the Isle could house so much civilization? As she sees rows of buildings and colorful awnings that indicate the possibility of a marketplace, Medusa begins to fully process the depth of the illusion presented by the front side of the island.

As they get closer, Medusa can see crowds of people moving through the streets, and it is surprising how populated it is here. Medusa had assumed that the only ones here would be active members of the Allegiance, but there seems to be more. They are almost at the docks when the sounds of the island make their way to her. People at the docks shouting across to each other as they go about their tasks, murmurs of conversation interrupted by occasional bursts of laughter, and even... children?

What Medusa pictured as a small band of fighters, maybe some support personnel, is actually a bustling community with people milling about in the streets, the occasional child darting in and out of the crowd, sometimes with others in tow.

The Leviathan pulls up to the dock and the deckhands toss ropes to the awaiting men, who catch them and tie off the ship. A vessel this size would normally not fit in the presumably shallow water of the harbor, but considering the wards, there must be more magic at work.

One of the dock workers looks up to the ship after securing his line. He takes in Medusa, his eyes widening as he notes her golden-green skin, scales along her collarbone. At no point does he become hostile, but he watches her cautiously, suspiciously until she slips into the background of the docking process and waits for Psyche or Alec.

On her way to find her companions, she passes the captain again, and he narrows his eyes and continues his conversation. So much negative and suspicious behavior toward her has her rethinking if she should have left her island. At least there, the only person who loathed her was herself. That is a feeling that is always there, simmering under the surface for pretty much her entire life.

Her thoughts are still a storm cloud of emotion when she finally spots Psyche coming up the stairs at the back of the ship. When Psyche sees her, she smiles a bright smile and Medusa swears it can rival the moon.

Medusa has joined a rebellion against the Pantheon, completely upending what meager life she had. Is this really the time for developing a crush on a god? One that would likely fizzle out before it even had a chance to start if the god in question found out what she really almost walked in on.

Once she is in front of Medusa, Psyche says, "I'm sorry it took me so long to make my way to you. I had to discuss the transfer and care of Cadmus. That's all taken care of now and I would love to take you to get settled. How does that sound?"

Psyche was with Cadmus. Did he tell her the truth once the dangerous beast was safely gone? Medusa's stomach clenches at the thought of the goddess looking at her with disappointment.

Oh yeah, Psyche asked her a question. Right.

Medusa nods. "That sounds wonderful."

The thought of all the stares that will inevitably come once they step off the boat is unsettling, but Medusa cannot stay on board forever and if it is in Psyche's company, she can endure it. Psyche loops her arm through Medusa's and they walk over to the gangway and off the ship.

The Isle is gleaming in the golden hour of the setting sun. The tall rock formations that hide it from the front should block out said sun, but somehow it's still brightly illuminating the community. Medusa finds there are many things she wants to inquire about later and if magic plays a part in their function is high on the list. They make their way through a worn dirt street, and she closes her eyes and takes in the sounds and smells. The mild breeze coming off the harbor mixes its salty smell with scaring meats, roasting vegetables, metal being worked, and stables. The inaudible murmur of people talking, and the clanging of tools from the blacksmiths come together in a song of community. It has been so long since Medusa has been anywhere populated. She does her best to stay grounded and breathe deeply so the noise does not overwhelm her.

AN HOUR LATER, Medusa is in her new lodgings. Despite the initial shocked face of the dock worker, most of the people Medusa passed on the street were warm toward her. There was an occasional concerned face, even a couple of hostile ones, but it is not as bad as she had been expecting. No children ran away in terror after seeing her.

Psyche set her up in a room in a building up on the hillside, equipped with a bed with soft white linens, a modest dresser, a chair, a trunk, and a bedside table. The view out of the small window captures the buildings going down the hill and then the bay down at the bottom. The Mysts are visible as well and linger on the edge of the horizon.

With a little time to kill before she goes exploring the Isle with Psyche, Medusa hopes to bathe. Cleaning up would be a welcomed relief after their time at sea and Medusa misses the hot spring from her cavern. There's a washbasin in her room but she braves going to the baths down the hall. They passed them on the way to her room and the call of the warm water outweighs her anxiousness about being around people.

The towels are soft under her fingers as Medusa grabs one from a small stack on top of the dresser and a thin silk robe that is hanging on the back of her door. The bronze color is very appealing, and she wonders if it was random or chosen for her.

The hallway is thankfully empty on the way to the bath. The end of the hall opens up to a large area with five small pools of bubbling hot water, separated by stained glass for privacy, each with a view similar to the one from her room but with a much larger opening. They are all empty, so she chooses the one at the end that feels the most isolated from the others. Removing her dirty travel clothes, everything but the hood and talisman around her neck, Medusa makes a mental note to ask Psyche more specifics about the hood. Can it get wet? Are there any important things she should know about it?

The hot water caresses her skin, and she sighs out loud at how good it feels. The tension in her body slowly melts away, and she can feel her muscles slipping into relaxation. Bubbles gently massage the soreness away and an ache that she had not noticed in her bones finally recedes.

This is the first time bathing without the constant wriggling and hissing of her serpents and she relishes the quiet. In their absence, though, Medusa realizes she has more awareness of them than she ever noticed before. An unexplainable feeling, the quiet is unnerving and welcome. She can normally feel the presence of each of them. How much more is there to unlock with her serpentine companions?

Medusa crosses her arms over the ledge of the window and relaxes as she takes in the view. It constantly surprises her how much more is here than she expected. It has been eight years, but she has never even heard the mention of a possible resistance group. Can they have gained this much momentum and support in only a few years? Tired of the never-ending swirl of questions in her head, she tries to just calm her mind and focus on what is in front of her. The setting sun is almost below the horizon, and lights flicker on in the windows of the Isle as people light candles and prepare for their evenings.

A group of children play in an empty portion of the street. They are holding hands, skipping in a circle, and when she listens carefully, she can hear the hints of a nursery rhyme being sung. Conversation in the hallway, moving toward the baths, quickly drowns out the sounds of the Isle, getting closer every second. Medusa reaches for her towel to leave, but it is too late. A group of three men come in, chatting amongst themselves loudly about their most recent exploits. Quietly moving to the back of her tub, stays as quiet as possible, hoping to escape their notice. Once they settle in their tub, she can leave.

The men seem like they are about to get into the tub on the opposite side of the bathing room when one of them scans the room and his sights land on her.

17

MEDUSA

Panic rears its head at the look in his eyes, and Medusa's serpents sluggishly come out of their slumber in response. The energy coming off of the men has every instinct telling her to run, but she knows she is cornered. Immediately, she curses herself for ending up in this situation, warranted or not.

"Well," he says with a smile on his face that looks anything but friendly. "Heard you were here. Didn't know if the rumors were true."

His friends follow the direction of his stare. They look equally excited about their find, and she doubts their intentions are cordial. Medusa has no choice but to stay in the water, keeping her vulnerability as minimal as possible. If she does not humor them with a reply, they will get bored and leave her alone.

"I'm talking to you." The first man says. "Wouldn't expect some half-snake *thing* to know basic manners, though." His friends laugh raucously.

"I don't recall hearing a question," Medusa answers with a stare that is getting more hostile by the moment. She tries to reign in the fear and her temper, having just arrived on the Isle and not wanting to cause trouble until she at least has some answers. If they force Medusa out because she has to defend herself against these men, she will spend the rest of her life in isolation, driven mad by the barrage of questions that she knows will never leave her.

Apparently, this is the wrong response and the man's expression goes from cruel humor to being indignantly offended that she would dare address him this way. "We are just having a friendly conversation here. No need to get all emotional."

"Look at you," the first one spits out, disgust painted all over his face. "The rumors are that Athena did this to you in a fit of jealousy. Supposedly you were some great beauty. You don't look so beautiful now, do you?"

She wants to respond angrily. Defend herself. It would fall on deaf ears. Medusa's pulse races as her frantic mind scrambles for a solution. What does she do? Besides wishing she was dressed and not exposed right now? Getting out and at least being in her robe would be preferable to this. Maybe she can slip away if she plans it right.

Before she processes, they are at the side of the tub, standing above her. Medusa raises her hand, without thinking or hesitating, reaching for the hood to defend herself. A strong grip latches on to her arm and stops her just before she reaches it.

"I don't think so. See, we are just going to continue our friendly chat, and you're going to sit here and pretend to be civilized," the first man says, as if she is being some unruly child. "Now tell me, I'm dying to know, are those scales all over?" His companions snicker, content to leave them talking to the first man. He is clearly the one running their dynamic.

Medusa tries to pull her arm back out of the man's grasp. He laughs as if restraining her presents little challenge as the third man grabs her other arm and they jerk her out of the water, up onto her feet, standing naked in between them, facing the first man. He leers at her, looking her up and down as she struggles in vain against the grips of the men holding her.

"Get your hands off me."

They all laugh. "C'mon now, we're just havin' some fun," rasps the man restraining her left arm.

"Exactly," the first man responds. He takes a step back to get a better picture of her and she wants to scream with rage. Rage over how defenseless she is at this moment. At herself for letting her guard down long enough for something like this to happen. Mostly at the cruel people in this world who are only happy as long as someone is under their heel. Her serpents start to hiss and shift aggressively, even under the hood.

The head asshole steps back toward her and says, "You almost look like a real girl. Let's see if you feel like one, too."

A bright light fills the room behind her as a female voice booms, "DO NOT PUT YOUR HANDS ON HER!" The man holding her right side panics, flailing and grabbing wildly and chaotically. His hand grasps her hood and pulls it down. One moment, she goes from struggling to free herself from her would-be assailants, to looking at three more in a long line of stone statues. She looks into their faces, wrenched in horror for eternity. When her eyes land on the frozen face of the first man, she feels no guilt, no shame. She can only muster disgust for him and every person like him who just takes and takes. She spits on his face and turns to put on her robe, pulling up her hood as she does so.

Psyche stands in the doorway and they stare silently at each other until all Medusa can think to ask is, "How were you safe when my hood was down? Poseidon said he was the only one who could look at me."

"It's my magic that makes that hood work, so naturally, the source of said magic would likely be immune," she answers with a warm smile. Then, with a mischievous glint in her eye, she adds, "Plus, the things Poseidon thinks he knows but actually doesn't could fill The Great Library and then some."

This draws a laugh from Medusa, and she is grateful for the moment of brevity. Medusa looks at the statues and remembers the incident with Cadmus on the ship.. If Psyche knows about Cadmus, she will never look the other way at this. Then it is a pattern. She quietly asks, "what's going to happen?"

Confused, Psyche asks, "What do you mean? Only the Fates know the future, well sometimes an Oracle gets glimpses, and then," she trails off and Medusa interrupts her.

"No, what's going to happen to me? I killed three men and just got here. You can't possibly still want me to stay after this." Despite Medusa's best efforts, desperation is present in her voice and she knows Psyche can hear it. She hates being so weak and needing this place and these people, but this is the first time she has begun to hope that there can be a life beyond her island. That is not something Medusa is ready to give up yet, but there are three lives she must answer for.

Psyche walks over and places her hand on the silk shoulder of Medusa's robe and looks earnestly into her eyes. "Absolutely nothing is going to happen to you. Even if you didn't have a literal god as your witness that it was self-defense, no one reasonable would think that in the bath a lone naked woman would be the aggressor against three men. I will have someone come take care of our new decor," she adds with a smirk, "While you and I work on taking care of *you*. Before you object," she says, putting a hand up, "I have already ordered tea and food for us to have in the lovely private lounge near your room. I came in here when I did to tell you about it."

Medusa takes a final glance back at the men. She imagines how the scenario would have played out without her snakes and feels a small bit of gratitude that they were there.

AFTER A SOOTHING MINT TEA, an assortment of foods, and some little spiced cookies with a thin white icing, Medusa is feeling a little stronger on her feet. The conversation with Psyche has been light but stimulating. Invigorating and healing. They talked about everything and nothing. It is easy to forget that Psyche is a god, and Medusa could almost forget that she herself is a monster. Everything with Psyche feels natural, and Medusa is recognizing the romantic attraction she has for the goddess. The flirtation has been one-sided, but it is so hard to tell sometimes. While she has always been an over thinker, eight years of isolation will magnify that, making her question everything, often well past the point she still should.

There is also another factor to consider. Being around people again is still so new, and it easily overwhelms Medusa. With all the emotional unrest and questions swimming in her mind, it is ridiculous to be entertaining thoughts of romance and attraction. Even if Medusa acts on the feelings she suspects she has, how will she know if she is ready? Best not to think about it, she decides, as if it is really that easy.

The conversation shifts to the soul oaths and the Oasis. Psyche is telling Medusa some of the most entertaining reactions people have had when they see the Oasis for the first time. Before she can stop herself, Medusa is saying the pun that immediately comes to mind, "or should I say OATHasis," and immediately regrets it. She cringes internally, but Psyche laughs. Only to humor her. "Have you tried to go back to the Oasis just for yourself since we talked about it?" Medusa asks.

"I haven't," Psyche replies, shaking her head. A quizzical look comes over her face and she asks, "Do you want to go there now? I was going to take you on a walk through our city here, but I'm very intrigued by this."

Medusa nods vigorously. "Yes!"

They hold hands and close their eyes. The contact is sinful and decadent., illicit. Something Medusa can cherish in these split -second moments and get lost in her infatuation with a gorgeous goddess. When they open them again, they are in the Oasis once more. Nothing has changed, and Medusa is once again getting lost looking up at the starlight. The fireflies are still here; they have just scattered more on the periphery, glowing brightly. The Oasis is an absolute dream.

The familiar presence of Medusa's constant companions has a soothing effect, surprising her. Holding up her hand to one of them and a snake coils itself around her fingers.

"Can you change things while we are in here, or do you even control what it is at all? Is it something that's just attuned to your magic?"

Psyche chuckles. "So many questions! I have only really used this for the oaths. I've never tried to make changes. This is just the way it was when I first conceptualized it."

Medusa and Psyche lie down in the sand to look up at the stars better. The ground feels nothing specific, which is nice because as textures go, the grainy roughness is not one of her favorites. The earth feels solid beneath her. As she runs a hand over a scaly spot on her arm, Medusa does not find it as unpleasant and grating as usual.

Together, they point out constellations in the sky that they know, discussing the legends and histories of them. Whichever one they talk about glows brighter than all the others until they move on to the next one.

During the conversation, Psyche laces her fingers through Medusa and squeezes gently. Medusa closes her eyes and savors the contact that is dimmed on this plane. Unlike when other people shake her hand and touch her shoulder back in reality,

Psyche's touch never feels like too much. Every time Medusa holds Psyche's hand, it feels like it is not enough. Medusa looks into the labyrinth of Psyche's eyes and earnestly looks for any clues that Psyche is enchanted with Medusa as well. Flashes of statues and death fill Medusa's mind and she looks away abruptly, not waiting for the sting of Psyche doing so first. They lay there in silence, fingers intertwined, until Psyche squeezes Medusa's fingers and their time in the Oasis ends.

They are back in the lounge, and it has gotten quite late. Psyche says goodbye and Medusa avoids making eye contact, still raw from the emotional trials and inner turmoil. Despite her racing thoughts, Medusa climbs into bed, determined to be well-rested because tomorrow is the day she will meet the Oracle.

18

HESTIA

Looking around the table at the gathered members of the Pantheon, Hestia wonders how many know how bad things are. Do they know how the mortals are suffering? How many of the gods are complicit in murder and trafficking? Zeus, Aphrodite, Athena, Poseidon, and Ares are wading so deep in corruption it is amazing the Fates themselves have yet to intervene. Hestia has to wonder sometimes if the Fates aren't just a myth. How can they be real and allow so much evil to thrive? Not interfering with natural orders is one thing- droughts, famines, diseases - but for them to completely ignore the bondage, the abductions, the executions, the children ripped from families to serve the Temples. She can only hope that they are the ones moving the pieces, and that they are using the Allegiance as their sword. Even if they are not, she knows every rebel will do their damnedest to see it done.

She tries to stay focused as Demeter drones on about crop supplies, but she stops paying attention once she hears this year's harvests have been bountiful. The rest is just background noise to her thoughts as she keeps replaying the injustice of it all.

121

"Hestia," Apollo whispers, nudging her arm from the seat to her right and snapping her back to the present.

Everyone is staring at her, and Hestia realizes someone must have asked her a question.

"My apologies," Hestia says demurely. "My thoughts were wandering away from me. Would you mind repeating?"

Demeter clears her throat, possibly in annoyance, and says, "I asked if I could come by the library this afternoon. My farmers have been looking for new ways to harvest what our earth has to offer and I was wondering if I might browse your agricultural section?"

"Oh, of course, you needn't even ask," Hestia replies, wishing she were invisible at this moment as she feels her ears turning red.

The conversation moves on without her as they wrap up the last bits of Pantheon business, say their salutations, and file out of the room. As she nears the door, Hestia notices that Zeus, Athena, and Aphrodite remain seated. They cannot be lingering for any good reason and Hestia hovers just on the other side of the door, straining to hear their conversation. She freezes, breath catching in her throat, when she hears Zeus talk.

His low, raspy voice barely carries to her, "Is everything set for this month's auction?"

Auction? Hestia's brows furrow in confusion. A *monthly* auction which sounds like happens regularly is not something she has heard anything about, which is very surprising.

"You know it is. Have we ever not been more than prepared for one of these stupid things? Honestly, they're so boring," Athena answers.

"Oh, they are dreadfully dull," Aphrodite admits, but adds, "The coin they bring in is plenty shiny, though."

Hestia's stomach is in knots as she waits to hear what they could auction in secret. This is something she wishes she never needs to know about, but lacks the luxury or privilege of remaining indifferent. Hestia's heart and soul will never allow her to stand by idly. Especially when hope is on the horizon in the form of the Allegiance.

"As you know, this month's event is at my Temple and, as it's the Temple of Love, this batch of nymphs will serve the role of sexual servitude," Aphrodite continues.

"I love it when it's your turn to host Zeus. When that rolls around, I'm generally in need of a new chamber servant, having typically disposed of the last already. Practically useless things," Athena laughs.

Nymphs? Hestia's stomach churns, and she fights to keep the contents where they belong. As she runs through what she just heard, her head spins. It is heartbreaking to think of the beautiful nymphs bound to slavery in secret. How far does the corruption run for there to be enough buyers for an auction?

Nymphs are rarely seen in developed areas, since they prefer the peace that comes from living in nature, connected to the elements they are bonded with. There have been rumors of nymphs being forced into chains, but those rumors are always rapidly hushed. The Pantheon has loudly denounced and decried the prospect of that kind of trafficking, yet they themselves are the ones perpetuating it.

Hestia tries to remain calm, expression neutral, lest anyone come down the hallway and see her as she gathers as many details as possible, tears rimming the edges of her eyes.

"How do we know that stupid group of rebels won't interfere?" Athena asks.

"My contact tells me they are unaware of the auctions still," Zeus answers. "He won't give me their location yet, but he's there with them."

Hestia stops breathing. *No.*

A gentle nudge on her elbow startles Hestia, and she has to stifle a gasp.

Spinning around, Dionysus is there with a finger to his lips, and pulls her into an alcove as the sound of footsteps close in. They duck behind a large urn, dropping out of sight as Poseidon and Ares round the corner of the hallway and go into the room, rejoining Zeus, Aphrodite, and Athena.

"I'm glad I was the one to find you snooping, and not one of those three." Dionysus says, jutting his chin toward the door.

"I wasn't snooping." Hestia huffs defensively.

"Don't bother, it's ok. We all have our reasons for what we do." He gives her a pointed look, and she wonders again if there is more to Dionysus than meets the eye.

They part ways and Hestia walks to her quarters, breathing deeply to keep it together until she can be somewhere private.

Rushing into her chambers, she goes straight for the bathing room, where she immediately drops to the floor. Her lungs scream for air as sobs overtake her, chest tightening as Hestia finally allows herself to react to everything she has overheard. Her stomach threatens to revisit today's lunch, and she fights to rein herself in.

The Pantheon's callousness should not surprise her anymore. But to hear just how far they are delving into their own depravity has her truly scared to think of the depths to which they would sink to get what they want.

When enough time has passed, and her nerves and stomach have finally calmed, she heads for the library, eager to share what she has learned with Alec and the Allegiance.

THE STONE IS GLOWING AGAIN as Hestia pulls it from the cubbyhole. His presence makes her smile, even if it may contain bad news. There is always that risk. The reward of Alec's voice is sweet as it fills her mind.

For the first time, the message contains no news. Alec only wanted to talk to Hestia.

Alec tells her about his past few days and how happy he is to be back at the Isle, even if it is never for long.

When he finishes speaking, Hestia takes a minute to bask in the glow of joy that sparks in her with each new message, then steels herself to deliver the gut-wrenching news. The Allegiance has no clue about these auctions. The thought of what else the Pantheon could be hiding makes Hestia shiver. Especially as they seem to be getting bolder and discussing these things in more public spaces. They do not seem to care if anyone catches them, but that cannot be the case. If it became known, the people would resist.

Does she tell him about the possible traitor amongst them? Does she have proof that there is one? Maybe all that information will do is rip the rebels apart with suspicion. No. Definitely better to wait until she has more specifics.

As Hestia tucks the stone away, she pauses. Hestia neglected to mention her feelings. She does not want that declaration tainted by the news she delivered. A separate message should be all right.

Once again, she closes her eyes and speaks.

"Hello one more time, my dear friend. There was no place for this in my last message, so I want to say it here. I couldn't go any longer without telling you I, too, think of you. Quite often. It seems silly. We have spent little time in each other's company, but your eyes follow me everywhere I go. I look forward to the day when I get to see them in front of me again, instead of only in my heart and dreams. In the meantime, I will make a deal with you. I'll do my best to be careful as long as you do the same."

Content, she puts it in the nook and slides the board closed over it, her magic making the seam disappear.

Dragging a cart behind her, Hestia walks through the library.

After a few minutes, it is filled with books on nymphs. Hestia must keep her research to nighttime and put the books away each time she is done, lest the Acolytes get too curious. This may be her temple, but this close to Zeus, one never knows where anyone's loyalties truly lie.

19

MEDUSA

It is a beautifully sunny day, but Medusa finds little joy in it as her nerves take over and the weight of her impending visit to the Oracle crashes over her with every step she takes The crowd now has more sets of eyes that have shifted from curiosity to suspicion. A lot less than she expected, though, after last night. They must not know about the men she killed yet.

A group of small children are playing tag, weaving in and out of the people walking, neither group paying each other any mind. One of the boys slams into the back of Medusa's thighs after not watching where he was running. He cries with a hand to his head and she crouches down to check on him. He looks up at her and his eyes widen, but not entirely with fear.

"You're the snake lady," he says, barely louder than a whisper.

Medusa answers, prepared for the horror that is sure to sweep across his face any moment, "I am. Is your head okay?"

He nods, forgetting to blink. "I think it would be so cool to have snakes growing out of my head. I love animals! It would be like having a *hundred* new best friends. WOW."

Medusa's jaw drops. He is not afraid of her? And thinks these cursed serpents are a *good* thing?

The boy's friends return with a woman who appears to be his mother. Concern is etched on his mother's face. As Medusa scans the children's expressions, their eyes focused on her in fear, she wonders if the boy's friends were protecting him from *her*. She braces herself for what she knows is coming. The mother grabbing her child and pulling him away in horror, dragging him off while scolding him of the dangers of being around someone so treacherous.

Much to her surprise, the woman says, "Joshua! Milo and Jeorge came to get me and said, you're hurt!" She turns to Medusa and adds, "Thank you for looking after him until I arrived. I hope he wasn't too much of a bother."

"Not at all," Medusa replies genuinely. "We were having a lovely chat about animals." She winks at the boy, who is looking back and forth between Medusa and his mother. He beams despite the growing bump on his head. One of his friends tugs on Joshua's arm and he they run off.

Joshua's mother leans in closer to Medusa and says,"I won't speak much on the subject because, frankly, I don't think they are worth our time." A passion comes through strongly in her voice that catches Medusa off guard. "I was very sorry to hear about what happened to you last night. Don't worry," she quickly adds. "The whole isle doesn't know about it. I work up at the compound where you are staying. They'll all know by the end of the day, though. I think you'll find more people here than not will feel angry about what happened to you. What we have here, this community, is fragile and there's no home here for people who would treat another person that way."

A Person.

Not a monster, not a beast. But a person.

Medusa expected the people here to riot against her when they heard what happened to three of their own. It never occurred to her for a second that any empathy would be spared for her and the realization makes tears stream from her eyes despite her best efforts to conceal them.

Saying nothing more, Joshua's mother gives Medusa a nod of solidarity, and walks away, leaving her there in shock over what had just transpired. The walk to the Oracle resumes with Medusa keeping her head ducked down, afraid that she will see evidence of horror in the eyes all around her, regardless of the kindness just shown to her by a stranger. The few gazes she meets, though, only convey more of the same warmth and compassion and Medusa continues to mull it all over as they reach the stone steps and begin their ascent to The Observatory.

The view from the top of the steps is nothing short of spectacular. "I would say this is breathtaking," Medusa huffs out. "But the steps took care of that." Looking over at Psyche, Medusa rolls her eyes internally, when she sees the goddess is not even slightly winded. *Gods.*

The entrance to the Observatory is near the top of the stairs. All that is visible is a glass dome with reflective window panes filling it out. The structure seems modest, but Medusa is not sure what she expected. Anything grand would likely be visible from the front of the Isle, defeating the purpose of the stealth measures in place.

The front of the dome has side-by-side glass doors, but instead of the mirrored glass, a beautiful stained glass design depicting the night sky sparkles in the daylight. The colors and constellations are clear and vivid. It is absolutely beautiful. Psyche opens the door and they enter a chamber that is dark despite the light that should come in from the glass dome above them. Candles along the floor show a set of circular curling stairs going down to their right. Psyche immediately descends and Medusa follows.

At the bottom, there is an impossibly large room. Instead of making the building taller, they carved it down into the rocks.

Rows and rows of shelves fill the room like a library, some holding books and scrolls, while others hold an array of crystals, jars of herbs, and possibly every mystical or academic ingredient someone could wish for. A long time ago, when she enjoyed learning, this place would have been a dream.

As they walk through the rows toward the back of the seemingly never-ending room. a disembodied voice weaves through the shelves and darkness.

"You have traveled far to be here, Medusa. Have you come to see what the Fates have in store for you?"

"Really, Cass?" Psyche asks. "Being a bit over the top, aren't we?"

Coming to a stop in front of a curtain along the farthest wall, a hand from the other side pulls it open dramatically, and Psyche rolls her eyes, making Medusa very curious about the dynamic between these two.

"My dear!" She exclaims, looking at Medusa. "I have been waiting for so long for this opportunity to speak with you. I have so much to tell you, and some that I still cannot, but I will reveal all I can. Please call me Cassandra, or Cass."

Full, voluminous hair frames her face like a cloud. Her orange and yellow robes make her rich walnut skin glow in the dim light of the sconces. The Olympic Oracle is much older. Medusa had only met her once, and even back then, she seemed ancient. Cass is in likely in her twenties, early twenties at that.

A narrow hallway leads to a small room with several armchairs, a couple of small tables, and a stack of books. It looks like a quiet nook to escape to. Medusa finds it oddly soothing and notices her nerves settling.

"Where would you like to begin?" Cass asks as she plops down in one of the armchairs, much more casually than one would expect from an oracle. Seeing the confusion on Medusa's face, Cass says, "I'm sure the Oracle at the Pantheon was prim and proper." She wrinkles her nose and continues, "Being raised outside of the Pantheon, I didn't exactly get their etiquette manual." The sarcasm in her voice is unmissable, but instead of finding it off-putting, Medusa feels like she has found a kindred soul.

"That's fair," Medusa responds. "And I'd like to start with my parents. What do I need to know about them, what they kept from me?" She and Psyche sit in the remaining two chairs that are next to each other and settle in to hear Cass's answer.

"I can't tell you everything that's been withheld from you. It's complicated, but the short version is, I was given this information when I was only a child. Only parts of it have been revealed to me, and I was told that we would know what was important when the time came."

"What could that possibly mean?" Medusa asks, resisting the urge to slap her palm to her forehead in frustration. "Why can't anything ever be a direct answer?" She tries to shove down the irritation, lest she push away the only person who can give her answers.

"I understand your confusion. All I can tell you about it is that when I was eight, the Fates came to me in a dream. They told me that one day I would meet a woman wronged by the gods, like so many others, except this one would be different. This one would be a very important piece to one of the most critical puzzles our society might collectively face. I was told that relevant information would reveal itself to me and when all the pieces come together, the tides of this world will shift and the gods will tremble."

Medusa just blinks in response, unsure of what to say. There has to be an error. She's positive about it.

"There's no chance I could be that important. I had my entire life stripped from me as they forced me into exile."

"It's not a mistake, Lyra," Psyche says, reaching out from one chair to the other to take her hand. A gesture that does not go unnoticed by Cass, who raises a quizzical brow. The goddess continues, "Destiny is here and pulling the strings. Something for which I, for one, am especially grateful." With that, she pats Medusa's hand and puts it back in her own lap, allowing Medusa to once again focus on the Cass.

"Your parents," Cass begins, "were actually the start of The Allegiance. They weren't involved, but it was their deaths that sparked it. Your uncle, Alec, was so enraged at what the gods had done, not only to your parents but to all the people they had stomped on, taken advantage of, and harmed all in the name of status and power.

"Your mother wasn't simply a god. She was in control of an extensive region and was beloved. The region itself hasn't been revealed to me yet, so I think that may yet play a part in all of this. I don't know how they did it, but when the Pantheon removed your parents from the history books, they somehow also made most of the world forget about them, and the people who *do* remember them all have conflicting stories. The only thing that could pierce the fog that hid their memories was true, unyielding love for them like your uncle bore and even then I question how accurate his own memories are. This game of information will be long and strategic, but in the meantime, we will do all we can to strike against the Pantheon with what everything we have."

"The Fates did reveal to me that you have a half-brother. He is unaware of you, as you have been of him. I hope we will know soon, as I am positive he will be an equally important factor in the time to come."

"Your mother was so much more than what they taught you. The Fates told me she was kind, fair, and compassionate. They flooded my mind with images of her, small visions of her helping people, ruling her region in a way that had her beloved by all. The Pantheon would never have gotten away with what they did to her if the public had known. They loved her so much that when she introduced her new husband, your father, they welcomed him to her side, despite the fact that mortals and gods are not supposed to form romantic attachments… physical ones are a different matter of course." O says with a smirk.

"Surely they didn't kill my parents just because of a relationship?"

Psyche's story about Selene flashes into her mind. Maybe they would.

"That is how it would appear to the only person who even remembers them, your uncle. The Pantheon wasn't concerned because they didn't believe anyone could ever have escaped their glamour. What your uncle doesn't know, what I only know because of the Fates, is that when you and your brother were both very young, the official Oracle at the Pantheon had been delving into dark magic. She used her sinister abilities to extract a prophecy from the universe. I don't yet know what that prophecy is, but I know it made the Pantheon nervous enough to go through the trouble of removing such a prominent figure in our society."

"A prophecy?" Medusa asks, startled.

Medusa's head is swimming with even more questions. Every answer leads to fresh lines of inquiry, and it is all too much for her. She gets up to leave the room, but Cass grabs her wrist.

"Sit." Cass says, but her voice is changed. It is deeper than before and sounds ancient.

"The spider hides
many lies.
A great power
hidden from time.
Only when the
three are united
May this wrong
be righted.
Hold fast. Stay true.

For we will
guide you through."

Cass slumps over, groaning. She reaches up to rub her temples.

"I always forget how bad the post-prophecy headache is," Cass says, her voice back to normal. "The Fates know how to leave a girl with parting gifts."

"Why do the Fates insist on communicating in riddles and rhymes? Why can't they just tell me what any of this means?"

"They might not even fully know themselves." Cass says with a dismissive wave of her hand. "There are secrets in this world kept even from the Fates."

Medusa wrinkles her forehead. "How is that possible? They know all. See all."

"It would shock you to know how many things slip past them. Don't let their vanity fool you, they can be bested, at times," Cass says.

"This is a lot to take in. I need fresh air," Medusa says. She does not wait for a response before jumping out of her seat and heading straight for the winding stairs.

20

HESTIA

Hestia rubs her eyes, trying to stave off the slight stinging that comes from reading for hours. She has been compiling information on how to best care for any nymphs they rescue. A full-scale plan is forming to free the captive nymphs, and it is astounding how much energy the Allegiance is expending on nymphs. Not because she did not think they would care about protecting beings that were neither mortal, demi, nor god. Some of the more pathetic people see them as lesser, but Hestia and the Allegiance would never see them as such. The surprise comes from how risky it will be. As far as Hestia is aware, the Allegiance has never planned a mission directly in the face of the gods.

Hope blooms in her chest at the thought of them pulling this off. She will have to be vigilant in her surveillance, as every detail will be crucial to this going smoothly. Anxiety and concern try to slam against the wall of optimism, but she shoves it down. It must be done. If they fail, then they fail. Doing nothing would be the biggest failure.

The absolute tantrum Aphrodite will throw if this goes well will be extra satisfaction. Maybe Hestia will even be present to see it, even though she plans to be nowhere around if possible. The others have training and skills. All Hestia has is a convenient location from which to steadily eavesdrop.

The clock in the library chimes, indicating she has worked until two in the morning. Hestia jots down some notes but is not ready to send the information yet. There are a few more tomes to give a quick pass through. Tucking the note next to the stone, Hestia deflates a small bit when its surface is not glowing, the cloudy swirling magic seeming dull when not bringing word from Alec. Things can get hectic when planning missions, so she hides the sadness away along with the worry lingering on the edges.

Once Hestia is satisfied that the evidence of her late-night study session is successfully hidden, she flicks her wrist and the library falls into darkness. She closes the door and heads to bed.

THE MOON BEAMS down through her open window as Hestia is ripped awake from a nightmare that is already fading.

Peeling off her nightgown, the silky material of her nightgown is clinging to her skin from a cold sweat.

The spring-fed tub in her chambers greets her with cool water. Hestia doesn't take the time to warm it, wanting the frigid shock to yank her out of her emotions.

Details of the nightmare are vanishing from her mind, but an uneasy feeling lingers with her. Dunking her head, the jolt of the icy water on her face helping to calm her nerves.

The feeling remains, even once her pulse is even, and her heartbeat is steady. It must be lingering from her dream, but a nagging voice in the back of Hestia's mind says something is wrong.

Avoiding the cold wet puddle of her sheets, she lays down on the sofa, tossing and turning there before falling into a fitful sleep that is thankfully devoid of any nightmares.

WHEN SHE WAKES, the looming dread is still present, clawing and nagging quietly in her heart. It plagues her throughout the day, and has her looking over her shoulder and monitoring everyone closely, certain at any point her world is going to come crashing down.

The clock on the wall in her chambers ticks and the normally soothing noise is grating. With twenty minutes left to get to the grotto to meet Dionysus, it is time to get moving. The investigation into Hera id slow going and tedious, but Hestia hopes that someone would do the same for her if she disappeared one day.

The walk through the compound is nerve-racking, and as she makes it to the outer walls of the Temple and through the gate, she breathes a little easier.

While walking below a series of windows, Hestia hears Aphrodite's voice coming from the room above. What are these rooms? Security outpost?

"Make sure every soldier has their eyes peeled for rebel activity at the Love Temple event. If anything goes wrong, I will hold you personally responsible, Commander."

"Yes, goddess." A voice answers. Hestia recognizes it as Orpheus, second in command of the Heroes, and personal security to Zeus.

"Nicodemus should be checking in shortly. He has proven his usefulness thus far. Let's see where that can take us."

Nicodemus? Nicodemus.

The captain of the Leviathan, Nicodemus. Allegiance Council member, Nicodemus.

Hestia has to warn them.

She abandons her route to the grotto. Dionysus will understand.

Each second ticks by agonizingly slow as the walk back the way she came takes forever.

When Hestia bumps into Ares, he chuckles at her with his usual menacing air.

"I think you should be careful where you're going there, don't you? Accidents can happen too easily."

Is there more meaning behind that? Is he on to her, or is he being himself?

The uncertainty is driving her mad. She needs to get to the library the moment it will be empty. Her heart is in her throat as she races to deliver this information. After, hopefully Hestia can make another attempt at getting some sleep.

As expected, the library is silent and vacant. Hestia feels weak and shaky as she trembles with anxiety. Her intuition is screaming. If only it would be more clear. What does it mean?

She tries to focus on getting the message sent to the Allegiance. The stone is flashing and her heart pauses, ready to shatter at any moment if this feeling has anything to do with what is about to come through the stone.

"Hello, My Fire." She blushes at the silly nickname. A joke between them regarding the constant misinterpretation of her sacred duty, maintaining the Flame of Knowledge.

The splintering cracks that have started to form recede and Hestia's heart is momentarily safe from shattering as Alec's voice comes through, the jovial tone soothing her even if only a little.

Alec keeps the mood light for a minute, and Hestia is grateful for the slight reprieve. The message ends on a more sobering note.

"Preparations are heavily underway and even though I'm thrilled to be back on the Isle, I'm itching to get going. Every second I think of those nymphs being held captive, and what they will be forced to do, I can't stand it," he says and she can hear the pain in his voice. It is one thing that allows Alec to hold space in her heart. His anger at injustice and desire to right it matches her own and makes her think *he* should be the one nicknamed "Fire."

"As always, please be careful. It's difficult having one's heart be so far away."

Hestia blinks at those words. *His heart?* Could he possibly love her? Does she love him? Her head shakes at the silly thought. Of course she loves him… is she *in* love with him as well?

The auction details spill out of her as she tries to be as clear and concise as possible. So much care is going into making sure the nymphs have everything they need until the Allegiance can get them home.

Too often, despite everything being risked spying on the gods, Hestia feels like an imposter amongst the rebels. They are out there getting things done while she sits in the lap of luxury, disgusted by all of it.

One time Hestia mentioned this to Alec and his next message was full of reassurances of the importance of what she is doing. He reminded her that being inches from the wrath of the gods every day and working against them in secret is equally as dangerous as everything the Allegiance does, if not more so. Hestia is as much a member of the Allegiance as anyone else who has taken the oath, and for the first time Hestia felt like she really was a part of everything, not just an informant bystander.

"There is one last thing I have to tell you. There's a traitor amongst the Allegiance. It's-"

The door bursts open, startling her. Hestia freezes when she sees members of the Guard filing in, Aphrodite bringing up the rear with a victorious smirk on her face.

Hestia closes her eyes and says, "They found me out," and then drops the stone, watching from the corner of her eye as it rolls out of sight behind the curtains.

"Seems like our little bookworm has been naughty," Aphrodite tuts.

Hestia rapidly tries to come up with a lie that will get her out of this, anything to cover for what she's actually been up to. Her mind, so full of information, fails her and comes up empty with any excuses. She stays quiet and sees what they know.

They all stand there in silence, and the tension builds to an unbearable thickness. Aphrodite's face is the picture of evil satisfaction. The surety on it warns Hestia that they must be certain of their accusations and she truly does not know what to do.

Zeus walks into the room, his silver cloak billowing behind him.

As Hestia opens her mouth to say something, anything, Zeus holds a hand up to stop her. Shaking his head, he snaps his fingers, and a jolt of electricity shoots through Hestia and her body seizes before crumpling on the floor.

21

APHRODITE

The doors to the dungeon fly open as Aphrodite strolls in, Zeus and Guards behind her with an unconscious Hestia in tow.

They walk their prisoner past the long rows of cells until they reach a large one at the end. Dropping Hestia on the ground unceremoniously, Aphrodite smirks at how pathetic her rival looks lying there in a heap.

The lock clicks in place and the Guard passes the key over to Aphrodite as she admires the white stone bars. The granite hums with the millennia of magic it has been infused with, designed to keep even a titan in check if one could get them into it. Fortunately for Hestia, Zeus is hesitant to upgrade to a god cage, so this will do for the moment.

Disgust rolls through Aphrodite as she pictures a fellow god working with those rebels, that *scum*. Would Aphrodite betray everyone herself? Of course, but for purely selfish reasons, like a craving for more power, or to get Andromeda back. These pests are disrupting the entire ecosystem just because mortals refuse to accept their place.

Aphrodite is still standing there, staring at Hestia's still form with loathing when footsteps sound behind her.

Poseidon, Ares, Athena, and Demeter walk her way, whispering amongst themselves in hushed tones. Everyone Aphrodite summoned. Excellent.

"What is the meaning of this?" Ares asks, voice full of annoyance over being dragged down here.

Aphrodite hides her inner satisfied smile, instead fixing an expression of grave concern across her features before answering him.

"I received urgent information that I felt was imperative I act upon swiftly. I am in contact with someone amongst those impudent rebels. He claims he can give us Medusa. I was hesitant to trust him, insisting he present me with actionable information that corroborates his knowledge of the rebel movements."

Pausing, Aphrodite assesses their reactions. This needs to go her way, so she waits to tailor her response to what she knows they will want to hear. Should she appear outraged? Hurt by the betrayal?

Demeter shakes her head. "Get to the point."

Aphrodite fights a biting retort, and instead sadly replies, "I couldn't believe what I discovered. It was outrageous. He told me we have a member of our inner circle who has betrayed us. He went through the different messages that had made their way to the rebels from the Olympic Temple. I went back and worked out the only people who would have had access to that information. The only person who was always just outside, always nearby when we discussed these matters, was her."

Aphrodite points a shaky finger in Hestia's direction.

Pushing betrayed emotions into her voice, she asks the group with a raised eyebrow, "Unless it was one of you?"

"Leave her here until I've reviewed these findings. Having her in the dungeon while we evaluate is one thing. I'm going to make damn sure she's guilty before we condemn her to a traitorous fate," Zeus commands, and Aphrodite has to resist the urge to roll her eyes at his swaggering authority.

"Of course," Aphrodite replies demurely, gesturing for them to make their way back out of the dungeons.

Once they are gone, a final glance is thrown over Aphrodite's shoulder for one last look at her slumbering rival.

In the hallway, whispers meet Aphrodite before she turns the corner. Certain words come through, but she cannot hear everything. Something about a witch.

The conversation stops once Aphrodite rounds the corner and finds Zeus and Athena. Zeus's face is red in anger and Athena's expression is masked irritation.

Aphrodite lays in the enormous bed in Zeus's chambers, satisfied, lazily staring at the ceiling. Zeus and Ares are already getting dressed again, but she is in no hurry, choosing to take this time to relax in post-coital pleasure.

Ares says his goodbyes, the door closing quietly behind him as he leaves.

Once Aphrodite and Zeus are alone, she turns to him, fixing a pout on her face.

"What is it, my pet?" He asks, pausing from combing his long grey beard.

"Well," Aphrodite answers coyly, eyes widening to convey the youthful innocence that she knows he has a weakness for. "The search of Hestia's rooms found pages of coded notes that appear to line up with everything our informant said. You can't possibly be thinking of releasing her."

Zeus shakes his head. "I'm not sure what I want to do with

her, aside from making sure she can never contact those fucking rebels again."

His eyes simmer with anger at the betrayal, likely more to do with his bruised ego than any sense of loyalty to their institutions.

Moving to the edge of the bed, still naked, Aphrodite begins lightly caressing up and down Zeus's arm.

She leans up onto her knees, bringing her lips to his ear, allowing her warm breath to stoke his desires and make him more compliant.

"Let me play with her," Aphrodite croons. His gray hair is rough as she threads her fingers through, letting her lips brush the edges of his earlobe.

Zeus groans and grows hard again, making Aphrodite smile at her skills.

While lightly stroking his erection, she continues, "I will make sure she suffers, I promise."

He reaches for her breast but she pulls back, not letting him have his fun until he gives her an answer.

"Fine," he replies, and she nods, giving him access to her body, nothing more. It is fortunate that Zeus cares little for feelings, since Aphrodite will never have any for him.

He wraps his arms around her, lifting her up and placing her on his cock in one swift movement.

The sudden penetration makes Aphrodite yelp, but she enjoys the slight sting that comes with it. Zeus grips her hips, and her arms circle behind his neck for support, as he slides her up and down roughly.

Moans spill from her lips as he hits a steady rhythm. She adjusts the angle of her hips slightly, crying out when she finds that perfect angle.

Zeus roars his orgasm as he comes inside of her. She stays in place until he is thoroughly spent.

Dropping her onto the bed, indelicately, Zeus moves to his bathing chamber, apparently finished with her.

The hint of rejection fails to take root. She lies back, twirling her flaxen hair in between her fingers as she plots just how she will make Hestia miserable.

22

MEDUSA

Psyche catches up to Medusa at the top of the stone steps, staring out at the Isle city silently as the wind whips around her. She turns to Psyche, struggling to breathe, as her heart races. This has just been so much. Three days ago, Medusa woke up on her island the same as every other day and almost every moment since has been filled with chaos, confusion, violence, questions, upheavals.

Psyche takes her hand. "Close your eyes."

Medusa silently complies, clinging to the feeling of Psyche's touch. "Open."

They are in the Oasis, and all is quiet, calm. The wind is no longer whipping against her skin, her breathing steadies, and she finally begins to recenter. Medusa is so grateful for the abrupt lack of excess stimuli, and Psyche knew that is exactly what Medusa needs.

Looking into each other's eyes, hand in hand, Medusa is back on solid ground. They turn and look around and both gasp at the same time. Neither of them noticed the sky is no longer twilight and now has a sun that is either a rising or setting, the deep orange color with hints of maroon blending with pinks and purples.

"It's never changed before." Psyche turns back to look at Medusa with a startled but excited expression. "It might have something to do with you. I've never been here more than once with the same person. Sometimes I come back on my own - which is very nice, by the way. I can't thank you enough for the idea - but the scenery has never changed. I'm curious to see what other changes we might see."

"You're not worried about it?" Medusa asks, concerned she may have caused a problem. How can she so easily mess things up, even in her own mind?

Psyche waves her hand dismissively. "Not at all. I'm positive something would feel off if anything was wrong. I think this is simply our minds interacting with each other on this plane."

"Thank you for bringing me here. I'm finding myself constantly overwhelmed, my emotions, my senses, everything. There never seems to be a reprieve, except when I'm here. In fact," she says, feeling bold, taking Psyche's other hand. Maybe the goddess will tolerate this small contact from Medusa without being too horrified. "Here, the thought of touching another person isn't terrifying. This acclimation to people and physical touch is proving to be a challenging one. Every touch is magnified by the fact that it's one of the first in almost a decade. If I want to, say, hold someone's hand, that's an overwhelming concept out there. In here, it feels right, it feels safe."

Waves of shame cascade through Medusa. This is going to chase off the one person who seems to *see* her. Feeling self-conscious and vulnerable, Medusa tries to pull her hand away, but Psyche holds tight.

"Please, don't," Psyche says. "You don't have to be so quick to shut me out after letting me in for the briefest moment. Thank you for sharing this with me. I imagined it would be an adjustment, but

I will admit, I hadn't even considered that aspect of this for you. I will do my best to keep that in mind from now on, especially as someone who also has ideas about things like holding hands."

Relief floods Medusa's entire body. Such a small gesture of consideration has her feeling warm, acknowledged, and valuable for the first time in a long time. If only Psyche could have seen her *before*. The thoughts of what could have been circle and swirl in her mind, reminding Medusa just how much has been taken from her.

"I think the connection to my snakes is stronger here," Medusa says. "Everything else is dulled, but my connection to them is heightened. Do you know why?"

"I imagine it's because in here, the Oasis strips your senses away and bares your soul. No matter how you got them, they are an intrinsic part of you."

"Oh." It is all she can think to respond at first. Anger builds in her chest. "I never asked for this! To be so cursed that it alters my soul!" Tears threaten to fall, but she will not let them.

Psyche shakes her head. "I know, it's not fair." Psyche gently cups Medusa's chin, making her look into her eyes. "But what I also know is you aren't the monster they've made you out to be. The one you now believe yourself to be. I see someone who was horribly wronged but didn't give up. You even saved Cadmus. What kind of monster would do that?"

Medusa's cheeks burn with shame as Psyche's words confirm what Medusa already knows. If Psyche knew Medusa tried to kill Cadmus, she would be ashamed and disgusted.

"Maybe the curse wasn't the serpents! Maybe it was to make my appearance as ugly as my soul!" Angry tears continue to well up in her eyes.

Psyche grabs her by the shoulders and forces Medusa to look at her again. "Stop that! I know you've been alone, and you've truly suffered, but that doesn't define you. Poseidon is an evil god, who did a horrible thing to you. You didn't deserve it, and it certainly wasn't a reflection of your soul or your heart."

"But-"

"No. No, but. I have seen you show kindness and generosity to every person you meet until they give you a reason not to. *Despite* everything that has happened to you. Fates be damned. I wish you could see yourself the way I do."

Medusa is speechless as emotions build into a storm inside of her, fighting each other's currents. She closes her eyes and just breathes.

This shall not break me.

"Can we sit for a minute?" Medusa asks. "Just one more moment in the Oasis before we return?"

Psyche responds by sitting in the sand facing the sun, and patting the ground next to her. Medusa sits down shoulder to shoulder with Psyche and they sit there, hand in hand, once more, taking in the scenery and the comfort of each other's company.

BACK IN THE REAL WORLD, the sun sets as another warm day turns into early evening. Once they make it down from the Observatory, they find they both worked up quite an appetite on the trek. A stall with freshly grilled fish makes Medusa's stomach rumble. The smell of the spices is too alluring to refuse - although Medusa would normally be fine never having fish again after such a steady diet of it.

When they have eaten the last of the fish, Psyche purchases a couple of frozen berry desserts to eat as they walk to a council meeting.

The Allegiance Council meets once a week to discuss

current movements and map out any new plans. Psyche gives Medusa the shorthand version of what to expect in between bites. The group is efficient and to the point, the only conflict being where to allocate resources. There are so many areas of need and only so much the Allegiance can accomplish at once, so they do their best to keep chipping away at the never-ending list.

The Council Room where the meetings are held is back in the Compound where Medusa and Psyche are currently residing. Hopefully, that means Medusa can easily slip out and retreat to her room if things become too much. It is doubtful anyone will mind if Medusa is not there for all of it.

When Psyche had told Medusa about the mission being planned, it flabbergasted her to know the depths of the Pantheon's depravity. She has heard of the illegal markets where anything can be purchased for the right price and knows they are horrific, but these auctions are a new level of atrocious.

Conversation comes to a halt as Medusa and Psyche walk into the room, before slowly resuming. A large oval-shaped table dominates the space and is piled with books, maps, and charts. Charts keeping track of forces on both sides of the equation cover the walls. *Do not linger on them.* That may make her appear too nosy and seem suspicious. Everyone will be as hesitant to trust her as she is of them. There have been a few pleasant surprises so far in her interactions with people, but not enough to allow Medusa to let down her guard easily.

Men and women of varying ages fill the half-full table. The rest file in as they finish their chatter amongst each other. Once everyone is seated, there are twenty-two people at the table in total.

Medusa and Psyche sit at the end closest to the door. Psyche sees Medusa making note of the door's location, leans over, and whispers with a wink, "I figured here would be good, in case we need a quick getaway."

A woman at the other end of the table stands up and everyone goes quiet. She looks like she is in her forties, with chestnut skin and deep amber eyes that land on Medusa, who cringes internally, waiting for what the woman will say.

"Welcome, everyone. It's always nice to see the faces that made it back once again this week, as we all know that isn't guaranteed." A few heads nod silently in agreement. "We were successful this week. We brought in three groups of refugees, two from the War Temple and one from the Iron Temple. I am grateful for every soul we spare from their misery. Another tick in the win column is sitting at the end of this table."

Everyone turns to look at Medusa, who braces herself, making eye contact with every person at that table one at a time, despite wishing a hole would just open up in the floor and swallow her. Most of the faces that meet her gaze are warm, neutral, or curious, allowing Medusa to breathe easier. One man looks somewhat unsettled, but the only real negative energy is coming from the captain of the ship that brought her here, Nicodemus. He was being rude on the ship and is now giving her a look that insinuates he would like to feed her to one of the leviathans his ship is named after. Medusa meets his glare and returns it, making it clear that she will not allow him to bully her. His nose pulls into a sneer and Nicodemus turns his attention back to the woman running the meeting, much to Medusa's relief. The woman is glaring at the captain, presently not in the mood to put up with whatever his problem is. Hopefully, Medusa will have time to ask Psyche or Alec why Nicodemus has so much animosity toward her.

The woman continues, "Welcome, Medusa. I know this is a lot to take in. Cass has told me that while the Fates have not given her the full extent of what role you will play in the grand scheme of our plans. She could not stress enough that you are vital to the success of our mission. My name is Isadora, but you are welcome to call me Isa or Issi, and I invite you to take the time you need to settle in and learn about what we are doing. You will find-"

Alec bursts into the room, alarm on his face, and everyone's attention snaps to him.

"They've got her, Issi! We have to go get her!"

Medusa is eager to know who would evoke so much emotion from him, terrified it will be someone close to him, her heart already breaking for him, knowing the answer will not be a good one.

Isadora walks over, puts her arm around Alec's burly shoulders, and turns him away from everyone, whispering something to him as his shoulders heave and he struggles to find his breath.

Is he crying?

He composes himself and turns to address the council once more.

"Hestia was sending me her weekly transmission when it was interrupted. Her last words were, 'They found me out.'"

The people around the table gasp, Medusa included. Hestia is secretly working for the Allegiance. Their cause may have hope after all if multiple gods are siding with them.

A man in the middle of the table asks, "How solid is this intel? How do we know this isn't a trap, and she hasn't been playing us all along?"

"It's solid, Devid, you know it is," Isadora bites out, not allowing the seeds of doubt to be sown for even a moment.

Isadora addresses the rest of them again. "I know this news is shocking and we have little time to put a plan into place. We must continue our current course of action until we have any intel about where they are keeping her. This news also means that more than we know has been compromised. This plan may go south, but we can't just sit by and let them do it, anyway. The risk is always worth it when the alternative is the permanent black mark on our souls that comes with the knowledge that we did nothing."

The fire in Isadora's voice is unmistakable. Everyone at the table nods in agreement. Not a single person hesitates or blanches at the thought of the cost and it inspires Medusa to declare to herself in that moment that she will do whatever is necessary to aid them in this mission and any others.

"Planning must resume," Isadora continues, handing lists of assignments to the different people at the table. She directs people to assess the readiness of whatever they handle, asks the smiths and armorer to do a thorough weapon inventory, the captain to see how soon his ships can be ready to sail, and so on until all tasks are assigned. The council members head out to begin preparations, and the only people remaining in the room are Medusa, Psyche, and Alec.

"I'm glad to have you here, Lyra. Your parents would be so proud if they could see you," Alec says to her with a warm smile. He opens his arms for a hug but waits until Medusa does the same to step in and closes his arms around her. She breathes in the scent of him and gets a citrus smell that has a hint of cinnamon to it.

When they separate, Medusa grasps his bicep and looks him in the eye, doing her best to convey the sincerity in her heart. "I am so sorry to hear about Hestia. I don't know what she means to you, but she is clearly someone you care about deeply, so I hope we can locate her swiftly and get her to safety."

"Thank you" Alec squeezes Medusa's hand in return, as he hangs his head and wipes his hand across his face. "She means the world to me. I… love her."

The declaration cleaves Medusa's heart in two as puts herself in her uncle's position, imagining how it would feel to have someone she loves ripped away.

The three of them leave the Council Room and walk the short distance to the lounge near Medusa's room. There is nothing that can be done immediately to help get ready to leave, so they stay together until the late hours of the night talking. At one point, Psyche slips away for a moment and returns with a sweet wine that has the most refreshing flavor, which she informs Medusa, comes from a unique concoction crafted by Dionysus using pomegranate, elderflower, and a secret ingredient that when asked, he simply declares it proprietary and that the matter closed.

Needing a moment of brevity, and eager to learn more about her parents, Medusa spends the evening lounging on the sofa with Psyche listening to Alec tell funny stories about all the shenanigans he and Medusa's father would get into growing up. With her head on one arm of the couch, Psyche's on the other, and their feet in each other's laps, they listen, drink, and giggle until it is time for bed.

23

MEDUSA

The next morning, Medusa wakes up and lays awake in bed, staring at the ceiling as if it will suddenly provide her with answers. She spent the night before tossing and turning while trying to think of how she could best be useful for the upcoming mission. Are they going to insist that she stay here on the island? Why can no one tell her how she is so important?

Stretching her arms and getting out of bed, Medusa walks over to her mirror, ignoring the robe for a moment, allowing the air to caress her skin. She leaves her hood off as well, allowing her serpents full access to the world. They slither around and Medusa tries to focus on them. Can they be more than just a curse?

She picks up hints of emotions - happiness, and curiosity. And maybe some sadness. Cool scales slide along her neck and she reaches up, gently running a fingertip along the top of its head. It lets out a long, low, non-threatening hum and Medusa smiles. Her reptilian gold eyes catch her attention in the mirror and her heart drops. What does it matter what *they* feel, what *she* feels? No one is going to see past the monstrous exterior to care

155

about the person underneath. Sure, the people here are being kind to her, but that is only because they need her. As soon as this is over, should she live through it, Medusa will probably end up exiled to another island. At least maybe then it will not be adorned with the evidence of her sins, like the last one.

Returning her attention back to the window, the bay is bustling with activity as preparations are heavily underway. Medusa wonders how soon they will leave and hopes they will include her. It is risky to do this, but she cannot stay here and do nothing.

The warm cloth rubs against her skin as she gives herself a quick mediocre cleaning in the washbasin. The baths are not as appealing now that they are overrun with the memories of the altercation. In the dresser, Medusa finds fresh clothes and puts them on. The soft linen of the pants and shirt is gentle on her skin. The material is light and breezy, causing it to flutter in the constant breeze of the Isle that is now flowing into her room from the large window.

As she leaves to search for breakfast, Medusa finds Psyche waiting in the lounge, sitting on the sofa with a tray of food on a cart in front of her. Have they tasked Psyche with chaperoning her, monitoring her?

Medusa sits down beside Psyche, who squeezes her hand. "Good morning."

Unlike in the Oasis, where her senses are diminished, this touch is tangible, real. It never fails to give her goosebumps and butterflies simultaneously. Medusa doubts she will ever get used to it, but this is exhilarating, even if it is torturous at the same time.

She can almost pretend that when they touch and Psyche gasps, that Psyche is feeling the same jolt, can almost pretend that the look of shock is not Psyche reacting to how horrible it feels to touch Medusa's scaly skin. Almost.

"Good morning," Psyche replies with a warm smile. "I was

hoping you would have a day or two to settle in before anything urgent came up. I hate the idea of you being here alone."

So there it is. They expect Medusa to wait behind.

"There's no way I'm staying here. I don't know how I can help, but I can." Medusa hopes her tone is as firm as she is intending. The thought of siting here while they go off and put themselves in danger is excruciating.

Psyche does not look surprised and says, "I had a feeling that would be your attitude on this matter. I can't say Alec and Issi will agree, but also can't say I don't see where you're coming from and would feel the same way. I'm going to discuss the plan so far with them in an hour, after I can fill you in and we can put our heads together and see what we think will be your best shot at being able to be useful enough that we can justify risking you being discovered. It's a tall order, but we will do our best and hope the Fates are smiling upon our wishes."

MEDUSA SLIDER her fingers through the rough, short mane of a newborn foal. The Stable master, Philip, was extremely welcoming to her and took her through introducing her to each horse. He noticed that the horses all took to her immediately and even noted that they were less restless when she was there. Upon this discovery, he proclaimed she was welcome in the stables any time, day or night, for he not only enjoyed her company, but it made his job that much easier. She had a good-hearted laugh at that and felt some of the stone that had been forming around her heart for so long begin the slow process of chipping away.

Psyche is discussing the possibility of Medusa going with the Allegiance and she spent the time in the stables sitting in the hay. Waiting is tedious, so she has spent most of it in here, the animals helping to calm her anxious mind. She plays out the scenario in her mind over and over.

Medusa can picture it so easily, Psyche talking to Isadora.

"Issi, she wants to help. And think of how useful she could be."

"She's a liability, Psyche, and you know it."

"And you also know that in the blink of an eye, she can eliminate an enemy threat."

A rustle of hay pulls Medusa from her daydream, and Psyche stands before her.

Before Medusa can get up, Psyche drops into the hay next to her and also pets the foal, giving him concentrated scratches on his forehead and behind his ears as he tilts his head in delight.

"The plan is complicated," Psyche begins. "We are taking a small group and one of our mid-sized, stealthy ships. We will infiltrate the gala, slip away and find where the nymphs are being kept, and then hopefully free them and lead them to the awaiting ship and be gone before the last note from the orchestra."

"Infiltrate? Do you mean sneak in unobserved or go incognito and present yourselves as guests?" Medusa asks.

"Ideally, a mix of both. We would like to have a few people going in pretending to be wealthy buyers - we have our ways of getting an invitation - and being loud and noticeable, drawing attention away from the dark corners the rest of the group will be slipping into. The 'buyers' will keep an eye on things while everyone else is finding the nymphs and guiding them out to the awaiting ship. If all goes according to plan, the 'buyers' will disappear in the chaos once everyone is ready to start the auction and discovers their 'merchandise' is missing."

Medusa takes a moment to mull over the plan and tries to find an opportunity to insert herself that will not slow them down and be a detriment to the entire operation. She wants to help, but is not selfish enough to want to do so at the expense of the entire Allegiance. Her gut is telling Medusa she should be there.. Are the Fates guiding her? Or is it just her anxiety?

"I suggested to Issi that you be with the group that is finding and freeing the nymphs. They are going to be terrified and you have a way of adding a calming presence amongst the innocent and vulnerable. The ignorant few aside, it's easy to feel safe with you," Psyche tells her earnestly, stroking the forehead of the foal as she speaks as if to emphasize her point with an example sitting right in front of them.

Psyche actually convinced them to let her go. But not as a weapon? Medusa was certain the only way she could have been an asset was to be a deadly one.

"Besides," Psyche adds. "Alec said he doubted we could stop you from going and wouldn't want you anywhere other than by his side."

Medusa is stunned by this assessment of her. Even before that day in the garden with Poseidon, after Nikolas' passing, so few kind words were directed her way. It can be a shock to the system to have someone believe in you again.

Doubt comes charging back in with force, extinguishing the glimmer of optimism expeditiously.

Psyche is only being this kind because Medusa serves a purpose to their cause. It is a mirage. One that will fall away and reveal the empty wasteland that was always there to begin with.

IT TURNS out they will leave the next day and Medusa and Psyche spend the afternoon hastily making preparations, which include trips to both the tailor and the armory. The former to select attire for the gala, and the latter to collect what weapons they will want with them.

The tailor is full of beautiful dresses. It comprises three connected buildings and is only steps away from the armory. The entrance, at the first building, opens to a room with staple clothing of all types, sizes, and colors. There are tunics, robes, pants, undergarments, everything that someone might need for the day-to-day. The second, has leather armor, the padding to wear underneath, and boots. The last building, somewhat smaller than the others and tucked farther back, is their destination for this quest.

Elegant garments fill the room. Silken fabric and beads sparkle in the sunlight filtering into the window. One dress catches Medusa's eye but is beyond impractical, so she focuses her attention on something that will fit in but not stand out.

Medusa lands on a dark green dress and black cloak to match her hood. The dress looks like it is made from a green metallic liquid that drapes and tucks in ways that are flattering on her generous curves but not restrictive. One side has a high slit that allows for freer movement but is low enough that she can conceal a dagger under the folds of fabric at her hip. The neckline is one-sided and comes up over her left shoulder.

She runs her hands over her exposed scales. This will not do.

As if reading her mind, Psyche speaks up. "The thought process is to play up the reptilian parts of your appearance to pass them off as a costume for the event." The final piece to her ensemble was a bronze mask that covered the top half of her face and had horns that extended out past the edges of her hood.

Medusa almost looks beautiful again. She can start to see the person she was before, simmering under the surface.

Unfortunately, there is another task required of them, but all Medusa knows is that they will check in on a patient. It turns out to not, in fact, be a routine checkup, as the patient in question is Cadmus.

Tension bubbles to the surface at the mention of him.

Medusa has forgotten about him entirely and is reminded that Psyche and Cadmus have been spending time together as she heals him. If Cadmus had told Psyche the truth about what happened on the ship, Medusa would know, right? Maybe he is just holding this over her head until she can take it no more.

Medusa bristles when she sees him lying in the bed, and turns to Psyche, saying loudly enough for him to hear, "I don't trust him. Why is he here?"

"He's here," Cadmus interjects for himself, "because he was trying to get here all along."

Medusa narrows her eyes suspiciously. "And what is that supposed to mean? All it sounds like to me is an intelligence mission for the Heroes and they carted you right in to tend to you."

At that, Psyche steps forward and respectfully, but firmly, says, "I need you to give us a bit more credit than that. I know you don't know us all too well, but trust that we don't take the security of this place lightly. He hasn't left this room, he's been monitored, and he has been oathed."

Oathed. Supposedly there is no way to get around those, but why would he agree to that? Why does he want to be here? She sees no reason to pick this battle but sets an intention to watch him closely and keep her guard up around him.

"I will respect that you have a better understanding of what is better for The Allegiance than I could. But," she adds, looking Cadmus in the eye, "you can't possibly expect me to trust you easily. I will wait outside until you're ready, Psyche."

Medusa turns and makes her way out of the room. She is almost out when she catches the beginnings of their conversation and is surprised to hear she is the topic.

"I... I've heard so many legends about her, including her beauty, *before*. How is it no one has mentioned how absolutely stunning she still is?"

Psyche chuckles. "She is one of the most beautiful creatures I have ever beheld. Besides, how many people aside from Poseidon have even seen her the way she is now and lived to tell about it?"

Medusa keeps walking and lets their voices fade, having already heard more than she knows what to do with, and wants a few minutes of quiet. How dare he talk about her beauty as if it is something that has anything to do with him? However, it may have been worth hearing him say that, to hear it echoed on Psyche's lips.

There is a bench right outside of the infirmary and Medusa sits down, content to watch the people stroll by while she waits.

By the time Psyche comes out fifteen minutes later, two stray cats have found their way onto the bench, with one even curled up in Medusa's lap. The gentle purring comforts her soul and soothes the edges of her nerves. With so much going on, so much to process and to prepare for, these gentle moments ease the difficulty and give Medusa the strength of spirit to keep from crumbling.

Psyche sits next to Medusa on the side that is not currently home to a snoozing feline. "I understand it will take time to trust him if you ever can at all. That's for you to decide. He is a very useful tool to us, and we are confident that the situation with him is under control. I wanted to give you a heads-up. He will come on this mission. Not only is he originally from a region near the Temple, he did his initial Heroes training regiment at the Temple of Love and knows it better than any other person here in The Allegiance. We need every advantage we can get with something like this. And again, he's oathed."

"I understand. I'm sure I can be civil and even work with him if and when necessary. I can't say I will be perfect at it and I'm certain I will make missteps, but I will do my best."

Psyche smiles and nods, and they rise from the bench, making their way back through the streets to the Compound. When they reach their floor, Psyche says, "I have an idea! Can you go wait in the lounge for just a moment? I want to put something together for you."

Medusa tilts her head with a smirk and curiosity. "Oh? Should I be afraid?" She asks, but they both know she is joking. Conversing with Psyche is becoming so easy, even though it has only been a few days. Psyche feels like someone Medusa was always supposed to know, and that invisible string of Fate has finally come into play. Medusa sits down and waits for Psyche to return, but does not have to wait for long. Psyche comes back and motions for Medusa to hop up and take her hand. When she does, Psyche tells Medusa to close her eyes and leads her out of the room. Trying to work out which way they are going, Medusa stiffens when their path indicates their destination is the baths. Before she can open her eyes though, as if sensing her discomfort, Psych squeezes her hand and says, "Please, trust me. If you don't like it, I promise we can leave."

Medusa holds her eyes closed even tighter in a display of trust and consent, even if it may have only been perceptible to herself, and nods.

Continuing, taking gentle steps led by Psyche, they do indeed get near the baths. The smell of lavender fills her nostrils and has an immediate calming effect. As they get closer, citrus smells intermingle with the soothing herbal aroma.

They come to a stop, and Psyche tells Medusa she can open her eyes. The view before her takes Medusa's breath away. Psyche has transformed the baths into something new. There is an illusion of a willow tree separating them from the area of the altercation, reaching across the ceiling, covering it will branches. The cascading leaves hang down like vines, transporting Medusa somewhere else entirely. Every other bathing nook is dark except for their private one that is filled with candles, their flickering flames casting light and shadows that dance along the walls and the surface of the bubbling water, which is filled with flower petals.

Medusa turns to Psyche, mouth agape, speechless. Psyche smiles, "I wanted to make this a safe place for you again, form fresh memories here that hold a more loving place in your heart." She reaches up and cups Medusa's cheek in her palm, and it is exhilarating and wonderful at the same time. Medusa is still adjusting to her reaction to Psyche's touch, but in a much different way than she does with Alec. While this one is unfamiliar to her, it also makes her heart race in anticipation instead of fear and anxiety. Having experienced so few opportunities to be attracted to someone, Medusa is hardly an expert, but it is becoming so clear, even to her cautious sensibilities, that she is falling in love with Psyche. She knows it is not something she should do, but does not know how to make it cease.

It is impossible for Medusa to wrap her mind around Psyche's reactions to her. It is becoming harder and harder to write them off as masked disdain. Is it possible that Psyche does not see her as a monster? Or even that Psyche *does* see her as a monster, but maybe monsters deserve to be loved, too?

Feeling emboldened by what she hopes are pretty clear signals, Medusa slides her free hand around Psyche's waist and takes a step closer to her until their faces are inches apart. Should she do this? She is tired of every touch being a violation or too much for her. This time, it feels invigorating and the welcoming look in Psyche's eye has her throwing out every reservation. She leans in and their lips meet.

Heat floods through her body as she closes her eyes and they both lean into the gentle kiss. They stay there, wrapped in that moment for what feels like an instant and an eternity. They both step back at the same time and stare into each other's eyes for a few heartbeats as the moment settles in. The air around them feels charged and the significance of the kiss caresses them in an afterglow that makes Medusa feel radiant.

Psyche smiles warmly and walks over to the bath. There is a glass bottle on the ledge and the goddess pours a pink liquid into the water that fills the bath with bubbles and more of the same heavenly combination of citrus and lavender.

"I'm going to step into the hall to give you privacy to undress. Then you can get into the bath, beneath the bubbles, and once you're comfortable I can join you... if you'd like?" Psyche sounds nervous that she might actually say no, but Medusa is pretty certain after that kiss, there may not be many things this literal goddess can ask of her that she won't gladly do with a smile on her face. She nods her head and Psyche beams and steps out of the room.

Medusa slides into the bath and settles into a comfortable seat before calling for Psyche to return, who comes back in wearing a white silk robe, her long hair up in a twist with two elaborately beaded sticks. Medusa is once again taken aback by Psyche's beauty, something that is bound to be a recurring problem.

Psyche is not as modest as Medusa and turns and faces away from the bath. She slips her rope off, slowly revealing her back, the curve of her backside, and her lean, long legs. Medusa spins her head and looks away when Psyche turns around to step into the bath. She feels foolish and uncertain about what their pace should be. Without any kind of experience to base this on, aside from a few flings here and there, nothing that had this much spark and passion. She does not want to mess things up by moving faster than she is ready for or misinterpreting the level of reciprocation. As usual, Medusa is over-thinking everything.

Once Psyche is in the water, she sits next to Medusa and places her head on her shoulder. "Is this okay?"

Medusa smiles, "Absolutely," and leans her head against Psyche's, finding Psyche's hand next to hers in the water and lacing their fingers together. They sit in their newfound peace with each other until the bubbles die out.

24

MEDUSA

The next day, Medusa wakes early in the morning, despite hoping she would get more sleep. The night had been restless, but in the best way. She kept feeling the silk of Psyche's robe under her hand, their fingers intertwined, her soft lips. Has she ever yearned for someone this way? She can't recall any time someone's touch set her on fire and she wanted more.This is a torture she can't seem to get enough of.

She lays there in bed replaying the night before. Her hands travel up and down her body as she caresses her hip, stomach, breasts. She may not know what to do when she's with Psyche, but her own body, she knows well. She knows exactly where to touch, where to apply more pressure, where to be gentle. Her left hand is on her left breast, pinching her nipple firmly but not hard as her right hand trails back down and between her legs.

Medusa slides her finger over her core and finds it already wet as she teases her opening, gently gliding her fingers over it before dipping a finger in, then another. Thinking about how soft Psyche's skin had been and the electricity when they touched, Medusa continues to slide her fingers in and out, putting pressure against her clit every time, building the pressure until, with Psyche's lips on her mind, she brings herself over the edge. She continues to stroke herself, slowing her speed and easing out of the moment. Feeling both sated, and still full of lust, Medusa slides her fingers back out and walks over to the washbasin to clean herself and get ready to start her day.

Since it is so much earlier than she has been waking up, Medusa wants to be the one to surprise Psyche with breakfast this time. She quickly dresses in a clean light blue tunic and brown leggings, her boots, and hood, then makes her way downstairs to the kitchens.

The smell of breakfast is wafting heavily out of the open kitchen door and it's bustling with people hurrying to make sure they packed enough provisions for the journey. Medusa pokes her head in tentatively, wanting to assess the room and make sure she won't be in the way or an imposition.

A short man with a handlebar mustache and bald head sees her and seems very excited by her sudden appearance.

"Hello! Welcome to my kitchen," he says to her as a woman in the background lightheartedly chimes in with, "Ha! YOUR kitchen. Like you'd get anything done without us."

He laughs a full belly laugh. "Well, you're certainly right about that, Lorena."

He returns his attention to Medusa. "Like I was saying, welcome to THE kitchens. We have heard so much about our new guest and we were hoping to get to meet you before you're off. It's hard to get away from the kitchens sometimes."

Medusa isn't sure how to feel about that but shoves down

the feeling of being a novelty and focuses on the warm welcome she is receiving. She has to admit, this isle has definitely defied her expectations. Sure, there have been a few people less than thrilled to see her, and a truly awful encounter, but mostly, everyone here has at least been willing to give her a chance. It makes her want to be more open and find a place amongst them.

"I'm pleased to meet you as well. I am so happy to put faces to the absolutely delectable food I've been having. My name is Medusa, but it seems you might already know that," she says, dipping her head slightly and blushing.

"My name is Oren. The mouthy one back there is Lorena, and then there's Janus, Dela, and Rochelle." The last three raised their hands in turn when he said their names. "Don't worry though, we don't expect you to remember them all immediately," he winked. "How can we help such a lovely lady today?"

"Well…" Medusa begins. Every morning, Psyche has had a tray of food ready for me at breakfast time every day that I've been here. I was up earlier than usual today and wanted to… return the favor?"

"Splendid! Oh! I'll get right on it!" His bubbly attitude is infectious, and she realizes she's grinning ear to ear as she watches Oren race around the kitchen, grabbing foods and dishes. By the time he's done, Medusa has an elaborately filled tray of foods, a few of which he swears are Psyche's favorites. She takes the tray from him and backs out of the kitchen, thanking him profusely and insisting that she can manage the tray on her own. She bumps into Cadmus on the way and almost drops the entire tray, but Cadmus catches it and helps her to right it.

She sighs in frustration but tries to keep her response as reigned in as possible. She's tired of her knee jerk emotional responses prevailing in situations, leaving her to regret her rashness later. Her voice is as neutral as she can muster through obviously gritted teeth, "um…thank you."

He smiles. "You're very welcome. It seems fortuitous that I was here."

"I wouldn't go that far," Medusa snaps out despite her best intentions. "Dropping the tray may have been preferable to having this conversation."

She sets her shoulders back and pushes around him, holding the tray tight, and heads back up the stairs, rolling her eyes at the smug chuckle she hears behind her.

WHEN PSYCHE COMES out of her room a short while later, Medusa is waiting for her on the sofa in the lounge. The tray of food is on the cart they have been using every morning, along with a small cup with freshly picked flowers. The Isle, and The Compound, have so much greenery all around providing an abundant supply of flowers for her to gather from, only taking from a plant that had plenty of other blooms and snipping at the stem junction to make sure the plant didn't expend unnecessary resources where a snipped bloom would be.

She stands up and walks over to greet Psyche, who is taking in the scene with a sleepy smile on her face. "You did all this for me?"

"Yes, I hope that's alright? Oren gave me what he claims you usually like, so I hope he knew what he was talking about," she answers with a smile.

"I see pastries, jams, and jasmine tea for starters, and that sounds absolutely perfect this morning." She opens of the domed dishes. "Oh! Are these moonberry tarts?"

Medusa shrugs and chuckles. "I have no idea. He didn't tell

me what he was putting on there. I've only known him since this morning but I get the feeling he knows exactly what every person here prefers and if that's the case, based on your reaction to the thought of them, I'm going to guess, yes, those are moonberry tarts."

"I will never not be astonished by that man," Psyche says with a tone of admiration and awe. Medusa finds that response curious but then Psyche continues, "Moonberries only grow around the Lunar Temple. A place I haven't been able to see for five years, ever since my involvement with The Allegiance became known."

"We don't have to talk about it," Medusa says, sitting back down on the sofa and gesturing for Psyche to join her. "But I would love to listen if you do want to."

Psyche smiles warmly and accepts her invitation. Once she is seated, they settle in and get comfortable. Medusa crosses her legs, resting her right ankle on top of her left knee. Psyche tucks her legs beneath her, knees bent toward Medusa.

"I was already heavily involved in The Allegiance the day they showed up at my Temple. I knew I wouldn't be able to stay under their radar. I'm not as good as playing both sides as Dionysus is."

"Dionysus?! The drunken buffoon who only shows up to drink wine and stumble through his duties?"

Psyche chuckles. "Puts on a pretty convincing cover, doesn't he?" She raises an eyebrow and continues. "He and Hestia are the only members of the Pantheon that we have within our ranks that aren't known to them, but I will get more into that once we set sail."

"I'll start at the beginning. What brought me to Alec, Cas, and The Allegiance. About twenty years ago, I had a lover. Her name was Selene. Yes, I know. The irony of a moon goddess falling in love with someone named Selene. She was mortal, like your father. Unlike your parents, we were not public about our closeness. We regarded it as a closely guarded secret, and it was - only a select few of our closest, most trusted, inner circle who knew. It turns out your closest, most trusted people can have their own motivations and duplicitous intentions."

Psyche is looking forward but Medusa can tell that she's far, far away, temporarily trapped in a memory, a look and feeling Medusa knows all too well. She gently takes Psyche's hand into her own, causing Psyche's attention to come back to the present. She smiles and squeezes Medusa's hand and continues.

"One day, I woke up and Selene wasn't in bed next to me. I thought nothing of it at the time. She regularly would wake up before me and go walk the gardens, often with a book in hand. I was starting to be concerned when I didn't see her for breakfast, but there had been no note or anything. All of her possessions were still in our chambers. I was frantic by dinner time. I had searched the entire Temple, scoured the grounds, asked the Acolytes. There was no sign of her. An Initiate came running to me and delivered a letter from Zeus himself," she says, biting his name out. "It merely said, 'Did you think we wouldn't know?'"

"No," Medusa whispers, mouth agape.

"Yes," Psyche continues. "I raced to the Temple of Olympus, but they had such a head start on me. What could I have even done, anyway? By the time I arrived, they told me I was welcome to retrieve her body from the dungeons and give her any burial I saw fit, for they did not care." Tears stream from her eyes.

Medusa wraps her arm around her back and pulls Psyche into a comforting embrace. She merely says, "Shhh..." and strokes her hair as her weeping turns into sobbing. Medusa holds space for Psyche's grief, allowing her to take a moment and mourn someone she clearly cared for deeply.

When Psyche's tears subside, and her breathing becomes steadier, she says, "I haven't even told you what happened the day they came for me."

"We don't have to talk about it anymore. If you need time, take it. I will always be ready to lend an ear if that changes," Medusa says.

"No. I'm ok. I want to finish. I want you to know why I'm here. After what happened to Sel, I went back to the Lunar Temple and was a complete shell of a person. The Acolytes were the only reason I didn't wither in my own self pity. They diligently cared for me and while I can't say I was even close to happy, I was at least functioning every day, going through the motions, when Alec arrived here one day. He introduced himself, offered his condolences, and then took a tremendous risk. He told me everything about The Allegiance - they didn't have the oaths yet- and said they were a small group of rebels, doing what they could to save people here and there when they could. They had little in the way of resources, but every one of them had a powerful reason to be there. He said they were tired of barely being able to help anyone while also gaining no traction in any way that could actual hurt The Pantheon. He thought I might be interested in joining them and I think he knew before he finished giving his grand speech that was going to say yes.

"I joined them and helped when I could, from the inside. I played nice with The Pantheon and ferried information over to The Allegiance, as well as going on missions and using my powers as subtly as I could to stay under the radar. Fast forward to five years ago and you will get the reason that the soul oaths were created."

"There was a man who was a member of the Allegiance. We found out he had been playing both sides and he confirmed the existence of us to The Pantheon and even revealed that they had a god amongst their ranks." Psyche pauses and takes a breath. A piece of hair falls into Psyche's face and Medusa reaches up and tucks it behind her ear with a warm smile.

"The Pantheon sent a group of Heroes to raid the Isle of

Remembrance, and my temple. I returned there the next day as I had been away. In lieu of me, The Pantheon slew every single Acolyte, every Initiate no matter how young. My Temple was a bloodbath, and it was all meant for me."

So much violence and destruction. Medusa's heart aches as she thinks about Hestia. Would they hurt or kill another god? If they will go that far with Psyche, what are they going to do with Hestia, who had been spying right under their noses?

"I went into a rage but had no where productive to direct it. I vowed to find a way to ensure that no member of the Allegiance could ever betray us again. I snuck back into my temple and threw myself into the library. I searched text after text, every pile of dusty scrolls, until I was positive I had pieced together enough magic to attempt an oath that was bound to your soul. With my abilities, I thought it would be doable. I crafted the Oasis in my own mind. Alec insisted on doing a test oath so we came up with one that would have minimal consequences if broken. I wrote out an oath that made him swear he didn't like pistachios, something I knew to be a favorite of his, and the consequence would be that he stub his toe once randomly during the next hour." Psyche chuckles at the silliness of the moment in the memory. A whimsical, bright spot in a tale of pain and horrors.

Medusa wonders what it would have been like spending the past eight years with these people, instead of alone.

"We finished the oath, and he made his declaration. Alec told me he felt a twinge in his rib cage as soon as the oath was broken. I asked him to report back once he stubbed his toe to make sure it worked, but we didn't have to wait long. He stood up from his chair and went to leave, and immediately slammed his toe into the side of the table. Once we knew it worked, I wrote the oath for the Allegiance."

Psyche wipes another tear from her eye and finishes, "and now you know why I haven't been to the Isle of Remembrance in so long, and why moonberry tarts would be extra special to me. Thank you. I think I needed this." She picks up one of the tarts and takes a bite. "Oh," she says through a mouthful, "perfect as usual, Oren."

They eat their breakfast, lightheartedly chatting about the items on the tray and why Psyche likes the ones she does. They keep the conversation easy to counteract the prior heaviness. By the time their bellies are full, their hearts are much lighter, and Medusa knows their bond has strengthened. She doesn't know where things with Psyche will go, but this is one uncertainty that she finds she's welcoming with open arms.

25

HESTIA

Pain rips through Hestia's exhausted body as she finally opens her eyes. Her vision is blurry and her head is throbbing in a rhythm that feels like her pain has its own pulse.

When her sight clears, Hestia sees the bars that surround her, their rusted color telling her exactly what that pulse is - the heartbeat of a god cage. It takes all the energy she can muster to lift her head and try to get a better gauge of the situation.

She doesn't have the strength to be shocked that these barbaric cages exist. Gods start out as children, like mortals. Also, like mortals, gods have their own scary tales told in whispers to keep children from getting into things they shouldn't or as a manipulation tool to make them behave.

She can almost hear one of the old crone's voices saying "naughty little goddesses end up in god cages. Do you want that, or do you want to be a good girl?"

She can't make out anything beyond the perimeter of her cage. The magic in the bars emanates a light glow, but there's nothing to be seen in the dim light it casts.

With no way to know how long she was unconscious, panic

creeps up on her. How long has she been in this cage? The second Hestia crossed the threshold, her clock started ticking whether or not she was conscious of it.

The magic continues to pulse, and the feel of it is stifling. She feels weighted to the ground, the pain never ceasing for even a moment of relief. She doesn't know what to do, so she lies back down, trying to conserve any energy possible in case there's a miracle and she needs to run.

Hestia closes her eyes and, when she opens them again, yelps as she sees Aphrodite's face as she crouches down next to where Hestia's head lay.

Hestia glares at her through the bars but doesn't bother to lift her head. This bitch isn't worth the wasted strength. Hestia shifts her gaze and stares off into the distance, looking at nothing.

Aphrodite decides this is the time for a monologue.

"You've been out for thirty-six hours."

No. So much time lost already.

"Was it worth it?" she asks, her eyes viciously cruel to match the twisted smile on her face.

"Spying on us for those Fates forsaken rebels. You couldn't possibly think they stood a chance?"

Hestia says nothing in response, but Aphrodite doesn't care and continues rambling.

"They have been such a nuisance and somehow always one step ahead of us. Who would have thought anything could pull you away from your books long enough to care about anything?"

The root of the centuries long conflict between the two of them finally rears its ugly head. Seeing the two of them now, no one would ever suspect that when they first joined the Pantheon, they were very close. They had gone everywhere together, spent their evenings laughing together, the best of friends.

They were inseparable. The Love Temple hadn't been built yet. All the gods used the Temple of Olympus as their home, but as the realm grew, everyone needed more space to conduct their affairs, and so they erected the temples, allowing different regions to focus on different things.

There was so much for Hestia to learn, and looking back, she realizes she didn't notice what her friend was going through.

She had been so thrilled to hear that Aphrodite was in love. Hestia only got to meet Andromeda once, but thought she was lovely and the two of them truly seemed madly in love with each other. Aphrodite had kept the loss of her lover to herself, and by the time Hestia knew of it, her friend was already bitter. She tried to reach out a few times, but she had missed her opportunity and Aphrodite had already shut herself off from the rest of the world, devolving into the toxic, jaded god she is now.

Hestia always feels a twinge of guilt when her intrusive thoughts pop in to torment her and ask her if she's *positive* she's not the reason Aphrodite went down the path. If she had paid better attention, she could have been there for her friend. She always shakes that voice off to the best of her ability, reminding herself that she is not responsible for the actions of others.

When Hestia still does not respond to anything she is saying, Aphrodite sighs, but doesn't appear flustered or frustrated.

When Hestia still fails to respond to anything she is saying, Aphrodite starts talking. "It doesn't matter. Soon you will be one of the stupid mortals you love so much. Zeus said I can play with you until then, here on my island. Once you're just as fragile as they are, he wants to ask you a few questions. I doubt you'll have the strength to withstand him for long. You should've said no to working with those traitors, Hestia. Tick-tock."

Aphrodite walks away, and the first spark of hope ignites in the back of Hestia's mind. She's on Love Island. They must have brought her here to keep an eye on her during the auction. He won't know to look for her here but her heart, her fire, will be here and might be able to rescue her. Clinging to that narrow chance like a lifeline, Hestia uses it to push back against every magical pulse of the cage. She wishes she had the stone on her, but the rags Hestia is currently wearing mean they likely would have found it on her if she had tried to conceal it. The Allegiance's communication method is hopefully still a mystery to the Pantheon, and she is glad she will not be the reason it is revealed.

Forty-eight hours. She closes her eyes and plays his voice on a loop on her mind while she sent silent prayers to the universe. Please *let him find me.*

26

ICARUS

Icarus stands outside of the dungeons of the Temple of Love, bored out of her mind. So far, her elite group has done nothing but go back and forth between the War Temple where their barracks are located, and the Olympic Temple where Ares has been having meetings.

The last few days, though, they have been in Aphrodite's domain, setting up for a gala. They have been guarding the main entrance to the dungeons in shifts, two at a time. The Heroes not on duty during the ball may be in attendance and Icarus is exhilarated at the thought of such a fancy evening. Icarus already has her dress and is excited beyond words, the opportunity for events like this never arising where she grew up. She is finally settling into who she is as a person and figuring herself out. Icarus daydreams of the music and the elegance of getting lost in someone's arms - even if just for the night.

Her shift started thirty minutes ago and is dragging. No one will tell them who they are guarding, and so far, it has not been enough of a temptation for anyone to get caught snooping. According to the last set of guards, Aphrodite has been in there for at least forty-five minutes, and that definitely has Icarus's curiosity piqued.

She turns to the Hero on shift with her, Lysander, and asks, "Who do you think we are guarding?"

He chuckles. "Do you really want to risk legion placement to find out?"

No. She does not.

The doors open, and the rumor is confirmed as Aphrodite walks out. Aphrodite's attention snaps to Icarus suddenly, catching her off guard.

"Who are you?" Aphrodite asks shortly.

"My name is Icarus. I'm part of the legion that accompanied Ares here," she answers.

Aphrodite stares into Icarus's eyes, as if searching for someone she knows.

Despite her heart being in her throat, and not wanting to get in trouble, Icarus is deeply attracted to the god before her. Everyone must feel this way in the face of the goddess of love. Her beauty is staggering, and it takes an effort for Icarus not to say that out loud. It is just the allure of Aphrodite.

A wall shutters behind Aphrodite's gaze and she turns on her heel, leaving the two guards in confused silence.

HER EYELIDS ARE heavy and close on their own as Icarus keeps falling asleep on her feet. A light slap to the face has her jolting awake, only to find an amused smirk on Lysander's face. If anyone other than him had done that, they would be on their ass before they can blink.

Lysander's room is just down the hall from hers in the

barracks and they had become fast friends over meals and card games, finding similarities in their rural upbringings.

A loud cry of pain comes from the dungeons and Icarus and Lysander glance at each other, questioning if they should go in.

"Don't even think about it. We need to mind our own business," Lysander argues, giving her a pointed look.

When Icarus does not respond, he furrows his brown in frustration, pinching the bridge of his nose. "I'm not going in with you."

Icarus shrugs her shoulders and pushes the door open.

Lysander curses under his breath and follows closely behind her.

They pass a long line of empty cells before they come upon a large cage in the back, a hunched-over figure inside groaning in agony.

Moving closer, Icarus gasps when she recognizes who is inside, the god Hestia.

She would recognize Hestia anywhere from the textbooks at school and the many paintings of her across the realm. The goddess of knowledge has a reputation for being good and kind, and Icarus cannot fathom what Hestia could have done to receive this fate as punishment.

Icarus knows the god cage from lore as a child and cringes in horror.

Lysander comes up beside her, his expression mirroring the shocked repulsion on hers.

"We need to get back to our post," he breathes.

Her head nods, but Icarus does not move, unable to pull her gaze from Hestia, who is in so much pain that she has yet to even register their presence.

"C'mon," Lysander urges and at last her feet listen.

When they return to their post, Dionysus is stumbling down the stairs, singing a bawdy off-key tavern song.

Dionysus puts his hand on Lysander's shoulder. "Tell me

why a couple of young, promising Heroes such as yourselves are down here?"

The god hiccups and burps at the same time.

Icarus and Lysander exchange a glance. Is this guy for real?

"Whatever Ares tells us to, sir." Lysander gives him a placating answer as he puts his arm around the god and tries to direct him back up the stairs.

Dionysus brushes off Lysander's arm and faces the dungeon door. "I'll just go see for myself." Hiccup.

He walks in and closes the door behind him.

"What do we do?" Lysander asks in a low, frantic tone.

Icarus shrugs. "He's a god. We take orders from them, not the other way around."

The door opens again, and Dionysus walks back out. Hiccup.

He makes it back up the stairs and out of sight right as the next shift arrives to relieve them.

27

MEDUSA

Medusa looks for something to do as Psyche oversees final preparations. Medusa has nothing to bring. The Seamstress has already sent the clothing they are bringing to the ship, informing them when they were leaving yesterday that the gowns, armor, and a few days' worth of regular clothes will be onboard. Medusa has no possessions to pack, so she finds herself idle this afternoon and is wandering the Isle City until the tide is favorable for them to leave.

The important buildings of the Isle look similar and have wooden signs hanging from the exterior as identifiers. The one before her has a book carved into it and piques her curiosity. Perhaps the shop owner will allow Medusa to browse?

A small bell rings as the door opens. The man who steps out of what appears to be a back room is not who Medusa was expecting. Older people had operated and maintained every library and bookshop she had ever been to growing up. She does not remember seeing anyone who ever looked to be younger than eighty. This man is young, twenties maybe? He also lacks the wiry frame the scholars always had. He has broad

183

muscular shoulders and is easily taller than she is, and she is not exactly short.

He smiles wide at her, "Welcome to The Little Library. My name is Jonas. Are you seeking knowledge? Adventure? Romance?" He says with an eyebrow wiggle.

Medusa's walls immediately start coming down and she quickly feels at home in this shop and with this man, returning his smile. "I was hoping maybe I could just look around. I don't have any money, but I would love to just see what books you have here and spend some of my afternoon here. Would that would be alright?"

Jonas shakes his head. "That's not how it works here. We don't operate on that kind of system. I am not a bookseller, I am a bookkeeper. My job is to be the caretaker of these books until the right person comes looking for them, and to help you find exactly what kind of story you need right now. My job is not to sell you books."

He sees the confusion on her face and continues, "The Isle doesn't use currency. Everyone who can, contributes, and everything we have other than a few personal possessions, is shared. I am in charge of the books, that's how I contribute. Allegiance members frequently pick up books on their travels and when they go on their assignments. Then they are deposited here for people to enjoy. If you go into the many bakeshops, you will find that as long as the system isn't being abused, anyone can come in and leave with a treat. People work in our shops, perform their crafts, and find ways to give back to the community that saved them. It's very rare that anyone violates the spirit of the Isle."

Medusa nods her head as she processes this. It sounds like a utopia; she hopes it does, in fact, turn out to be so. "Ok... thank you. So far, this place has proven to be mostly wonderful. You have added to that and I'm grateful for the warm welcome."

"I know not everyone here has been kind to you. I'm sorry

about that. Please know that we don't tolerate that here, and I hope you continue to be met with the kindness you deserve. And with that, I'll leave you be to the books. If you need any help, there's a bell on the desk here. You'll pretty much just find works of fiction in here. The Observatory houses everything academic, but if there's ever a topic you need more information on, I go up there routinely to fulfill requests. O just has the most use for them, so we found it more efficient for those to be up there with her."

"Thank you," Medusa smiles genuinely.

"I should also warn you, the shop cats like to pop in randomly on people, so I hope they don't startle you."

Jonas walks back into the rear room from which he first emerged, whistling to himself as he does. Medusa would normally find the sound grating, but her spirits are too high for it to bother her.

Surveying the shelves of books, Medusa walks over to the first one. She scans the titles absentmindedly, running a finger gently along the spines as she goes, hoping one will catch her eye. The variety of subjects is staggering, but Jonas seems to have done a surprisingly decent job of sorting them into loose categories.

The section labeled 'adventure' catches her eye, and Medusa pays a bit more attention to the titles here, thrilled at the idea of some exciting escapism. Many of the books she sees here she has never heard of. Were they produced in the last eight years? If they had been around, they certainly escaped her attention. Medusa spent almost all of her free time as an Acolyte in the temple library. The Masters rolled their eyes when they caught her lost in another fantasy or romance novel, but mostly they were grateful when Medusa was quiet and stayed out of their way.

Most of the books are worn, some tattered, with very few having any descriptions on the back or inside the front cover, but some titles reveal what the books might be about - pirates, dragons, love. She is trying to decide between two books when Jonas re-emerges from the back room.

"Ah," he says, eying the books in her hands, "You have excellent taste. Those are both wonderful books, if I say so myself."

"Well, I'm trying to decide my mood. This mermaid book looks very entertaining, but I feel like I might also enjoy this seemingly darker book about some creatures they call Fae. I've never heard of either story."

"I think you're going to be away for a bit. How about you just take both?"

"Are you sure? I don't want to impose, really," Medusa starts, but Jonas puts his umber hands up in objection.

"I insist. We aren't a proper library per se, but if you care to bring them back when you're finished, it would be most helpful." He answers, smile still beaming.

"I will definitely do that."

They chat a little more as Medusa makes her way back out of the shop. He hands her a cloth bag to carry her books with as he waves goodbye.

With nothing left to do, Medusa walks over to the docks to find out if Psyche or Alec are there yet. Perhaps she can even make her way on board and get settled or assist with preparations. Despite offering to help at every opportunity, Medusa was told that it was well in hand and to take it easy. They mean well, but she is restless. The waiting feels like a minor form of torture.

When she is almost at the harbor, Medusa sees Psyche standing there talking to someone, coming to a halt as she realizes it is Cadmus. He is going to tell Psyche. Maybe not today. Or tomorrow. But he is going to tell her.

Frozen in place, Medusa watches Cadmus say something to Psyche, causing Psyche to double over with laughter. The pang of jealousy is unmistakable, and she tries to root out its origin.

Is she jealous of their friendship? How carefree Psyche seems with him right now? Or is Medusa worried that she might have misread where things stood between them? This differs from the fear of Cadmus telling Psyche the truth. Emotions rattle around, weaving in and out of each other as Medusa's stomach churns. The inner war in her head is still raging when Psyche turns and sees Medusa standing there.

Psyche waves excitedly, calling Medusa over to them. Cadmus looks toward Psyche's attention and a smile blooms across his face as well at the sight of her, which is utterly confusing. As she takes tentative steps and walks over to where they are standing, Medusa reminds herself repeatedly to be nice to the Hero... should she even still call him that?

Taking Medusa's hand, Psyche says, "It's time to go. The First Mate told me we can board anytime."

"I'm eager to get moving. I always get so antsy when I have to wait for anything important. I used to drive the masters absolutely mad with my fidgeting before an exam or evaluation."

"I'm the same way," Cadmus responds.

Medusa tries to keep her expressions as neutral as possible. He has said nothing wrong, but she has the urge to snap at him and tell him to mind his own business. She knows the hostility toward him is valid, but for the sake of the Allegiance and everything they are trying to do, she will do her absolute best to put that aside.

He continues with an amiable smile, "they always put me on patrol duty right before anything major. They didn't bother telling me to rest instead, they knew it was futile and if they didn't give me something official to do, I was likely to find myself in a spot of trouble."

"The Masters would do the same. They would assign me the most mundane tasks that they knew would keep me busy, lest they find me sneaking into sealed areas or pilfering elderflower wine from the kitchens." Medusa responds, feels herself softening with the easy conversation.

Cadmus smirks. "I bet you were fiercely mischievous under the influence of spirits."

Her patience with him frays and snaps. "What in Tartarus is that supposed to mean? Of course, you would assume I was a delinquent."

"I… uh…" At a loss on how to respond, Cadmus opts to leave the situation altogether and turns and walks away.

Medusa immediately kicks herself.

We JUST talked about this. Why are you like this?

Feeling like a petulant brat, Medusa is embarrassed to look Psyche in the eye. Psyche simply takes Medusa's other hand and pulls her attention to her.

"Hey, it's ok. I only know a fraction of your history with the Heroes but what little I *do* know tells me that this will take time and even then, you never have to like him. No one, including Cadmus himself, would blame you for that."

"What do you mean, Cadmus wouldn't blame me? I haven't given him a moment of kindness. Why doesn't he hate me?" Medusa asks.

"He's not like any of the other Heroes I've ever met. I hope my trust in him isn't misguided, but my gut says he's different." Psyche replies. "And I've seen his soul."

Medusa thinks for a moment, then says, "I have been trying to be patient around him, but I'm failing. I will keep working on that and see if I can't give him a chance because if you say he's alright, who am I to disagree with that?"

Psyche smiles warmly in response and leaves it at that. They both turn and face the ship, taking in the bustling activity as people carry supplies on board, unfurl the sails, and make all the last-minute preparations.

After they take in the scene, Psyche says to Medusa, "I have one more thing to discuss with you before we head aboard." She pauses and almost seems nervous. "cabin space is limited, meaning people have to share. I thought I would be whom you might be most comfortable sharing quarters with and volunteered us for that," Psyche finishes and awaits Medusa's response.

"Oh," is all Medusa can think to say, swallowing awkwardly. "That… that should be alright."

Neither of them looks each other's way for the discussion and Medusa wonders if Psyche is nervous. Was she concerned Medusa would say no, or be angry at the assumption? Also, what does this mean? Her brain is walking the line of trying to assess if the gesture meant more, and also trying not to read too much into it. Regardless, the upcoming time at sea with Psyche is something Medusa very much looks forward to.

28

MEDUSA

Once they board the ship, Psyche and Medusa make their way to their cabin. Deonn waves when he sees her and Medusa is grateful there will be another friend on board.

Deonn guides Medusa and Psyche below deck to find their cabin. As Deonn opens the door, Medusa discovers sharing a cabin on this voyage also means sharing a bed.

Medusa's eyes widen with surprise and Psyche flushes and quickly blurts out, "I'm so sorry, they didn't mention we would share beds. I promise you, I wouldn't have sprung this on you."

Psyche being flustered makes Medusa smile. The thought of sharing a bed with Psyche is terrifying and exhilarating, but in a way that is romantic and exciting. Even if nothing new occurs between them, it is a relief to not be distraught by the mere idea.

"It's alright," then, feeling a little spunky, Medusa adds, "It won't be our first time being close to each other. Somehow I think we'll manage." Medusa follows it up with a wink and has an immediate internal rush of awkwardness. Who is this person being bold and flirty? Whoever this new Medusa seems to be, hopefully she stays around a while.

MEDUSA AND PSYCHE walk up to the upper decks to watch as they leave. The sun is setting as they are leaving, timing Medusa finds curious, but was told by Isadora that their departure time had been carefully calculated by Nicodemus, who would be the one sailing us there. It does not thrill Medusa to know it would be the same captain who had been rude to her on the way here and was then openly hostile to her in the meeting.

According to Isadora, no one can handle the seas as swiftly as Nicodemus, aside from Poseidon himself.

The ship moves away from the Isle and Medusa watches as it shrinks in their wake. A few minutes later, they have to go back through the Mysts and Medusa remembers what happened last time.

Turning from the railing, Medusa makes her way back to the cabin, hurrying to make it back before they go through the Mysts. There have been more people kind to Medusa than scared of her, but she does not want to press her luck by frightening them with something has no explanation.

She rushes through the door and is surprised to see Psyche has followed.

"You didn't have to come back down here with me. I'm alright." Medusa says.

Psyche asks, "Something isn't right. You can tell me. You don't have to, of course, but like you, I'm an excellent listener."

Medusa answers, "I had an interesting reaction to the Mysts last time we went through. You weren't there with me and I forgot to mention it with everything else that has happened. I don't know how to explain it, but I'm pretty sure it scared the people who saw it, and I don't want that to happen again, so I came down here."

"What kind of reaction?" Psyche asks gently.

"The Mysts began to glow and dance around my skin. It didn't hurt, but it tingled, like static energy."

"I've never heard of anything." Psyche replies but stops when the ship enters the edges of the Myst and she gets to see first-hand exactly what Medusa means.

The cabin fills with the dark mist, just enough so that they can still see each other. Psyche's mouth drops open when tendrils of Mysts snake up and down Medusa's arms and legs, glowing brightly in a beautiful shimmering silver.

Psyche reaches over for Medusa's hand, but she hesitates to take it.

"It might not be safe," Medusa urges. "I don't want to hurt you."

"I am a god. If I can't withstand whatever this is, you have my permission to take it up with the Fates."

That logic is questionable, but Medusa takes Psyche's hand, hesitantly.

Psyche immediately glows, as the energy makes its way up to her head and her hair floats ethereally around her.

They stare at each other with shocked expressions when all of it suddenly vanishes, and they have made it through the Mysts.

Psyche breathlessly says to her, "I think coming down here might have been a good idea."

MEDUSA LOUNGES IN THE CABIN, reading one of the books she brought with her. She is a few chapters into the Fae book, *The Borderlands Princess*, finding the alternate world fascinating and an excellent escape from the stress of the past few days. Her eyesight struggles a bit in the dim lamplight of the cabin, but that has never deterred her from diving into a good story before.

She is so engrossed in the novel that she jumps and lets out a small shriek when Psyche walks in the door. Psyche giggles at Medusa's reaction. "I'm so sorry. I didn't mean to startle you."

"It's what I get for being so engrossed in a silly book." Medusa chuckles, closes the book, and sets it on the bedside table.

"It must be a pretty good one," Psyche continues. "What's it about?"

"It's about a fictional world where these people called 'Fae' are at war against a great evil, but the more I read, the blurrier the lines seem to get between good and bad, except for the villain who is evil. It's really quite fascinating." Medusa stops herself. "I'm sorry, I don't want to ramble. How was your evening?"

"It's not rambling. I enjoy hearing about things you enjoy, or thoughts you want to share."

Psyche sits down on the bed next to her and Medusa is suddenly acutely aware of the fact that they will share this bed. The rapid beating of her heart is synced with the flapping wings of the butterflies in her stomach.

"My evening was good. I went over some things with Nico, making sure we are still on course."

"I'm sure he loved that." Medusa rolls her eyes, making Psyche laugh.

"The ego isn't lacking on that one, is it? He's fine if you just ignore him. Can't argue with him being the best captain on the seas, but that doesn't mean I will not be double-checking things when I can."

Psyche walks over to the washbasin and pours some water in from the bucket they have in the room, taking a cloth and bathing herself lightly. Medusa watches as Psyche's hands rub the washcloth against her shoulders, her collarbone, and her neck. Medusa continues to watch her dip the cloth back in the water, bringing it up her thighs between the slits in her dress. She turns around when she's finished and Medusa quickly looks up at the ceiling, embarrassed to have possibly been caught staring.

Psyche walks over to Medusa, who is sitting with her legs over the edge of the bed, and gently grasps her chin, tilting it up until their eyes meet.

"If I had a problem with you looking, I wouldn't have done it in front of you," Psyche says while gazing into her eyes.

Neither says anything for a moment as they merely stare into each other. Both of them move their faces closer until their lips are almost touching. Suddenly, they are in the Oasis once more.

Medusa looks at Psyche, confused. "Why are we here?"

Psyche shrugs her shoulders and looks somewhat sheepish, "I... I know touch can be overwhelming for you right now so I had the thought that maybe if I kiss you here - and I mean really kiss you- that it would be easier for you?"

Medusa is shocked at the level of consideration but quickly offers Psyche a warm smile. "That's one of the kindest things anyone has ever done for me. You're absolutely right. It has been a complete overload for my system. However, and I mean this sincerely. With you, I want to feel everything. Fully."

Psyche smiles and squeezes her hand. Then they are back in the cabin. Medusa on the bed, Psyche standing there between her legs. Their lips meet almost immediately and Psyche's lips open for Medusa, where it's reciprocated. When their tongues meet, Medusa moans. Psyche pushes down to deepen the kiss, one hand on either side of Medusa's cheek. Medusa's hands circle around Psyche's waist and caress her back. When Psyche's lips trail down Medusa's neck, shivers erupt down her spine, sending a shockwave throughout Medusa's Has she felt truly adored like this?

Psyche pulls her head back and halts the kiss. Medusa looks up at her curiously as Psyche reaches for the hood.

Medusa's eyes go wide with surprise and Psyche continues, still fiddling with the hood, "May I?"

Medusa nods slowly, remembering how Psyche had been unharmed in the baths when Medusa's hood had been ripped off. She is afraid to even breathe wrong because this moment is both entirely too perfect and terrifying.

Psyche gently pushes the hood back, and it falls slowly. The serpents slither slowly but are still lulled into a daze by merely being in Psyche's presence. She runs her hands up the back of Medusa's neck and once again tilts her head up to her. When their lips touch again, they devour each other with fervor, and Medusa consumes the feeling. Psyche grasps the hem of Medusa's tunic and lifts it over her head, breaking the kiss only when necessary.

Once her tunic is on the floor, Psyche straddles Medusa. Her core is molten with desire for the goddess in her lap.

Medusa's hands roam up Psyche's thighs and then cup her behind, squeezing. Psyche raises her arms behind her head. One hand removes the clip from her hair and Psyche's raven locks come cascading down around her shoulder, stirring up her scent of jasmine. Medusa's other hand goes to the back of Psyche's neck and undoes the clasp holding her dress together, causing it to fall down, the silk fabric pooling at her waist.

This time when they kiss, it is slow and tender as their hands explore each other. Medusa sighs into the kiss as Psyche's touch skims all over, gently bumping over Medusa's scales and sliding across her skin. Then, Psyche kisses Medusa's cheek, and her jaw, until she lands on the spot where her neck meets her ear, and Medusa moans again. With every stroke of Psyche's tongue comes waves of pleasure.

Psyche's kisses make their way down to her shoulder, and then to her sternum as her left hand cups Medusa's left breast and her thumb slightly grazes over Medusa's nipple. The sensation is overwhelming but wonderful, and her breathing kicks up a notch. All hesitations and thoughts are gone from Medusa's mind as the kisses make their way to her right breast and then Psyche's lips are on her right nipple while her left thumb still has the other as an ecstatic hostage.

Psyche's tongue gently flicks over Medusa's nipple, and she closes her eyes, leaning into every sensation fully as it continues to fuel the inferno between her thighs. The pleasure is coming in waves that are timed to the rhythm of Psyche's tongue. Before Medusa can stop herself, an orgasm comes crashing over her. Psyche holds her tight as she continues to pull the climax from Medusa.

As the pleasure subsides, Psyche moves back up to Medusa's lips and takes her mouth for another deep kiss. Medusa's eager response is all the indication Psyche needs to continue. She breaks the kiss and stands up, grabbing a pillow from the bed. Psyche plops it on the floor in front of Medusa unceremoniously and then before Medusa can process what is happening, Psyche is on her knees between Medusa's legs, using the pillow as a cushion.

Psyche doesn't say a word, just stares into Medusa's eyes as she trails her fingers from each knee, up both inner thighs, until they are resting on her waistband. Psyche pauses again, another opportunity for Medusa to make sure she wants to do this. She does and nods her head yes again.

Medusa leans back onto her elbows and lifts her hips so Psyche can remove her pants. Once they are on the floor, Psyche stands back up and leans down, and kisses Medusa. As she is trailing kisses down Medusa's neck and collarbone, she lingers over Medusa's scales, kissing them tenderly. With her heart pounding in her chest, uncertainty makes its way into

Medusa's mind. Shame churns her stomach while a goddess is up close and personal with Medusa's flaws and imperfections.

Psyche is on her knees between Medusa's legs. Medusa watches Psyche's every move, waiting for the inevitable disgust at Medusa's reptilian form. It never comes and tears threaten to fall from Medusa. A day when someone looks at her in her current monstrous state and still wants her is something Medusa imagined would happen in her wildest dreams. Psyche puts a hand on Medusa's thigh and with the other hand lightly traces up and down between Medusa's legs using the tip of a finger. The touch is so delicate, but it sends shivers across Medusa's body. When it's almost too much to bear, through hooded eyes she meets Psyche's gaze as the goddess takes the same torturous finger and puts it in her mouth to wet it. Psyche's dark eyes continue piercing through every part of Medusa's being as she inserts her finger inside of her.

Medusa moans and throws her head back as Psyche tenderly slides her finger in and out. Medusa writhes her hips in rhythm with Psyche's movements. Psyche removes her finger and brings it to her lips once more, and moans when she tastes Medusa. A second finger goes in her mouth and then she is at Medusa's entrance with both fingers, which slip in readily and begin their work, driving Medusa mad. Her heart feels like it is pounding out of her chest and it peppers her skin with goose-bumps. Her hips are rocking in time with Psyche's sensual torment, and Medusa feels close to shattering again. Medusa whimpers as she nears the edge and Psyche's thumb is on her clit causing the world explodes into ecstasy.

Medusa closes her eyes and soars as her body finishes riding the high of the orgasm. When she opens them again, Psyche climbs into the bed to lie alongside her. Medusa rolls over onto her side and kisses Psyche deeply, planning to reciprocate the pleasure, but Psyche stops Medusa, taking her hand.

"There will be so many opportunities for that. I just want to lie here and be with you for a while, is that alright?"

More than happy to spend the rest of the night near Psyche and bathe in her closeness, Medusa nods and moves to lie properly in the bed, pulling Psyche's hand to join her. Psyche settles in, putting her head on her shoulder as Medusa wraps her arm around her.

Medusa cups Psyche's cheek and draws her into a sweet, soft kiss that deepens into something soul-shattering.

They lie there wrapped in each other's embrace, Medusa twining her fingers through Psyche's hair until they fall asleep.

29

MEDUSA

They have made swift progress, according to Psyche, as she returns from conferring with the captain. Until the source of Nicodemus's animosity toward Medusa is revealed, she wants to remain out of his sight.

Medusa sits on the deck with Psyche and they watch the waves slap against the hull of the boat. Iris, the first mate, approaches them.

Iris looks in their twenties with shoulder-length dark hair that has the slightest wave to it which they wear tied back with a cord. Their piercing blue eyes are kind when they speak. "Just wanted to give you both a heads up. We will be at The Siren Strait in just under an hour at our current speeds."

The Strait fascinated Medusa when she was growing up. Countless hours of free time were spent in the library learning about the devastatingly alluring, wicked vicious beings. Entire ships were lost without a single sailor remaining.

The Siren Strait is the stretch of water between Sparta at the tip of the main continent and the Isle of Remembrance. That small channel of water allows for more ship trade and commerce, creating a faster alternative to slower transport on

199

land. The only downside is the terrifyingly beautiful beings that inhabit it.

According to Psyche, there had been much debate about the Siren Strait during the planning stages of this mission, but The Allegiance came to the consensus that the time it would take to go around them would cause too great of a delay.

Ajax, one of the crew members, adds, "We have Psyche's protection, though, so nothing to worry about."

He has broad, muscular shoulders and long, shaggy blond hair, a beard, and tattoos covering his arms. Ajax looks like he can handle himself in most situations, but the Strait requires more than strength and grit.

"How does your magic protect the entire ship?" Medusa asks Psyche.

"When the sirens sing, it is to the soul, stirring up emotions and unrest, sowing chaos in their victim's mind. I will use my powers to keep souls calm, making them resistant to the draw of the sirens." Psyche places a hand on Medusa's shoulder in reassurance.

Official Pantheon ships have a seal that allows safe passage, but the rebels have Psyche.

Psyche's abilities are impressive, and Medusa does not doubt them, but everyone knows the dangers of the Strait.

"What would we do to make it through if Psyche weren't with us?" Medusa looks at Iris and Ajax.

Iris's chest heaves as they exhale loudly, and Ajax scoffs. "Try your best to not go over." His muscular hands clench tightly around a coil of rope as he gathers it before leaving in search of more.

Medusa and Psyche make their way back below decks to ride out this treacherous part of their voyage.

Nonessential crew and personnel will stay below decks while going through the Strait, still needing to remain silent, but at least safer behind locked doors. The crew members unlucky enough to be the ones operating the ship through the Strait will have a harder time. In the past, sailors would try to block the sound from their ears. This also meant they couldn't hear the captain's directives and ships crashed against the jagged rocks.

"I have to find Alec. I'll be right in to join you," Psyche says, taking Medusa's hand in her own and kissing the inside of Medusa's palm before walking away.

Medusa's foot touches the top stair to go below deck when Nicodemus' voice sounds behind her, sending a shiver down her spine.

"Ah, there you are, Medusa. There are some logistics that Isadora asked me to discuss with you."

Medusa's heart pounds, and she forgets how to breathe. Something is off. Beneath the hood, her serpents stir. Excuses fly through Medusa's mind and she tries to come up with any reason not to follow Nicodemus.

"All right." Medusa's chest tightens at the thought of being alone with the captain, and she wishes Psyche was still with her.

"Excellent, come with me and we will have a quick chat before we get to the Strait." Nicodemus gently grabs Medusa's upper arm to guide her.

Her instincts scream that something is wrong, and she bristles at his touch, yanking her arm from his grasp. Nicodemus glares at her through a clenched jaw but does not reach out to touch her again. Is Medusa confident enough to jeopardize the mission? If only Psyche were still with her.

They reach the back of the ship, and the aft deck is empty. No Isadora, no other crew members. Just a dinghy, ready to drop into the water. Medusa spins around to find Nicodemus invading her personal space, close and threatening.

"Medusa, your role in this mission has changed. Get in the boat."

"No." What is Nicodemus doing? There is no chance the plan would have changed like this without Psyche knowing.

Reaching into his pocket, he pulls out a vial. Medusa takes a step back, bumping into the railing. She is cornered. Subtly adjusting her feet, Medusa strengthens her stance. She will fight this man if it comes to it.

But what if it did? Indecision claws at her, pricking her skin with shards of doubt.

Pain stings Medusa's waist, and she finds a dagger digging into her side.

"I can make this easier and kill you right now, but that's not how he wants you."

Nicodemus thinks Medusa will be easy to subdue? Good.

Medusa brings her knee to Nicodemus's groin, and the resulting groan is satisfying. He hunches over slightly and Medusa tries to slip around him.

"She's not going anywhere, Captain. What is the meaning of this?" Psyche says.

Distracted by Psyche's presence, Nicodemus twists Medusa around and holds the dagger to her throat. Before she can process the absence of pain in her side, the blade is digging into her throat. Nicodemus digs the blade in deeper and a warm trickle of blood trails down to her collarbone.

Using the hand not holding the dagger to Medusa's throat, Nicodemus uses his teeth to pull the stopper out of the vial that he still holds, dropping it to the ground. Black smoke billows from the broken shards of the bottle and Nicodemus pulls a cloth out of his pocket, covering his face.

Psyche shoves Medusa, causing her to fall several feet away, clear of the vapor.

"Run!" Psyche yells, but Medusa it rooted to the deck as Psyche loses consciousness.

No. How did this go so wrong, so fast?

Nicodemus lifts Psyche up and hoists her into the lifeboat.

Reaching into his pocket, he pulls out his pocket watch and curses.

No! He can't have Psyche!

"Well, you're not the one I was after, but I'm pretty sure they'll be happy to have you, too," Nicodemus says to Psyche's body.

Medusa lunges but has no weapons and is completely defenseless. Again.

Except she isn't.

Her snakes hissing in a rage as Medusa pulls her hood down. "Let her go!"

But he has already dropped the lifeboat below her line of sight.

Nicodemus calls back over the railing. "You can come after me, or you can go inform the crew that they have no captain or protection for the Strait. Maybe they'll have just enough time to improvise and pull it together. But if you follow me, Viper, every one of these people will die because you abandoned them."

This can't be happening.

Does Medusa go after them? Save Psyche? Her serpents hiss loudly as the internal war rages. Clenching the railing, Medusa watches the boat's descent as guilt overwhelms her.Tears fall freely from her face as she realizes Nicodemus is right. If Medusa tries to save Psyche, there is little chance any of the crew will survive. They are heading into the deadliest waters in the Olympic Isles without a captain or a god's protection.

This is my fault.

Silence washes over her mind as Medusa puts the hood back on, turns, and runs back to the front of the ship, asking everyone where she can find Iris.

Deonn leads Medusa through the chaos of the ship to Iris. She tries frantically to tell them what happened, but she cannot find the words to say that Psyche is gone. That Medusa failed her and allowed Nicodemus to take her.

Medusa sucks in rapid, shallow breaths of air. *He took Psyche.* A wail escapes her as the reality of Psyche's absence hits Medusa. The hardwood of the deck is solid when her knees slam into it.

Looking around at the crew of the ship, all staring at Medusa with confusion and curiosity as she sobs, she knows she made the right choice to save them, but her heart shatters every second she is away from Psyche.

A shout comes from the crow's nest announcing their arrival at the Strait. Medusa does not have the luxury of wallowing in her failure. If she cannot pull it together, Psyche will be gone and every person on this ship will die. All because of Medusa.

Everything seems far away, and the murmur and shuffling of the crowd sounds muted. Someone drops in front of Medusa, cupping her face in his firm hands. As Medusa's eyes lock with Cadmus's, her breathing steadies and Medusa tells him what happened.

Iris shouts out orders to the deckhands, assuming the role of captain like they were born for it. Ajax jumps in as first mate and they adapt to the new command structure seamlessly.

"Hey," Cadmus says tentatively.

"Hey," Medusa replies, trying to look away from him in shame, but he gently keeps her facing him.

"Sorry about what happened with the captain. I wish I had been there. I would have thrown him overboard and let the sirens have him. The coward knew the rest of us would never let him take you, but he got you alone."

Medusa nods, as her rage returns now that her shock is wearing off. "There's still time. I'm going after her."

Cadmus shakes his head, holding up his hands, "No. We are too close to the Strait, it's too dangerous. We can't lose you, too!"

"I wasn't asking for your permission, Hero." Medusa spits out the last word. How dare he try to tell her what she can do? His approval is not needed or wanted.

Medusa turns to walk back to the small boats Nicodemus abducted Psyche. Maybe there was a second boat there and Medusa can follow Psyche, despite Nicodemus's unfortunate head start.

Cadmus steps in front of her, his tall frame blocking out the bright sun overhead, casting his features into shadow. "C'mon. Let's get you below deck. We're almost out of time."

He grips her upper arm, exactly where Nicodemus had his hand, and Medusa has had enough, yanking her arm from Cadmus's grip. "I can't just let him take her! I thought you cared about her!"

Medusa's eyes narrow with suspicion as she glares into Cadmus's golden eyes. "This seems too well orchestrated for the captain to have managed it alone."

Cadmus's jaw clenches. "I didn't do this! We don't have time to argue. I have to get you below decks."

The crew races around them, ignoring their altercation as they prepare the best they can to face this peril with no protection. The clanking of metal fills the air as the crew members, who are absolutely necessary to operate the ship, chain themselves to their posts with ankle shackles.

"Worry about yourself. I'm fine. Let. Me. Go." Medusa says through gritted teeth, daring him to challenge her.

Stepping around him, Medusa once again goes to leave.

The deck spins as Cadmus's arms circle around Medusa's waist, as he throws her over his shoulder with a grunt.

"I'm not losing you too." He grits out through the effort of containing Medusa's flailing as she hits and kicks him. Anything to make him let her go.

Medusa fights him through every step as he carries her down to a cabin.

"We have to go get her!" Every second that passes feels like a rope between her heart and Psyche's is being stretched and pulled.

"We will. We have to make it out of the Strait first."

The door slams behind Cadmus as he drops her on the bed. The bed where she and Psyche made love mere hours ago mocks her. Medusa runs her fingers over the coarse blanket. Cadmus sits beside her.

This is all Medusa's fault. Fighting Nicodemus was stupid. If she had gone along with what he asked, they would have been long gone before Psyche got there. Guilt consumes Medusa. What did she do to make the Fates consign her to a life of nothing but impossibly wrong choices?

The external lock clicks on the door, sealing them in together to ride out the Strait, and with Medusa's options completely out of her hands, the fight finally leaves her. Tears flow freely and Medusa lets them fall. Spasms wrack her chest as she struggles to breathe. Her grief is palpable — a gaping hole in Medusa's soul.

Cadmus watches Medusa patiently, saying nothing, as her sobs slowly subside.

When Medusa looks at him again, she softens. This man took care of her, kept her safe from herself. With danger barreling down on them, Cadmus made Medusa and her safety a priority. Accusing him of orchestrating Psyche's abduction was a low blow. Medusa knows Cadmus cares for Psyche, has seen the way he looks at the goddess when Psyche was unaware. But he let Medusa say all of those things, anyway. Let her rage and cry.

Cadmus is close enough that Medusa is within arm's reach if she needs him, but only just. Medusa reaches over and takes his hand, lacing his fingers through hers.

He turns to look at her with a shocked expression, but gives her hand a gentle squeeze, running his thumb along hers in soft strokes.

Medusa and Cadmus lean back against the wall in the bed, fingers laced together as they brace themselves for what will hopefully be an uneventful half-hour.

THE SILENCE IS EXCRUCIATING. The sirens know they are here, but drawing extra attention to themselves seems foolish, so they do not utter a sound.

Medusa's focus should be on surviving the sirens, but all she can think about is Psyche. Surely the Pantheon will not hurt her. She is a *god*.

It would hardly be the first time the gods have harmed one another, though. The Pantheon has proven itself to be unscrupulous. Fear for Psyche is all Medusa can think about, unable to stop herself from imagining all the ways Psyche could be harmed.

They are mostly through the fields and the light at the end of the tunnel is nearing when, suddenly, harmonic notes fill the air.

Medusa's eyes glaze over, and her jaw drops open as the ethereal voices flood her mind. They are singing a sorrowful tune. They are not words Medusa's mind recognizes, but her soul does, a cry escaping her as emotion floods through her and pictures of Psyche race through her mind.

She grips Cadmus's hand instinctively and the squeeze that is returned snaps her back to reality slightly. Turning her head, Medusa sees his jaw is set, his eyes closed as he, too, tries to block out their melodic torture.

Medusa reaches out with her free hand and cups his cheek.

Cadmus's eyes fly open and meet Medusa's. The song fades slightly and Medusa does not know if they are almost through the Strait or if the power of their eyes locked together is enough to slightly diminish the call of the sirens.

There is a loud thunk from the decks above, followed by, "Son of a bitch!" A series of crashing sounds follow.

Both Medusa and Cadmus stop breathing in fear of the source of the exclamation they just heard. There is a brief second of silence once more before the shouting begins. Medusa jerks as if to jump up, but Cadmus squeezes her hand and firmly shakes his head no.

Medusa's heart is in her throat as the noise continues, but it is extinguished soon after it begins. The silence left in its wake is heavy with dread. Tears are streaming from the corners of Cadmus's eyes and Medusa is paralyzed with fear and frustration. It goes against everything in her to hear someone in distress and simply ignore them, even if she knows that would help no one.

The silence stretches on for a few more minutes, and then there is a gentle knock at the door. It opens, and Chloe appears, eyes rimmed red from tears, choking back sobs as she informs them the ship has cleared the Strait.

"Who?" is all Cadmus has to ask.

Chloe's chest heaves with a large sob as she simply says, "Deonn," and leaves, closing the door behind her.

They sit there in shock.

Deonn was warm and had a bright personality to be around. He made her feel welcome when others wanted to shun her.

Another knock sounds at the door. This time, it is Iris.

"I came to check on you both as soon as I got the all-clear from Chloe. Glad to see you're both alright, at least physically. I bumped into Ajax on the way to you and based on what they told me, you're going to want to sit tight down here a bit longer. If you're restless, I'm sure it would thrill Zephyr to see your faces in the galley, but you should steer the decks clear of for the time being."

"What the Fates happened?" Medusa asks.

"I was up there," they start and take a breath, running their hand over their shocked face. "I've never been through before without being on an official ship," they gulp. "Their voices, they filled my head, and I immediately felt both at peace and desperately craving something. It was like my heart had both filled with elated air and left my body, and all that was left was a hollow cavern where it used to be. It was bliss, torture, ecstasy, and longing all at the same time."

A tear runs down their cheek, a monument to the emotion of what they just experienced.

"We were clinging to the masts, to each other, anything to maintain our grip on reality and remind us not to go. It was too much for Deonn. The shackle around his ankle was closed completely, and he got loose of his bindings. We tried to stop him, screaming at him not to listen to them, but he was gone, lost in their spell. Ajax even tackled him. They fought, but it was useless."

A shudder escapes them as they finish. "All he did was lean over the rail to get a better look. They yanked him over the edge, but he gripped the railing tight, hanging on for dear life. His fingers finally slipped, and he was gone, only to be followed by a forceful spray of blood."

Medusa pictures the scenario despite her best efforts not to. She thought she was struggling with not being able to help while she was just hearing what happened. The sirens viciously killed someone they cared about, right in front of them.

Iris exits the room, leaving Cadmus standing there, shifting his weight from one leg to the other awkwardly, unsure what to do with himself.

Medusa offers, "Would you like to stay here with me for a short while?"

Medusa tells herself it is because Psyche always seems to enjoy his company and because he was there for her during the Strait, but the voice in the back of her head suggests that Medusa might not mind Cadmus as much as she thinks.

Thinking about Psyche's interactions with Cadmus brings the reality of the goddess's absence crashing to the forefront of Medusa's mind.

"We have to get Psyche *now!*"

Cadmus rubs his hand across his face. "I know. We already are." At her blank look, he continues. "Think it through. Everyone is gathering for the gala. If Nicodemus is going to take her somewhere to hand her over to the Pantheon, the gala is the first place to start."

Medusa nods her head and breathes. *Deep breaths. He's right.*

Cadmus turns the lone chair in the room around to face away from the bed and sits backward in it, folding his arms over the back and resting his chin on them. The move is almost childlike and Medusa recognizes a boyish nature to him when he is nervous.

"I'm scared," Medusa says quietly. "We may not get her back, and it's my fault. I am constantly letting everyone down. I will never forgive myself if she isn't okay."

"So let's talk about it," Cadmus says. "I know the Allegiance values Psyche and Hestia, but I don't know if most of them would make Psyche's rescue their top priority. We can do everything like we are supposed to for the Allegiance plan, but you and I should be on the same page about how far we are willing to go to get Psyche back."

30

MEDUSA

Medusa listens to Cadmus as he and the other council members go over the plan. Knowing what they need of her is crucial to getting Psyche back safely, but it is hard for Medusa to concentrate on anything other than Psyche's absence.

Medusa tries to smile when she sees Alec, but the motion feels empty, hollow. He has kept to himself most of this voyage and she knows he is worried about Hestia.

Worry eats away at her. Worry for Psyche, for Hestia, for the mission.

The assembled party is a mix of Council members, and hand selected Allegiance members. Galen, Irene, Linus, and Alec comprise the representatives from the Council while Cadmus, Ajax, and Cyril round out the rest of the group. Everyone will dress for the gala and slip in amongst the masked guests. The Pantheon believes only those invited know of the party, so no one should check names, plus that increases the anonymity which is likely necessary for events like this.

Once through the doors, the Council members, minus Alec, who will be with Medusa's group, will disperse amongst the

211

crowd and loudly mingle as they pose as buyers while the rest of them look for the nymphs.

After establishing the broader plan, the group splits into two to discuss their separate aspects of the mission.

Medusa looks at the people standing around her and takes a moment to really observe them.

Cadmus has a smirk on his face that is both youthful and cocky. Medusa finds it annoying but does not miss the enticing glint in his caramel colored eyes.

Ajax and Cyril share a look of tired grief that Medusa sympathizes with. Ajax's blonde hair comes to his shoulders in wavy curls and Cyril's is ear length, darkly curly hair similar to Cadmus's.

It hits Medusa like a brick that she knows none of these people. Thinking of how much has changed between when she was on her island and now, anxiety surges. Closing her eyes and stepping away, Medusa steadies herself before anyone can notice.

Get it together.

Breathe in. Breathe out.

This shall not break me.

When Medusa opens her eyes again, nothing but patience and understanding greets her. She may not know them, but she knows what they are feeling. Knows how it feels to hurt at the injustice of the world. To rage against it until you want to scream. The look on their faces says they know that feeling all too well and give her the space to compose herself.

When Medusa rejoins the group, Cadmus slides a barrel over to the middle of where they are standing. He rolls a piece of parchment out across it and Medusa realizes they are schematics. In delicate script in an upper corner, she sees "Love Temple" and it clicks into place that these are layouts for their target.

"They weren't kidding when they said you know the temple, were they?" Medusa asks.

"I can't guarantee these are completely current. I acquired these… a long time ago," Cadmus says as his expression shifts to one of steel to stamp out any ghosts who may have been about to pop up and haunt him.

No one presses the matter and they go over the details of the building and assess what the best route will be and where they think the nymphs are being held until the auction.

A large part of the Temple is usually open to the public, with the exception being special events like the one tonight. Logically, the nymphs are being kept somewhere the public cannot stumble upon them, which limits the options significantly. They narrow it down to what had been an indoor market, but has been abandoned since Cadmus was a teenager. He remembers it being closed off but heavily guarded. He tells them about the many times he and his friends tried to sneak in there out of boredom, but always ran into resistance in the form of the Temple Guard. The boys chalked it up to being in dangerous disrepair, but his eyes glint with anger as they all make the realization that these auctions have possibly been going on longer than any of them could have fathomed.

"Why do we have these blueprints if you don't even think the nymphs are on the Temple grounds?" Medusa asks, breathing through the instinct to roll her eyes. Having trouble reigning in some of her negative responses to him is frustrating. Despite all the progress, will he always be her enemy deep down?

Ignoring Medusa's tone, if he detects it at all, Cadmus continues, "We have them because there is a tunnel marked on them, almost unnoticeable."

Cadmus points to the paper and they all follow his finger as he traces the faint line that is so thin it could be mistaken for a hair on the document. When the line ends, the path is directly in the center of the markets.

"We just have to keep our heads down, make it to this tunnel and hope they will assume no one will stumble into it and leave it relatively unguarded."

Nobody says a word, and Medusa wonders if, like her, they are hung up on the word "hope." So much at risk for a plan full of unknown variables with nothing but hope to get them through it. No part of her is considering backing out, though. Even if that was an option, Medusa could never sit back and leave Psyche in danger. Every second that Medusa cannot go after the goddess who has her heart is agony. The stakes are higher now than they have ever been for Medusa. It was one thing being the only target of the malicious gods, alone on her island, but now there are people she cares about, lives that Medusa feels she must stand up for. The nymphs, and what they are likely to be subjected to, are reason enough to make sure Medusa stays the course.

APHRODITE

The morning of the gala, Aphrodite goes through all the arrangements for the day, making sure nothing is out of place. It is lovely to be back at her temple for a few days, even if there is little time to herself before the other gods arrive.

The thought of her captive gives a spark of satisfaction. After bringing her here in the god cage, Aphrodite has had little time to truly torment her prisoner, but at least the cage itself is torture enough.

The real fun will come once Hestia is mortal. The loss of her godliness will magnify that pain.

Once this gala is out of the way, the gods can turn their focus on getting Medusa for Poseidon. Aphrodite is not sure what his fascination is with her, but it will at least be a worthy blow to the rebels after they went through so much trouble to rescue the beast. Athena has also been tight-lipped anytime Medusa is brought up, making Aphrodite wonder if the rumors of her friend's jealousy are the true root of Medusa's curse.

Aphrodite walks through the grand ballroom, mentally ticking boxes as she surveys the setup.

The blood red Greek peonies are interspersed throughout the room, their sweet scent carrying loosened inhibitions and heightened lust. Both should provide excellent bidding frenzies on their merchandise.

While their informant did not mention any knowledge of this evening's gala and auction, Aphrodite is less than confident that the event will not be interrupted. It had taken some coordinating, but she was able to switch up the order of events.

Normally, the gala would provide a reason for all the people with the deepest pockets in the Olympic Isles to gather. After, when the bulk of the attendees have gone home, they hold their auctions.

Fortunately, Aphrodite got messages out regarding the change of plans. Almost all the buyers replied swiftly, having no issue arriving early.

The door behind the stage slides open and closed smoothly. After it got stuck the last time she hosted the auction, causing an embarrassing delay, Aphrodite is not taking her chances, and is pleased to see it working.

It slides open smoothly again, and she ticks off that box, ignoring the wails of the nymphs being held there. Aphrodite's trusted Acolytes already moved them here, with only two hours to go before they get started. Their cries fall over each other, turning them into a cacophony of unintelligible noise. Pity creeps its way into her heart before Aphrodite shuts it down, sliding the door closed again.

ATHENA IS WAITING OUTSIDE of Aphrodite's chambers when she returns to get ready for the gala. Aphrodite smiles at her friend and occasional lover, appreciating the respect of her boundaries. Unlike Zeus, who barges into her space whenever he pleases. Perhaps Aphrodite will find out more about this witch and whatever secrets Athena and Zeus may be sharing.

"Shouldn't you be getting ready?" Aphrodite asks her, cocking her head in curiosity.

Athena smiles, dipping her head as her full red curls fall around her tiny face. Aphrodite chuckles at her, instantly spotting the timid behavior Athena exhibits when she wants to fuck. Always so shy and prudish. Aphrodite really does not understand what everyone's hang-up is with sex, but she humors her friend, gesturing for Athena to continue.

"You know I get stressed before these silly things. I don't know why. I'm always worried something will go wrong," Athena says.

Deciding to play aloof and enjoy the game, Aphrodite slyly asks, "What does that have to do with me?"

Athena gives her a look that says 'don't be stupid' but answers anyway, "I thought we could take our minds off it for a few minutes. No one can touch me like you."

Aphrodite smirks at the obvious play to her ego but decides it will suffice. She breaks out into a grin, extending her hand to Athena, who takes it, interlacing their fingers together.

They enter her room, and Aphrodite leads Athena over to the lush sofa, taking the lead because she knows that is what Athena responds best to. Aphrodite's magic makes it so easy to read the sexual energy coming off of people, allowing her to adapt and give them what they need.

She sits Athena down on the couch and then drops to the soft carpeted floor on her knees before her. Without breaking eye contact, the piercing green of Athena's eyes boring into her own blue ones, Aphrodite gently finds her way below the hem of her long dress. Athena's cool pink skin is silky smooth to the touch as Aphrodite lightly runs her hands up Athena's calves, her thighs, finding her warm center already getting slick for her.

Aphrodite gently teases Athena's opening, enjoying the breathy gasps that escape her. She inserts just the tip of a finger into Athena, as Athena's hips buck up, trying to get her to go deeper. Aphrodite pulls out and enters her again, stopping just short of going farther than the previous time.

Athena whimpers with need and Aphrodite steps back for a moment, enjoying the sight of Athena on full display for her.

Athena sits up but halts when Aphrodite holds up a hand to stop her.

Aphrodite walks over a set of drawers, rifling through them until she finds what she is looking for.

When she is back in front of Athena, she flips Athena over onto her stomach, bending her over the seat of the couch with her knees on the floor.

She pushes the hem of Athena's dress up to her hips, and before Athena can react, Aphrodite's face is between her legs. Her tongue strokes Athena's clit, sliding up over her slit and up to tease her ass, making her softly moan.

Pulling back again, she continues to toy with Athena's core with one hand while adjusting the straps with the other.

Once everything is secure, Aphrodite brings the tip of the phallus to Athena's center, rubbing it around her opening, getting it slick with her wetness.

When Aphrodite is satisfied she lubricated it enough, she pushes forward with her pelvis and slides inside of Athena.

Athena gasps as it fills her and Aphrodite pushes and pulls, in and out, in a slow rhythm, allowing Athena to adjust. She increases her speed, gripping Athena's hips and admiring the view of her back and her ass.

Aphrodite can tell that Athena is close to climaxing, so she reaches her hand around their bodies, finding Athena's clit and playing with it in time with her thrusts, enjoying Athena's screams of pleasure as she rides out her orgasm.

A knock sounds at the door. Aphrodite sighs.

"I'll join you in my bath in a moment?" She asks Athena.

Athena nods and leaves the room.

Aphrodite throws on a robe and yanks the door open. "What."

An acolyte is standing there, looking absolutely terrified of her. Good.

"Um, pardon the intrusion, goddess."

"The next words leaving your mouth will determine if I kill you where you stand for interrupting me."

He gulps and wrings his hands. "There's a captain here to see you. He said it was urgent and to come find you, no matter what you were doing."

She narrows her eyes at him.

"He told me it would be worth your time, and that not telling you now would get me in more trouble."

"Does this captain have a name?"

"Uh… oh geez… Nolan? Nigel? Nick?"

"Nicodemus?"

He nods his head vigorously. Aphrodite glances back at the bathing room. Her questions for Athena will have to wait.

APHRODITE FOLLOWS the Acolyte down to one of the receiving rooms where a small group of heavily armed guards stand outside. Curious.

Even more curious, one of them is her son.

"Oedipus, what are you doing here?"

He frowns. "Why are you never happy to see me, Mother? I'm always so invigorated by seeing you?"

Aphrodite hides her shudder. "Of course, dear. I'm always glad to see any of my children. I just wasn't expecting you."

He wouldn't cross a line here, would he? Out in the open, in front of others?

His broad grin does nothing to hide the sinister glint in his eye.

"I volunteered to work at this event. I told Apollo how it would be a great opportunity to see you and he was more than happy to allow this temple temporary use of your baby boy."

"Oh. That's lovely. I do hope we have time to catch up, but my schedule is tight getting ready for the gala. I'm sure you understand."

Aphrodite awkwardly puts her hand on his arm and brushes past him.

When she is almost to the door, Oedipus says, "I'll be seeing you, Mother."

In the room, Aphrodite finds Nicodemus waiting for her. Having never met him in person, Aphrodite is surprised when he is much more handsome than she envisioned. His devilishly handsome face looks like it was made for trouble. He will be a delightful distraction to remove the ick after seeing Oedipus.

On the couch behind him is Psyche.

"I see you brought me a present." Aphrodite turns to the Acolyte. "Leave. You live. For now."

"Thank you, goddess." He bows and backs out of the room at a break-neck pace.

Aphrodite returns her attention to her visitor. "How did you get her to cooperate?"

"It turns out she's rather attached to Medusa. The monster was my goal, but I figured a traitorous god would also be a hefty prize."

"Hmm... indeed."

Aphrodite finally addresses Psyche. "I guess I shouldn't be surprised. You always had a soft spot for everything weaker than us."

Psyche refuses to fall for the bait. "You did too. Once. Do you think we've forgotten who you were five hundred years ago? Back when *she* was alive."

"Don't. Leave her in the past. I have. Do you think appealing to the old me will save you?"

"Andromeda-"

"If I ever hear that name leave your lips again, you will *wish* I had merely put you in a god cage. Guards!"

They file in from out in the corridor.

"Take her and put her in with our other prisoner."

"Yes, goddess."

"Now," Aphrodite says, turning back to Nicodemus. "First, you're going to tell me everything you know about the rebels' plan for tonight." She runs her hand along his forearm. "Then we can talk about how you might like to be rewarded."

32

MEDUSA

The cargo hold of the ship is dark and cramped as Medusa dresses for the gala there rather than trying to lug everything she needs back to the cramped cabin.

The large space is empty of people save for Medusa, and she opens the container that has her evening wear. Psyche's gown is on the top and Medusa takes it out, carefully running her fingers over the thin bronze chiffon. The dress sparkles, even in the dim lantern lighting. Medusa stares at the dress. Psyche was supposed to wear this. She was supposed to be here.

Medusa lifts out the two masks- her bronze one and the other a dark, dusty gold.

A shiver spreads across Medusa's body as her bare skin meets the chilly air of the dank space. Stepping into her dress, one leg at a time, the silky green fabric feels smooth and cool as it slides over her hips and then clips over the right shoulder, leaving her left shoulder bare. The black cloak fastens at her collarbone. The velvety texture of it matches the black velvet of her hood, making it look like part of the ensemble.

Knowing she is alone, Medusa lowers her hood and slips the mask over her eyes. The strap is tricky to adjust comfortably around her snakes, who are slithering excitedly at not being covered. One of them coils around her finger and Medusa reaches up and pets the top of its head. "Hello."

A necklace is sitting in the crate, and Medusa picks it up. It's the same bronze as her snake mask that wraps around the base of her neck. She puts it on and gasps as Psyche's magic comes pouring out of it.

As sparkling particles envelop Medusa, she glows. It twines all around her, kissing her skin and sending the faintest shivers coursing through her body. Medusa's eyes widen when snakes appear. They are slithering around her arms, one around her neck, but she doesn't sense any presence from them the way she does with the ones attached to her head.

She looks into a mirror that someone set up for her. "They're illusions."

Standing before her is not a monster or a hideous beast. Medusa can almost convince herself that she is beautiful. Is this how Psyche sees her?

To blend in better, they had given Medusa an outfit with snakes everywhere. Very few people actually know what she looks like now, so this should help keep anyone from being too suspicious if they catch a glimpse of a serpent or two. Medusa did not love the idea at first, but looking at her reflection now, there is not as much shame as she expected.

Pulling her hood back up, Medusa makes her way up to the deck to gather with the others. When she emerges from the stairs, the Temple is looming on the hill and a wave of anxiety crashes through her. It seems stupid to go right underneath the noses of the gods, but Medusa cannot idly sit by, hiding. Especially as she hears more and more of how The Pantheon has wronged so many people, and destroyed so many lives and families. Even if her rebellion is short-lived, Medusa is going to fight back. Even if it means her death, which it almost certainly will.

The group that is going ashore huddles together near the railing where the large dinghy they will be boarding is located. The Council members are dressed lavishly but lack the luster that Medusa exudes. Ajax, Cyril, and Cadmus opted for more understated but elegant looks. They each wear black tunics, pants, and boots, with black cloaks. The only color to be found is from their bronze masks.

"Line up!" Cadmus says and they all do so. He goes down the line, handing each one a bracelet. By the time he finishes and they put them on, their party truly looks fit for a godly gala.

They all board the dinghy, and Iris and Chloe lower it into the water. Medusa's pulse races with every inch as they get closer to the surface of the sea, but she stamps it down defiantly.

I'm done being held hostage by my emotions. I AM stronger than this. This shall not break me.

Medusa controls her breathing until her heart rate slows to normal once more.

Cadmus takes Medusa's hand and mouths, "Are you okay?"

Medusa squeezes his hand and nods yes in response.

The landing party makes their way to the shore in silence, the only sounds coming from the water slapping against the sides and the effort of Cadmus and Cyril rowing.

As they get closer, they can see the main harbor in the distance, filled with ships of all sizes. People in robes and masks make their way along the main path to the Temple.

The Allegiance, however, will avoid that route until they get closer to the Temple, and slip in amongst the stream of gala goers unnoticed. They could not have asked for a better cover for their operation than the gala. Opportunities that allow them to slip through the door do not come around often.

The boat jerks a little as it connects with the soft mud of the shore. Medusa's stomach drops, but she holds her head up. Cyril takes his cloak off, hops out, and ties the boat to a small tree on the shore. One by one, everyone steps off the boat until it is

Medusa's turn. She pauses, and Cadmus reaches his hand out and helps her to neither fall nor destroy her dress.

Medusa puts one foot on shore, then the other, standing up straight and smoothing her dress and cloak while also being unable to take her eyes off the Temple.

33

Pain cuts through Hestia's body like shards of glass, reaching every crevice of her being, like death by a thousand cuts. Like her bones are shattered and stabbing Hestia every time she moves, breathes. It does not come in waves, or spurts. This pain is constant. There are so many things the god of knowledge knows, but Hestia did not know it was possible to hurt this much. Or which is worse, the pain itself or the psychological torture of its incessantness.

Unable to contain it, a tear rolls down Hestia's cheek, following a well-established path, and her breath hitches to prepare for a sob. The jerky movement is excruciating, and she opens her mouth to scream, but doing so hurts so much that no sound comes out.

Her stomach heaves, but it is empty, so nothing comes out. Every new movement is more unbearable than the last, as if being multiplied exponentially each time.

The life is leaving her body, Hestia can feel it. Her vitality, her immortality, and everything that could have been flashing before her eyes as her mind loops on the things she will never get to do now. A pair of steel-gray eyes keeps taunting her with the knowledge that she will never get to be held in his arms.

Alec.

Hestia imagines running her fingers through his gray beard and pictures the rough feel of it against her fingers, desperately clinging to him as her immortality continues to drain, despite the heartbreak that comes with it.

The daydream of them spending their days together has always been nothing but a fantasy, but Hestia cannot fault herself for having indulged in it.

In her mind, his hand cups her cheek and he whispers to her, "Hold on for me, I'm coming."

It matters not if the voice is a delusion, if it gives Hestia the strength to try. The cage will take the choice from her before too long.

Footsteps approach, but the thought of lifting her head to investigate is too much. Everything is too much.

The cell door opens, and Hestia still doesn't move.

"No, don't do this!" A female voice. Who is that?

A scream of pain echoes around the room and someone falls to the floor of the cage in front of Hestia.

"Psyche?" Hestia's voice is weak and drowned out by Psyche's wails of pain.

Psyche takes a few breaths, bracing herself through the pain, and looks over at her.

"Hestia. Thank the gods." Psyche reaches over and takes Hestia's hand. The pain is almost blinding, but Hestia welcomes the contact, refusing to spend her last few hours hurting *and* alone.

"I don't have much time left."

"Do you know where we are?" Psyche asks, fighting through the onslaught of the god cage.

"Love Island."

"That's great news. A rescue team is on their way. Help is coming." Psyche squeezes her hand gently.

"There's not enough time."

"Shh," Psyche says. "Just hold on. We will hold on together. They will find us."

34

MEDUSA

Medusa's thoughts cycle between everything that can go wrong, and if Psyche is okay. She looks at Cadmus and has to wonder, is he really safe to trust? Or is she falling into trusting him in the absence of Psyche? Should she put aside any uneasiness she has regarding him since the Allegiance trusts him? It could just be the stakes of the mission, but her instincts scream that this will not end well.

The Allegiance group reaches the procession of people walking to the temple. Medusa sucks in a deep breath and holds it as they step out into the street and merge with people walking, only letting it out when no one gives them a second glance.

They walk briskly, but make a point to not appear too rushed and out of place.

"How did you become so close with Hestia?" Medusa asks Alec quietly. "You don't have to talk about her if it's hard right now."

Alec shakes his head and says, "No, not talking about her would be a greater disservice to her. The world deserves to know how smart she is, how brave and beautiful."

"I know you are in love with her. We will get her back."

229

Medusa's heart shatters in sympathy for him. Alec has known Hestia longer than Medusa has known Psyche and Medusa will already burn the world down if anyone dares to hurt Psyche.

Emotion fills Alec's voice. "Her world is books, and I always think about how the story of us would look if it was written in one. I often lie in bed and flip through the pages of it in my mind. I imagined sweeping gestures where I am her hero and sweep her off of her feet. I'm worrying that it will be more of a tragedy."

The temple looms before them and Medusa looks up at the grand columns that adorn the front of the building. The architecture of the temples is something Medusa used to love and could easily get lost just looking at the carvings along their facades. Now when she looks at it, it is a pretty face on something monstrous. Will Medusa ever be able to look at a temple in awe again, knowing they are filled with horrors?

Medusa's legs feel like jelly when they reach the top of the temple steps. She laces her fingers together as she clasps her hands in front of her. Her pulse rises and her chest heaves with every step forward through the threshold.

35

APHRODITE

The sheer, glittery fabric of her auction gown is rough against Aphrodite's skin and she fidgets inconspicuously, counting down the minutes until she can change her dress for the gala. Technically, everything is covered, but the dress is so transparent Aphrodite might as well just have gems glued onto her body instead.

She likes to present a tantalizing package during these auctions. Sex sells, and that is exactly what Aphrodite wants on the minds of the buyers as they bid on the nymphs.

The last lot comes to a close, and the curtain is drawn over the stage.

"No, please!" A small voice cries out. The Acolyte handling the nymph grabs a livestock prod- enchanted with Zeus's magic- zaps the nymph, and she falls limp on the floor.

The buyers depart immediately, taking their purchases with them while the guests who ended the auction empty-handed start mingling until the additional visitors arrive for the gala portion of the evening.

Aphrodite steps into the small dressing room behind the stage, stripping off the scratchy dress.

231

Her blush pink satin dress is hanging on the rack and she reaches for it gratefully. The cool fabric is soothing on her irritated skin as it slides over her body. Looking in the mirror, Aphrodite admires the way the fabric gathers at her waist and under her breasts. The slit is dangerously high, coming up to her hip, creating the illusion of a long frame, despite her shorter stature.

Kicking off her heels in favor of bare feet, the plush carpet feels soft beneath her toes. Aphrodite has several reasons for the odd choice of footwear. In her opinion, it presents a more intimate appearance, as if she just rolled out of someone's bed. Her role and image are part of a carefully crafted game that Aphrodite adores. The high she gets when every person in the room wants to bed her is almost addicting.

The image in the mirror is hollow. Nothing about Aphrodite's appearance has changed, but looking at herself feels unrecognizable from when Andromeda was alive. Her face seems sharper at the edges, to match her heart. She straightens the rose gold mask covering her face, the intricate metal filigree similar to her lock box, vines and thorns weaving into an intricate pattern designed to lure someone in for a closer look and then leave them wounded.

Leaving the dressing room, her bare feet meet the cold stone tile of the hallway that connects the stage, dressing rooms, and ballroom. Feet are sore from her high heels, Aphrodite soaks up the soothing relief that comes from the cool floor, one of the other reasons to go without shoes.

The sound of the string quartet playing their first piece meets her in the hallway outside the ballroom, announcing the start of their decoy event.

Aphrodite mingles through the small sea of masks, cloaks, and dresses of varying degrees of decency. Some people come dressed demurely despite the odds being favorable that their body will end up on full display while being fucked by at least two people, their screams echoing throughout the ballroom for anyone to hear. Everyone shines and sparkles and it is easy to get swept away in the general splendor of these events.

Some people like to claim it is Aphrodite's Ambrosia wine that gets everyone particularly riled up. Others swear that something came over them and they cannot remember what happened and therefore are not to blame for their actions.

The truth is, being here naturally loosens their inhibitions. This is where they come to be free to express themselves sexually, where no one will judge them for what makes them orgasm.

Aphrodite rolls her eyes, thinking about how timid the general society is as a whole. Repressed sexual desires are one of the fastest ways to create a bunch of angry, miserable people.

The ballroom doors open and the new guests file in, greeting people as they work the crowd. The masks free them even further, allowing the liberty of anonymity to fuel their passions.

Aphrodite preens under the attention of the eyes glued to her body as she makes her rounds, eager to see who will share her bed tonight. She grabs a full wineglass off the tray of a passing server and drinks it all, enjoying the rush if the light buzz as she closes her eyes and lets it go to her head.

Tonight, Aphrodite is going to have fun. The auction is over, and those responsibilities are complete. She is going to drink, dance, laugh, and fuck. Tomorrow, her new toy might even be mortal enough to play with.

As Aphrodite is leaving the ballroom for some fresh air, a flash of gold catches her eye. Her breath stops at the source. The gilded woman with a golden-winged mask makes Aphrodite's mouth go dry, shining like sunshine itself. Her necklace shines like a thousand stars and flickers like a flame. Aphrodite's heart beats harder in recognition. Can it be *her*?

36

MEDUSA

The grand foyer of the temple rises high above Medusa's head as she takes in the extravagance. meticulously arranged tiles cover the floor in a collage of images, all depicting lovers mid-passion. Elaborate moldings adorn the walls and the ceiling has been painted with a mural that is like the floor except instead of individual couples, it portrays a group sex scene.

Candles are lit all along the sides of the walkways, in the sconces, casting the entire area in a soft, romantic glow, creating an atmosphere that makes one long to be between the sheets with a lover. Everything about this place screams seduction with the heady scent of the flowers filling their senses.

The other gala attendees continue straight through the foyer to the ballroom, and their group follows. They pretend to mingle as they work their way over to the hallway off the ballroom that has the lavatories. According to Cadmus's map, this hallway should continue in the direction they need to go to find the tunnel.

On the stage, the musicians are playing and the sound of the instruments soothes Medusa's nerves slightly. The sensual melody is hypnotic, but they have a job to do.

They go through the motions of using the facilities until no bystanders remain. The process eats into the precious minutes they have to linger, but it pays off when the coast is finally clear. They continue on, quickly disappearing around the corner before anyone spots them.

After they are a little way down the hallway, Cadmus opens his mouth to speak when a man comes stumbling toward them. He appears drunk, with his rabbit mask sitting haphazardly on his face, revealing whiskers and ruddy skin likely from years of alcohol abuse.

He sees Medusa, and slurs, "Ssswhat are yousssss doing here pretty ladiessssss," and belches.

They make to just ignore him and move past him when suddenly he grabs Medusa's arm and yanks her toward him.

"Don'tttt ignore meee, bitch," he grunts out the last word.

Medusa is done being grabbed and touched by people, twisting out of his grip and punching him square in the throat. Nikolas trained her well and knows where to land a hit. He makes a choking sound that is then accompanied by his wailing, bringing her more satisfaction than it should have, but she is done letting the people she cares about get hurt.

"Touch me again, and I will hurt more than your pathetic neck."

The man tries to regain control of his breathing, repeatedly gasping for air.

Medusa has put the mission at risk. Again. How does she let herself be constantly provoked into making the wrong decisions? Every time they back her into a corner, it leaves Medusa with nothing but impossible choices and people angry with her. It does not matter if it was instigated by someone else, or if her options we limited. Medusa always pays the price.

The man looks like he wants to say something back to her,

but before he can, Cadmus abruptly puts the encounter to an end by striking the back of the man's head with the hilt of the sword he pulls from under his cloak. The man crumples into a heap, holding his head. They continue down the hallway as he scurries off.

As Medusa watches his form recede, her unease grows with every stride he takes. Alec gives Cadmus an approving glance and once again, they are on their way to find the tunnels to the marketplace.

37

ICARUS

Icarus grabs a glass of wine from a passing server and closes her eyes as the sweet fruity flavors hit her tongue. This wine differs from the ales and meads at the barracks these days and she letting it carry her away, lightly swaying with the sound of a bow being pulled across the strings of a cello.

Growing up on a farm, Icarus dreamed of opportunities like this. The grand party is the stuff of fantasy, gilded decor in soft candlelight, beautiful people beautifully dressed, and food and wine flowing. She feels both out of her element and ready to embrace the new experiences her new life is affording her. Being in rotation for one of the elite legions definitely has its perks.

Shopping for the dress for this had been an utter fantasy. It was silly and girly going to the shops trying them on, and Icarus loved every second. The gold satin dress that slid over her body like liquid metal was the obvious choice, confirmed by the multiple sets of eyes that have been watching her. Golden wings fanning out from the sides of a matching mask drew Icarus in the moment she had laid eyes on them, like they called to her.

When Icarus opens her eyes, the first thing that is visible is rose gold, but when her vision focuses, there is an incredibly beautiful woman standing there. The metallic blush color of her dress compliments the golden yellow of the one Icarus wears. The vines and thorns on her mask frame intensely violet eyes.

Icarus's heart skips a beat. Even with most of the woman's face obscured, Icarus knows this is the most she has ever been attracted to anybody.

Perhaps there is an aphrodisiac in the wine, or maybe the flowers, but Icarus wants to get lost in this woman. A tug of something familiar simmers beneath the surface.

"It's you," the woman says, breathlessly.

What does she mean?

"Never mind that," she continues with a wave of her hand.

A small hand extends to Icarus, and the woman asks, "Will you do me the honor of a dance?"

Icarus blushes, taking the mystery woman's hand and accepting her invitation. Something seems so recognizable about the woman's voice, but Icarus is struggling to place it, too lost in the woman's trance to even really try.

They walk to the middle of the dance floor right as the song that is playing ends.

The woman raises her arms, bending her elbows and squaring her shoulders into a perfect frame, and Icarus places her left hand on the woman's shoulder and her right in the woman's left.

The music begins, slow and sensual, and the mysterious stranger leads Icarus across the dance floor. It is a good thing her father had taught Icarus how to dance. She matches the woman step for step, turn for turn. Everything feels right with this woman. Icarus's body feels both at home with her and ignited with desire. The pull is so strong that Icarus rethinks her entire life. Was she searching for a place in this world amongst the Heroes this whole time, or was she just searching for *her*?

The song ends with a flourish as the woman spins Icarus and finishes with a dip that they hold for several heartbeats, staring into each other's eyes.

The woman closes the distance between their faces and Icarus doesn't hesitate, lifting her head to meet her halfway, their lips coming together with so much passion, Icarus is certain hers are scorched when they separate. Desire soars through Icarus's body. This feels like a mirage. What Icarus envisioned as a night of drinking, dancing, and some flirtation is rapidly spiraling into something magnetic.

As Icarus allows the woman to lead her off the dance floor, through the crowd, and out of the ballroom, her pulse races, pounding in her ears. Going off with people Icarus does not know is likely a bad idea, but she can't bring herself to care, at least for this night she will follow this woman anywhere. Consequences be damned.

Neither of them says a word as they continue along several long, dark hallways until they reach large, ornate double doors.

Inside is the most lavish bedchamber Icarus has ever seen. This woman must be important. Something in the back of her mind says again she should know this woman. A part of her is screaming with familiarity, but Icarus is too enraptured to listen or care.

All the furniture in the room is white with gold accents. Vases with flowers in varying shades of pinks, reds, and whites flood the room with a divine scent. The four-poster canopy bed is in front of an open air window that takes up the entire wall. Icarus can see all the way to the bay and the view is magnificent.

Icarus is still standing in front of the window when the woman walks up behind her and puts her arms around Icarus's waist from behind. The gesture is so intimate, but it feels right. Icarus sighs and leans back into it and the woman's lips kiss the nape of her neck. Icarus gasps at the touch of soft lips on such a sensitive spot.

Icarus turns around to face the woman, and their lips meet. A whimper leaves the woman. Why is this sensual stranger so affected by her? Icarus opens her mouth, and the woman does the same, their tongues meeting, sending a shock to her soul.

The inclination to take off the woman's mask, or her own, is strong, but Icarus hesitates, not wanting to break the spell. Instead, feeling emboldened, she reaches for the strings holding her dress together behind her neck, untying them and letting it fall to her feet.

The woman inhales sharply at the sight of Icarus wearing nothing but her mask.

Cupping Icarus's cheek in her hand, a tear rolls down her cheek. Before Icarus can ask why she is crying, the woman's mouth is on hers again. She is kissing Icarus with a desperation that her own soul mirrors.

The woman backs her up to the bed, kissing Icarus deeply the entire time.

Once Icarus is sitting on the edge of the bed, the woman steps back again, taking her fill of the sight of Icarus's naked body. After a moment, the woman reaches behind her back, unzipping her own dress and letting it fall to the floor.

The woman's body is jaw-dropping. Her tight, petite curves are both soft and sexual. Stepping back up to the bed, she guides Icarus back to the headboard, straddling her once they are at the head of the bed. Pale blonde hair cascades down around Icarus, mixing with the golden blonde of her own hair.

Icarus groans as the woman kisses her deeply again, pulling away only to trail kisses down Icarus's neck and collarbone, lingering between her breasts over her heart. The woman's hands are roaming up and down Icarus's torso, sliding her hands down Icarus's hips and then slowly up her inner thigh.

Icarus raises her hips to meet her, needing the woman inside of her. Is she really in a stranger's bed not even an hour after meeting them? Is this woman really a stranger?

The woman's fingers make their way inside of Icarus, and the thought dissipates instantly. First one, then a second, and finally a third. The sensation is cataclysmic and Icarus sees stars when she closes her eyes, a soft moan escaping her lips.

The woman pumps her fingers in and out in a slow but steady rhythm that has Icarus's breath catching, an orgasm building faster than ever. The woman puts her thumb on Icarus's clit, driving her over that cliff in the blink of an eye.

When Icarus finally opens her eyes, she looks over to see a steady stream of tears on the woman's face and Icarus's heart crumbles for her, sensing a deep hurt.

She wipes her tears away and turns back to Icarus, then pauses before finally saying, "I will explain tomorrow, I promise. If you will allow me tonight, I will explain everything."

Icarus doesn't know why she trusts this woman, but with her whole heart, Icarus tells her it is okay, and she means it.

They take their time in each other's arms, the party lost from their thoughts entirely as they touch and kiss each other anywhere and everywhere.

An abrupt knock on her door interrupts them entirely too soon.

The woman curses and throws on a white silk robe, looking ethereal with her bed-mussed hair and lust-hooded eyes. "You've got to be kidding me."

After conferring with whoever came to bother them, the woman slips back into bed with Icarus, a conflicted look on her face.

"Will you wait here? I have to go attend to something urgent but I will be back in an hour, two at most. You can use the hot spring pool in my bathing chamber, and read any of the books I have lying around. I can even have some food and drink brought in for you," she says, her tone hopeful.

Icarus isn't due to report back to her detachment until noon tomorrow, and does not hesitate. This evening is hers and she will offer every second this woman wants to take. She nods, "Yes. I'll be here."

Relief washes over the woman's face, and she quickly throws on a much more simple gown than she had worn for the party. She leans over and gives Icarus another deep kiss.

She leaves the room, muttering something about sending up refreshments anyway, and Icarus thinks she heard something else. It sounded an awful lot like, "I can't believe I found her."

38

MEDUSA

Cadmus navigates around the turns of the Love Temple hallways without referencing the map. Medusa can picture him as a teenager running around here, likely when he was not supposed to be. The thought makes her smile slightly, but she clears her head of the daydreaming and refocuses on the task at hand.

They descend a set of stairs that becomes more poorly lit the farther they go down. There is a junction at the bottom. To the right is an illuminated tunnel that even has a runner along the floor. To the left is darkness and Medusa grimaces when Cadmus turns that way.

After a few moments, Cadmus stops and Medusa slams into his back. The rest of the group do the same to her and they all clash like dominoes. Cadmus grunts in frustration, but that is all she hears from him until the sound of the door's mechanism being fiddled with meets her ears. A few more grumbles and clinking metal sounds, and the door slowly slides open. Cadmus takes Medusa's hand in the dark and they walk forward, with Medusa taking Alec's hand behind her.

This side of the tunnel is dark as well, but light appears the farther they go provided by the occasional flickering sconce.

Soon they are at the end of the tunnel and, as expected, it brings them directly to the abandoned marketplace. What is unexpected is the fact that it is empty. Are they too late? Is this a trap?

Alec gets in Cadmus's face. "Well? This was your plan! Where is everyone?"

"I… I don't know." Cadmus looks stunned. "I told you, these are old schematics. Don't blame me. For all we know, they could have a shiny new dungeon somewhere. This was always a guess!"

Medusa steps between them, pushing them out of each other's faces. "Stop it. We need to come up with a new plan and then get out of here before we're caught. Fighting amongst ourselves will just get us killed."

The layout is a labyrinth, with stalls branching out in each direction. The group members wander separately, assessing the area so they can formulate a plan while Alec goes to see if Hestia is here.

Once almost everyone is back, minus Ajax and Alec, Cadmus addresses them, "I think we need to leave. This is on me. I gave it my best guess, and it was a bad call. We need to cut our losses and leave before we push our luck and are noticed by someone."

Everyone is nodding their heads, and Medusa is inclined to agree. All the time and resources wasted like this is frustrating, but dwelling on it long enough to further risk their safety does not seem like a wise course of action either.

Ajax comes jogging back over and interrupts Cadmus to say, "Hey! Looks like we weren't too far off. You're going to want to see this."

Rushing over to see what he found, Medusa gasps. They had converted the market stalls into cages. There are small pieces of tattered clothing discarded. When her eyes land on a pile of bloody rags, Medusa feels woozy and puts her hand on the nearest object to brace herself, which is one of the cages.

She startles when suddenly the bundle of blankets in the cage moves.

"Help! Quick!" Medusa shouts.

The others come running as she tries to find the door to the cage. A scared pair of eyes peeks out and stills her. Medusa calms her energy, not wanting to startle the nymph. She crouches down to appear less threatening and says in a soothing voice, "I'm so sorry for what you've been through. You're safe with us."

The eyes blink back at her and Medusa thinks she is going to have to try again when the blankets start to shift and the nymph emerges from them, eyes wide with fear, frail body trembling.

Medusa hears the sharp collective intake of breath when it becomes visible to everyone what kind of shape the nymph is in. She is emaciated, and her wrists and ankles have dark circles around them, indicating the use of restraints. Her skin is a dull slate gray, despite her being a water nymph who should be the richest of blues. The gills at her throat are dry and crusted over.

Medusa looks around all the empty cages. *Oh no.*

"We're too late," Alec says.

"How long has it been since you've been in the water?" Medusa asks.

The nymph merely holds up all five fingers on one hand.

"Five days?" Medusa asks, and the nymph shakes her head no.

"Five weeks?" No, again.

"No. Five months?"

The nymph sadly nods her head and Medusa has to do everything in her power to restrain her anger, not wanting to scare the nymph.

"Let's see if we can't get you out of there. Then we'll try to find you some water." Medusa says. The nymph nods her head and sits back down, pulling her knees up to her chest and putting her head down on them.

Medusa turns back to the group before her, "Can we get the cage open without the key?"

Cadmus pulls against the bars at the cage door, grunting as he strains.

"I don't think so," he answers. "I can probably use the hilt of my sword."

The sudden sound of footsteps that are approaching quickly interrupts Cadmus. There is no time to hide as Pantheon Guard members come rushing in from the way they had come.

The group stands there in frozen horror as twenty Guards file in from the tunnel entrance. More footsteps sound from behind them and another ten Guards come from what is likely the main front entrance to the marketplace, completing the semicircle that was formed by the first group, leaving them surrounded. Lagging behind the group, hands on his throat still, is the drunken rabbit.

39

HESTIA

Hestia can barely open her eyes when she hears footsteps coming her way. A blurry shape materializes through the bars. Even with her fuzzy vision, she knows that face.

Alec came for her. Either that or her mind is playing tricks on her to ease the torturous assault on her body and mind from the cage.

It does not matter which one it is. Hestia is happy to see him even as a figment of her mind, which feels nearly gone.

He says her name, and it slightly pulls Hestia out of the fog with how close it sounds.

Maybe he is really here.

"Alec," Hestia croaks out weakly.

"I've got you my fire. We are going to get you out of here," Alec says, stroking Hestia's hair through the bars.

The caress adds to her pain, but Hestia does not tell him to stop. She does not know how much time she has left on this plane, so Hestia will take any touch from Alec, even if it feels like a hundred knives stabbing her following the path of his touch.

247

Psyche asks, "Where is everyone else?"

"They are searching for anything useful here."

Alec stands and rattles the door to the cage, but the lock is firm and the sound of it sends more pain ricocheting through Hestia's head. He turns around and begins searching around for the key while Hestia continues to lie where he found her, not having the strength to move.

Suddenly, the pain kicks up to a new level and Hestia screams, the sound coming out raspy and raw.

Alec rushes back to her side but is helpless to ease her burden.

Hestia's body feels like it is being pulled in different directions and she imagines this is what being on a rack would feel like. The pressure builds with the pain and Hestia is pretty sure she is still screaming, but drowned out by the roar in her head.

Alec is yelling at her, but Hestia cannot hear any of it.

A loud popping sound precedes a blinding pain that feels like every bone in Hestia's body has broken simultaneously. She convulses and her consciousness fades, riding the waves of pain until she succumbs to the shock and passes out.

WHEN HESTIA WAKES BACK UP, she feels empty. The pain is still there, but now it is a dull nagging pain under the surface.

Realizing what happened, Hestia cries out, startling Alec. Looking at him, Hestia sobs harder. How does she find the words to tell him? Will he still look at her the same?

Everything has changed.

"What happened? I'm so glad to see you're awake," Alec whispers, the relief clear on his handsome face.

"My time's almost up, Alec. My immortality is gone."

"No." The horror on his face is not directed at her, but that they did this to her.

"Please, just leave me. I don't have much longer in here now that I'm mortal and I couldn't bear seeing something happen to you in my final hours because you were here with me. Go find the others, and get out of here."

Alec shakes his head no. "They can leave without me for all I care. I'm going to be here by your side until we either get you out of this cage or they kill me." His voice cracks with emotion.

Hestia is too weak to force herself to say the words to make him leave. Maybe she is selfish but Fates, it hurts so much and the only thing that has allowed her to breathe again since being thrown in this cage is him.

The metal of the bar is excruciating against Hestia's skin as she extends her hand toward the bars. Alec quickly makes up the distance with his own, their fingers intertwining. She grits her teeth as the movement feels like razor blades slicing up her arms, but it does not matter. Hestia can give him this. Give *them* this.

A whimper leaves Hestia as Alec's hand squeezes hers and she watches a tear run from his eye. Hestia hates herself for being the reason someone she loves, someone as strong and magnificent as Alec, is crying. Hates herself for being too selfish to make him leave. All of it is drowned out by the love she has for him and what his being with her for her final moments is doing to her soul. It will be easier to rest peacefully knowing, even if only briefly, that this great man loved her.

Hestia looks at Psyche, lying in this cage with her, immortality intact. There is still time for her.

"Alec."

"What is it, my fire?"

"You have to go find the others. For Psyche. You have to help her. Don't make this time with us together cost her life."

"I can't leave you."

"Find them and come back to me. Please, Alec."

He kisses her hand, letting his lips linger on her skin for several seconds.

"I love you, my fire."

"I love you, too."

His hand slips from hers and he disappears into the darkness of the tunnels once more.

40

MEDUSA

Medusa is lying in one of the nymph cages with her arms bound behind her. The stone floor is frigid and the thin fabric of her dress does nothing to shield her from it.

Well. This was a disaster. How could it have gone so horribly wrong?

Aphrodite had shown up right behind the guards, still wearing the blood-red lipstick Medusa remembers as a child.

Medusa recalls the way Aphrodite had called Cadmus "darling" and it makes her stomach turn. Did he betray them? Medusa has taken every opportunity to warn that he would, but she cannot bring herself to believe that it was him. Between Nicodemus and the man in the rabbit mask, this mission was doomed as soon as Nicodemus abducted Psyche instead of Medusa. How would things be right now if Medusa had gone with the captain? Deonn would still be alive. The crew would have still had access to Psyche's protection. Psyche would be safe and out of harm's way. How many people have to get hurt or captured because of Medusa's mistakes before it is no longer worth it? At least on her island, missteps did not snowball into full-blown crises that affected people Medusa cares about.

It is a struggle to sit up between her positioning and bound arms. Medusa finally makes it to a sitting position and looks around. There is little light to see much of anything and she squints, trying to make out anything, to no avail.

Screams pierce the silence, and Medusa's heart stops. *Psyche. No.* Medusa frantically looks for a way out of her cell until she hears approaching footsteps and stills.

There is the faint glow of a flame, getting brighter as the steps get closer and louder. Medusa braces herself for who might be about to greet her as her pulse thunders in her head. Will it be Aphrodite, or has Cadmus come back to gloat for fooling them all? The thought of seeing his smug face while being forced to hear Psyche's torment is enough to make her rage, but that will help nothing. Medusa needs to come up with a plan, and fast.

Her racing mind fails to produce anything actionable as the lone figure approaches. Too tall to be Aphrodite, so it must be Cadmus. She's imagining ripping him from limb to limb when his face materializes, and it's... Nicodemus?

Medusa's shock must be apparent because Nicodemus chuckles when he steps within a few feet of her cell, face fully illuminated now. The screaming has stopped, and Medusa hopes it is not merely a temporary reprieve.

"Why did you do it?"

Nicodemus laughs. "It is a pity I had to give Hestia and Psyche to the Pantheon, but it's the only way they would trust me. A worthy price to watch you pay."

"You did this because of me? You would betray the entire Allegiance because of ME?" Confusion courses through Medusa as she tries to put together the puzzle that is still missing pieces.

"But why? At least tell me that," Medusa asks, even though

she knows the answer is irrelevant and will not help get her out of there.

"Fine, you want to know why?" Nicodemus asks, rubbing his hand over his face. "Growing up, my family was the picture of dysfunctional. Both of my parents were abusive drunks," he starts, lip curling up at the memory of them.

"What does this-?" Medusa starts, but he interrupts her bitingly. "Do you want to know or not?"

When she nods, he continues. "My older brother was an absolute asshole. To everyone but me, that is. He was old enough to step in when either of my parents needed to be kept in line, and he took on the brunt of what they had intended for me. His name was Dorian."

Medusa is afraid to know the answer but asks anyway, "What happened to him?"

His gaze sharpens to a hateful point. "You did."

Medusa's heart rate accelerates. How can she be responsible for his brother's death? Is this another mistake from her past that Medusa now holds responsibility for?

"Did… did he attack me on my island? I hurt no one while I was there who wasn't there to harm me first, I swear it!"

Nicodemus's temper flares. "Do your kills mean so little to you that you can't even keep track of them? I'm not surprised you didn't even bother to learn his name. Maybe you really truly are the monster the stories claim."

"I don't understand," Medusa starts, but realization dawns on her. "Oh."

"Oh? Oh?? Is that all you can say to me?" He exclaims while rattling the bars, tears of both anger and sorrow welling in the corners of his eyes.

How did she miss the resemblance before? When his brother attacked Medusa, she had not exactly stopped to consider who he possibly looked like. The same eyes looking back at Medusa now with hate that had been in the bathhouse when she first arrived at the Isle.

This is a hate that will never see reason. Grief does not care if the death was justified or not, it only knows that the hole left in your heart feels like a void.

"You called me Viper before that happened, though. Why did you already loathe me?"

"Women like you disgust me. You think you can lead men on, even gods, and then refuse them? No. No more teasing and torturing. Harpies like you are going to start getting what's coming to them."

"Teasing? Leading men on? What on Gaia's earth are you talking about?"

"Poseidon told us everything. All of the Olympic Isles know about how you taunted Poseidon with your beauty, and then refused him when he couldn't take it anymore. Everyone knows what you made him do to you and why."

Everyone. Everyone thinks this? Is that what they see when they look at her?

One question keeps nagging in the back of her mind, though.

"How did you get around the oath? Do you think your brother would have wanted your soul in Tartarus for eternity?"

"Don't you dare try to tell me what my brother would want for me! You silenced him for eternity. And those oaths? Psyche isn't the only god with powers. Workarounds can be found if one is inventive enough."

"*He* attacked *me*. I know this means little, but I never intended to truly harm him."

"Save it. Once Poseidon gets here, I never have to look at you again, you fucking scaly monstrosity."

He spits on the ground at her feet and turns on his heel and retreats into the distance, the light fading with the sound of his footsteps.

ALONE IN HER cell once again, Medusa tries to stay calm, but it has been a losing effort. Every time she thinks she has a grip on herself, her thoughts remind her *HE's* on his way. It seems like Poseidon is right on her heels at every turn. Her thoughts cycle between impending doom, fear for Psyche, and guilt over assuming the worst of Cadmus every chance she got. Medusa thinks about Ajax and Cyril and says a silent prayer to the Fates that any of them see the other side of this.

Medusa hopes beyond hope Alec might still be free out there. Even if she does not make it out, knowing that at least he did would be better than the alternative.

Her thoughts wander back to her island and how much has changed in the few days since Medusa left. Was leaving worth it? Psyche's smile pops into her mind, pulling her back into the memories they have already made together, and she knows it was. It has been exhilarating getting to know Psyche. There seemed to be all the time in the world for her to court Psyche's soul, but now Medusa's own heart aches.

Finally, feeling less woozy from her head wound, Medusa stands carefully, taking it slowly to avoid vertigo. The exterior of her enclosure is still barely visible.

With her back to the cage door, her bound fingers brush over the bars as she feels for hinges or mechanisms, almost crying from joy when her hands find the lock. Shuffling across the floor with her feet, Medusa looks for anything that can break the lock.

Two passes over the entire floor finds nothing of use.

Medusa paces in the cell and tries to think, racking her useless brain.

More footsteps approach, much quicker than before.

Someone comes running in her direction, trying to see in the darkness.

"Medusa, Ajax, Cyril, Alec?" A low voice calls in a hushed tone.

Cadmus?

"Here!" Medusa says, careful not to be too loud.

Cadmus pauses to light a torch, then walks over to her door. Medusa does not miss the limp in his gait or the way he winces as he raises the torch.

"Is anyone else over here with you?" He asks.

Medusa shakes her head. "No one conscious, anyway."

No one alive.

"You're hurt." Medusa says gently.

Cadmus shrugs his shoulders. "I heard her screams. Even when she wasn't screaming anymore, it was all I could hear."

He does not need to say who.

Medusa nods in response, and neither of them needs to say more about it.

"Step back," Cadmus informs her, raising the sword in his left arm, and bringing it down on the lock once she complies. The lock falls apart and drops to the ground. Cadmus places the torch in a holder on the pillar near her cell and opens her door. He uses the sword to cut the ropes from her hands and she throws her arms around him.

"I'm so sorry, I rushed to assumptions," Medusa says before she can lose her nerve, determined to end the erroneous cycle of anger and hatred.

Cadmus chuckles and wraps his free arm around her waist.

"I didn't hold it against you. In your shoes, I would have done the same."

Medusa releases him and steps back, composing herself.

"Do you know where Psyche is? Is she okay?" Medusa asks, heart in her throat.

"I don't. You're the first I've found. I covered a lot of ground, though, so we should find them soon once we head that way."

"Alec? Hestia?" Any good news at all?

Cadmus shakes his head no, and her shoulders slump. It is better than bad news.

"What's the plan?"

"We have to make our way around and find Cyril and Ajax if we can. They can help with any heavy lifting if we need to carry anyone out. Hopefully, we will cross paths with Alec, but he knows how to take care of himself."

"Ok." The thought of leaving Alec does not thrill Medusa, but they still have time before that would happen. Best to focus on finding everyone.

Darkness descends as Cadmus puts the torch out, and Medusa grabs his forearm.

"One more thing," Medusa says. "Don't forget the promise you made me on the ship. Psyche leaves here. No matter what."

"I would rather die than see Psyche trapped here, but don't think for a second that sentiment doesn't apply to you as well." Cadmus's voice swims with an emotion that surprises her.

Medusa repeats, "You have to—,"

"No."

"Please. Promise me you'll do what it takes to get her out of here?" Medusa pleads. Psyche cannot pay for her mistakes.

"I promise."

41

MEDUSA

edusa and Cadmus scan the open area before them and see the god cage in the middle of the room. There are only two Guards. The only one with a weapon amongst them is Cadmus, but if they do this right, they should be able to handle them.

They found Ajax and Cyril after two empty rows of cells, with no resistance.

Toward the back, coming from another aisle, is a figure Medusa struggles to make out. He gets closer and Medusa internally jumps for joy at the sight of Alec.

Alec sees them and smiles. He takes in the party and the two guards before him and Medusa can see that he likes the new odds.

Cyril and Ajax quietly make their way to the outer guard and wait as Alec, Cadmus, and Medusa stealthily advance on the Guard near Psyche. Simultaneously, they attack their targets. Instead of using a weapon, Medusa steps into the Guard's line of sight and gets his attention.

His eyes go wide in recognition and he opens his mouth to

call out, but Cadmus brings his sword up through the back of the Guard's neck.

Shouting draws their attention to where Cyril has his arm wrapped tightly around the neck of the Guard he and Ajax were supposed to be fighting. Medusa looks for Ajax and sees him barely moving on the ground, blood pooling beneath his back. Medusa and Cadmus race to assist Cyril and Ajax but the last Guard succumbs to the choke hold Cyril has him in and suffocates.

Medusa drops to her knees on the floor when she gets to Ajax. His breathing is raspy and shallow. There is a dagger hilt protruding from his abdomen and Medusa rips a strip of fabric from her cloak, desperately trying to stop the blood flow.

Her heart sinks as his eyes stop fluttering, his chest no longer rising and falling.

Grief and guilt rack her body and she feels like she could vomit, but there is no time to process, no time to hesitate.

Cyril, eyes rimmed red, says to them, "Another Guard came in behind us. I was just about to run him through when I saw Ajax take the hit. He used that as his opportunity to flee and go get reinforcements, I'm assuming. I will tuck the bodies somewhere less conspicuous. You three get Psyche out of there so we can leave."

Medusa walks over and crouches down near the Guard by Psyche, digging into pockets until she produces a key.

Rushing over to the cage, Medusa tries to ignore the fact that Psyche is not moving.

Can't panic over that, have to get this door open.

"We've got you," Medusa says, reaching for the lock, but when her fingers brush the metal of the cage, pain tears up Medusa's arm. The pulsing pain is emanating from her wrist, at the site of her birthmark, causing the key to fall from her hand. What the Fates was that?

Cadmus picks up the key but yelps in pain when he also tries the lock, clenching his thigh.

Alec looks at the cage in confusion. He picks the key up from where Cadmus dropped it. "We don't have time for this. Hestia I've got you."

Crying out, Alec grabs the back of his neck. None of them can get in.

Cyril comes running in from moving the Guards. "What are you guys doing? Let's go!"

Alec throws his hands up in frustration. "None of us can get in the Fates' damned cage."

Cyril puts the key in the lock and Medusa holds her breath, waiting to find out if their last chance will work.

The lock clicks and opens, groaning as Cyril swings the door open.

"I'll be damned." Alec looks at Cyril with surprise.

"There's no time to question it. We have to move." Cyril responds as he picks Psyche up and brings her out of the cage and into Cadmus's waiting arms.

Psyche groans into Cadmus's shoulder, but her eyes remain closed. He shifts to position her better and grimaces as it strains his injury.

Medusa checks on him, but he dismisses her, "It doesn't matter. We have to go."

Cyril walks back into the cage and Medusa's heart drops when he collects a very still figure that must be Hestia. *My gods, how long has Hestia been in here?*

Once across the threshold of the god cage, Hestia finally takes a gasping breath before saying Alec's name and falling unconscious. Alec gently collects her from Cyril and feels for a pulse. Medusa can see the relief on his face, making its way directly into her soul when he finds one.

They move to join Cyril to leave when Medusa freezes. "Wait!"

Taking the sword from Cadmus, Medusa goes back to where the water nymph was. She had been in pretty terrible shape, but hopefully, they can still get her out of there. After breaking the lock, Medusa scoops up the bundle of blankets concealing the nymph, relieved when it rustles in her arms. The weight of the nymph is a hinderance to Medusa's speed, but she cradles the nymph and focuses on escaping.

Medusa returns the sword to Cadmus as they meet back with Cyril, who has the dagger that killed Ajax in his hand. Cadmus gives the sword to Cyril, taking the dagger from him and giving it to Medusa to use to cover them while he carries Psyche and Alec carries Hestia. They decide to leave through the main entranceway to the marketplace hoping it is not being heavily guarded this late at night.

Their hunch pays off and they swiftly make it to the front entrance, where only a few guards linger, on low alert. They whisper and debate the best approach and settle on trying to slip by them unnoticed. There is a wide perimeter around them, and if luck is on their side, they might make it.

They navigate around the Guards at the painstakingly slow pace necessary for a stealthier approach. Medusa is afraid to even breathe loudly.

Minutes tick by, but eventually they are almost clear. Shouting once again calls their focus and Cadmus swears under his breath as Guards pile out of the front entrance. Before the Guards can spot them, they take off running for the rendezvous point. They have no idea if it will still be an option, but it is the only one they know to try.

The Guards aren't far behind, the clashing sounds of their armor following close on their heels like a ravenous wolf.

Medusa's side is aching at the sudden exertion, but there is no time to slow down. Her chest heaves as Medusa runs as fast as she can, hoping the nymph in her arms is alright. They are halfway to the water when Medusa makes out the dinghy in the moonlight.

"There!" She directs their course more precisely.

A lone figure is near the little boat and Medusa prays to the Fates that it is one of their own.

The figure gets the boat ready to shove off and hope blossoms. They might actually make it.

Glancing back to make sure her companions are close, Medusa also finds the Guards too close for comfort. Cadmus seems to notice this at the same time and calls for Cyril. He shoves Psyche into Cyril's arms, grabbing the sword from him and shouting something into Cyril's ear that Medusa cannot hear, turning to face the horde of Guards on his own. Alec is by her side, Hestia still in his arms.

Medusa motions for him to keep running and Alec does not hesitate. With the shape Hestia is in, Alec needs to get her as far away from here as possible.

Medusa turns her attention back to Cadmus and takes the sword from his hand before he can react.

No more of this. No more suffering to save her. Psyche and Hestia are in horrific shape. Deonn and Ajax died. I can trace too many of these things back to my mistakes.

This shall not break me.

"What are you doing?" Cadmus yells.

"Go! Get everyone to safety. No one else is getting hurt to protect me." Medusa shoves the nymph into Cadmus's arms.

"No!" He screams and tries to stop her.

"Let me go." Medusa says. The drum of her heartbeat is frantic. They are running out of time.

This shall not break me.

"I can't get her out of here and just leave you. Either you come with me, or we all stay." Cadmus says to her.

Medusa faces an impossible choice, but Cadmus locks eyes with her and she yells, "Please! Go!" Voice cracking on the last word, Medusa's heart fracturing with it as she raises her hand to her hood. Her serpents are already in a frenzy, as her emotions override the magic of the hood. "Don't make me do this."

This shall not break me.

"Fuck." Cadmus turns and makes for the final stretch to the boat.

Medusa watches to make sure he is retreating before walking over to the flat boulder on the side of the path, sitting on it and steadying herself as she awaits her fate.

This shall not break me.

42

HESTIA

The hum of Alec's chest as he shouts is comforting, but the jostle of being carried as they run for their lives is excruciating. Hestia is so tired.

"We're almost to the boat, my fire. Just hold on."

A man hands Psyche over to the person manning the boat and then climbs in. Was his name Cyril?

"I'm going to have Iris hold you for a minute so I can get in, and then you'll be right back in my arms." Alec's voice is deep and smooth, so much richer in person than through the stone.

Cadmus situates the nymph in the boat and turns back to where they left Medusa behind. "I'm going after her."

Alec steps in front of Cadmus, blocking his path. "Don't be stupid. You're just going to get yourself taken, too. The best way for you to help her is by coming with us so we can make a plan and get her back, by force, if necessary.

Cadmus lets out an aggravated huff and shoves Alec. "Get out of my way! We can't leave her!"

Using his broad stature, Alec steps forward, getting into Cadmus's face and grabbing his shoulders, shaking them. "Pull it together. They would probably just kill you. We have to GO!"

"Medusa?" Iris asks Hestia.

"She stayed behind so we could make it out." Hestia answers, her voice still raw.

"Fine. But if the Allegiance takes too long, I'm going after her myself."

Alec's expression softens. "If they take too long, I'll join you. You have my word."

They row to the ship, and everyone on board hastily prepares to make sail. Hestia recognizes a few faces from the one time she was at the Isle of Mysts. The last thing Hestia sees on the deck before Alec carries her below is Cadmus standing at the railing, staring at the Temple.

Alec takes Hestia to a cabin and gets her settled in.

"I'm going to leave you here in my cabin until we are safe and clear, then we will get you situated wherever you'd like."

Hestia nods. Fatigue drags her down.

"I'll send a healer to look at you and Psyche as soon as I can."

Alec kisses the top of her head and walks out of the room.

A few minutes later, there is a knock on the door and Psyche comes in.

"I'm already feeling much better now that I'm out of that disgusting cage. How are you?" Psyche asks.

"I don't know, honestly. Everything feels different, wrong." Will Psyche understand? Or will she and the other gods look at Hestia as if she is a false god?

Psyche takes Hestia's hand and sits next to her on the small bed.

"I'm sure your soul is making room for something new, mortality." Psyche's voice is soft and patient.

Hestia is a mortal. Eons no longer span before her. There is so little time now. If Hestia has to be mortal, though, at least she can be mortal with Alec. The imbalance of their life spans will no longer play a part in their love story. It does not make up for having the rest of time stolen from her, but at least she will not be alone.

"Is Medusa going to be alright?" Hestia asks, wanting to change the subject from the topic of her mortality.

Psyche drops her head onto Hestia's shoulder. "I hope so. Poseidon is too enraptured with her to kill her. We just have to hope he isn't too monstrous before we can get to her."

"Another rescue mission? When this one went so well?" Hestia raises an eyebrow.

"There's nothing I won't do to get her back. If I have to risk everything, I will. If I hadn't been it that damned god cage, I would have been strong enough to at least try to save her."

A light knock and the door opens. Cadmus comes in and he drops to the floor before Psyche.

"Goddess, forgive me." His voice is choked up and full of emotion. "I didn't want to leave her."

Psyche runs her fingers through his hair. "It was an impossible choice. We will find her. Together."

Cadmus takes the hand that's in his hair and brings it to his lips. "I'm so glad we found you."

43

ICARUS

The morning sun streams in through the giant window, onto the cream-colored satin sheets that are entangled around Icarus and her mystery woman lover. They kept the masks on all night, but now it is morning and Icarus is owed answers. There is more going on here. Icarus can feel it, and her heart is telling her it matters.

Icarus takes off her own mask, setting it on the table beside the bed. She turns back, and the woman is awake, sitting up and removing her rose gold mask. Icarus gasps when she sees it is none other than Aphrodite. The shock is short-lived though as her heart pounds in her chest, as if it is trying to leap out and directly reach the goddess across from her. It should be confusing, but it feels right.

"What's happening?" Icarus asks, "Tell me you're feeling this, too?"

Aphrodite's eyes well up with tears and her voice is so soft when she answers that Icarus almost cannot hear it. What she says, though, sends an echoing shockwave through Icarus's soul.

"It's been five hundred years since I've held you in my arms,"

Aphrodite starts, putting a hand up to halt Icarus when she goes to ask a question.

"I'll start over. Five hundred years ago, I was with the love of my life, Andromeda. She was incredible. Everything about her was sunshine, and it was impossible to be unhappy in her presence."

Hearing the name Andromeda has Icarus's head once again screaming at her to see an answer that should be right in front of her.

"My beautiful ray of sunshine had a curse, however. I don't think even she knew the entire story, but her parents had done something stupid that royally pissed off the Fates, causing them to curse their daughter. They granted her mighty phoenix powers, making her immortal, but there was a catch. She will die in every life she lives, but she will be reincarnated. However, the gap in between death and rebirth was not a set amount of time, meaning we would never know when she came back."

Icarus takes Aphrodite's hand, intertwining their fingers.

"I still don't know what happened, but I lost her. She died in my arms, poisoned by a coward that I still haven't found to this day. I waited. Everywhere I went, I watched for signs that she had been born again, certain that if I was patient, she would come back to me. I knew when I found her, my soul would recognize hers immediately, even though I knew she wouldn't recognize me. It was a worthy price to pay to get to have her in my life again."

Aphrodite's voice is thick with emotion, and Icarus's mind reels as she puts together the pieces. Aphrodite's shocked reaction to her, the pull they feel toward each other, the electrifying lovemaking.

"Am I... am I her? Your Andromeda?"

"Only you can tell me that. Did last night feel different to you than previous encounters? Did it feel more magnified, more intense?" Aphrodite asks.

Icarus does not even have to think. "Yes. I have never felt anything like I felt last night."

Aphrodite gets out of bed and comes back with a beautiful box covered in thorns. Icarus watches as Aphrodite uses her blood to open it, pulling out a medallion that looks ancient and the sunstone around Icarus's neck hums.

Icarus holds the sunstone up to the disc, and it clicks into place in the medallion.

Aphrodite throws her arms around her, hugging her. "I'm so sorry. I know the distance isn't there for you, but for me it's been so long. Hundreds of years I've waited, and waited, convinced the Fates had kept you from me."

Icarus cries softy as well as she responds, "No, the distance may not be there for me but I feel something here. My soul feels like it's found something it lost that was very dear. I may not have the memories, but my soul and my heart clearly recognize you."

Icarus's mind briefly flits to what she saw in the dungeon. Should she ask about Aphrodite about it? Icarus will definitely keep an eye open, but there is no real benefit to bringing it up now.

Aphrodite explains some of the phoenix powers Icarus will manifest on her twenty-fifth birthday as Icarus lays in bed envisioning the beautiful golden wings she will have.

When Icarus boards the ship to leave the island and return to the War Temple with her regiment, she feels like a completely different person than the one who disembarked from this same ship a couple of days ago.

They will keep things between themselves for now, but with Aphrodite making plans to see Icarus soon. A relationship with a god will get out and complicate things for her amongst the Heroes, but it is worth the risk because Icarus's heart finally feels like it has found that missing piece. She just never would have imagined it would be in the shape of Aphrodite.

When she boards Ares's ship, Athena is there waiting for her.

"Hello, Icarus."

Icarus bows. "Hello, Goddess."

"That was quite an impression you made at the Trials."

"Thank you, Goddess."

"Is it true you have your heart set on the Pegasus Legion?"

Icarus's pulse thunders in her ears. "Yes, Goddess."

"Welcome aboard."

44

MEDUSA

The boat sways as Medusa sits in her tiny cage in the cargo hold of Poseidon's ship. It has been hours, or at least it feels like it, and Poseidon has yet to his face.

Aside from when he captured her, Medusa has not seen him at all. She is not complaining, it is just odd.

Medusa tries to shift to the right of the cage to avoid the incessant drip from a leak, but there is not enough room. Her knees ache from having to keep them bent.

Does this ship not have normal cells?

Voices carry from outside of the room, and Medusa sits up, ready for confrontation. The voices fade as quickly as they arrived, and she slouches back down.

He is doing this on purpose. Making her sweat. Trying to break her.

He can't. This shall not break me.

It will take more than the silent treatment and being caged like an animal to force her to ever want Poseidon. If he had been the one to find her on her island instead of Psyche, Medusa might have given in. Seeing herself through Psyche, and

Cadmus, has changed her forever. She is not unlovable. Not a hazard, or a monster. Just Medusa.

Sending up a quick preyer to the Fates, Medusa hopes everyone made it away safely. It is doubtful anyone will tell her otherwise, unless it is just to gloat.

Picturing Cadmus standing there, refusing to leave her, is still a shock. Cadmus tried to save her. Despite Medusa being cruel to him at every turn, and even trying to kill him, he cares about her. He and Medusa both care about Psyche, but she is a god. A breathtaking god at that. Who could resist her?

Voices approach again and this time the cargo hold door swings open.

Poseidon strolls in, looking entirely too proud of himself.

He walks over to where her cage is and snaps his fingers. An Acolyte rushes over with a bucket and places it upside down for him to sit on.

Poseidon says nothing. Simply sits there looking in at Medusa, observing her, like she is some precious bird in an aviary instead of a person.

After several minutes, he gets up and walks out.

The Twins come in as soon as he is out the door and Medusa's stomach drops. The low lighting in the cargo hold bounces off of the sharp features of their faces.

Each one is carrying a bowl, and they drop them down in front of her. Food and water. If you can call the mush in the bowl, food.

"Do you see the Master's new pet?"

"I do, brother. I've seen better if you ask me."

"Should we feed it?"

"Oh, yes. Definitely. It looks thirsty too."

They pick up the bowls and hold them upside down over the top bars of her cage as the contents pour down onto her. The sludge smells like porridge and clings to her skin. Medusa does her best attempt at wiping it off while the Twins laugh at her.

One of them finally addresses her.

"Hi, pet. We're going to have so much fun together."

45

HESTIA

The harbor at the Isle of Mysts is a chaotic scene as Allegiance members race to pack up the ships. With traitors in their midsts, their location is compromised.

"Mama, I'm scared of the ship. I don't want to go!"

A little girl is pulling against her mother's grip, straining with as much effort as her small body can muster.

"Rue, please. It's not safe here anymore." The mother drops to her knees and cradles the child.

Hestia keeps walking, slowly. Her body is still so weak, but she can feel herself getting a little stronger.

The Council members are gathered in a small pavilion, debating where to go, and Hestia joins them, sitting down on a stone bench.

"We should go to Corcyra. That's definitely off the Pantheon's radar."

"Corcyra? That place is overrun with spiders the size of houses."

"That's a myth, but surely we should go to Crete."

Everyone has their own idea of where they should go and after an hour, no one is budging. Isadora stands up at the front,

274

listening and weighing options. Her dark brown hair is in rows of tight braids against her scalp, and golden beads adorn them.

The night sky is cloudy, coating the Isle in darkness.

Isadora clears her throat and finally speaks. "There is merit to many of your choices, I will admit. I can't help feeling like we haven't found the right one yet. It will take us hours to get the ships loaded and the residents ready. I suggest we spend more time deliberating and less time arguing." She gives several of the council members a pointed stare.

Before Isadora can continue, someone amongst the council gasps. Everyone turns to find her staring up at the sky and follows her gaze.

The clouds finally part and the moon peeks through. Hestia sees the color and her heart stops. Orange. A Fire Moon.

Everyone turns to look at Hestia, and she cannot bear their pity.

Hestia's fate is sealed. A new Keeper of the Flame has been born. The Fates really waste little time, do they?

No part of Hestia really thought she was going to get her immortality back, but the confirmation rising in the sky feels suffocating.

Hestia turns to leave when the winds pick up.

Cass's eyes glow, and she throws her head back.

She stays like that for a few minutes before the glow fades and her head returns to where it was.

Cass opens her eyes and shakes her head a little. She looks around at the gathered council members, and then Isadora.

"I know where to go."

"Where do the Fates wish us to go?" Isadora asks.

"To the Under Temple, where we will seek refuge with Medusa's brother."

ACKNOWLEDGMENTS

Bear with me, this will take a few. I'm so unbelievably grateful to have so many people that contributed to this book getting written. The process was long, but it wouldn't have been possible without the following people:

Shannon, your unflinching belief in my ability as a writer and as a person helped me find something that has been missing for a while, but you saw it immediately once my story gained traction.

My daughter, I am proud of you every single day. Thank you for always believing in me. Your own writing is remarkable and I hope you continue to nurture it.

Renae, thank you for being my best friend, no matter what we have been going though. I can't wait to see what adventure are still in store for us!

Meg, Alora, and Lacey, we are really doing this! Love you lots like polka dots.

Shawna, I will never stop being grateful to have you in my life.

Taylor, keep making the whole place shimmer! Love to the moon and to Saturn.

Josh and Kris, thank you for reading this book even while it was still in its infancy. Your feedback throughout this process has been unbelievable helpful.

Thank you so much to my beta and ARC readers. You have been instrumental in helping me craft the best version of my story.

ABOUT THE AUTHOR

River Bennet is a romantic fantasy writer with a focus on queer stories. She lives in New England with her partner, teenage daughter, two dogs, and three cats.

From the rural farm where she grew up in TX, to the bustling city life of Manhattan, and now the serenity of the Berkshire Mountains, she has always had a love of nature, animals, and a good cup of tea.